"I don't know what you think you're doing, but I want to know why you've been following me."

Something sparked in his eyes, but he didn't speak.

"Fine." Maryanne stepped toward her car. "You can play Mount Rushmore all you want. Just remember, if I see you again, I'll call the cops."

"Go ahead."

"Quit following me and mind your business. There's nothing interesting about me. I'm a librarian."

He shrugged. "I am minding my business, and I'm good at it."

A shiver racked Maryanne. "Stalking's a crime, you know. They can lock you up for a long time."

As she went for her car keys, his hand shot out and grabbed them. Fear churned her gut, and she hoped he wasn't able to smell it on her.

He unlocked her car door then handed her the keys. In silence he strode into the darkness. Maryanne stood there for long moments, drenched in rain and sweat.

She tried to relax, but she failed. Miserably.

What did J. Z. Prophet want with her?

Maryanne knew he was keeping tabs on her. What she didn't know was why. But she'd better figure it out soon...before it was too late.

Books by Ginny Aiken

Love Inspired Suspense

Mistaken for the Mob #26

GINNY AIKEN

was born in Cuba, grew up in Venezuela and now lives in Pennsylvania with her husband, with whom she has four sons. After careers as a ballerina and a newspaper reporter, Ginny is thrilled to be writing romantic suspense for Love Inspired Suspense.

mistaken
for the mob
GINNY AIKEN

Steeple
Hill®

Published by Steeple Hill Books™

STEEPLE HILL BOOKS

Steeple
Hill®

ISBN-13: 978-0-373-87378-4
ISBN-10:   0-373-87378-6

MISTAKEN FOR THE MOB

Copyright © 2006 by Grisel Anikienko

www.SteepleHill.com

Printed in U.S.A.

"For I know the plans I have for you," declares the Lord, "...plans to give you hope and a future... and [I] will bring you back from captivity."
—*Jeremiah* 29:11, 14

ONE

Philadelphia, Pennsylvania

Mary Margaret Muldoon was terminated.

As were Helmut Rheinemann, Toby Matthias and Muriel Harper. J.Z. Prophet held the death certificates of the well-to-do seniors in his left hand. On a neat pile before him sat autopsy reports that identified the cause of death as natural in all four cases. But the papers in his right hand belied those certificates.

"E-mail," he muttered to his partner, Dan Maddox. "What self-respecting mobster orders hits through e-mail? But here they are: Terminate Mary Margaret Muldoon, and Terminate Helmut Rheinemann."

J.Z. could have read the others, too. But why? They said the same thing. And the same woman had sent them all: Maryanne Wellborn.

He flung the pages onto his desk and rose from his chair. He went for his coffeepot, which he'd brought to the office when he got tired of FBI sludge, and poured himself his fourth cup of the morning. It was only seven o'clock.

After another hit of caffeine, he asked, "What kind of librarian would order a bunch of hits?"

Dan, an easygoing guy, shifted in his chair and shrugged. "Hey, it's a great cover—if they were hits."

"Okay. It is. But I want to know how she's offing them. Pathology found no evidence of foul play. The causes of death are listed as asphyxiation from emphysema, congestive heart failure, liver cancer and pneumonia. We might be able to pin the asphyxiation on her, but how'd she kill the others?"

"I think it's our job to find that out."

"It's our job to get the evidence that'll lock her up."

"Hmm…a librarian. Maryanne Wellborn, you say?"

"She's behind these hits."

"Sure of yourself, aren't you? And letting it get personal."

The accusation slugged J.Z. in the gut. "Not at all. This is business. The other's past history." He set his coffee mug on the corner of his desk, then jabbed a finger toward Dan. "Don't forget. You were right at my side the last six months. You helped me track the Verdis and their mob pals as they scammed their way through these ritzy retirement homes. You counted the bodies they left behind, just as I did, and looked just as hard as I did for something to stick on them—"

"Something stuck. Joey-O's behind bars."

"Not for this. He shot Carlo Papparelli. Aside from those shaky connections to Joey-O and Tony the Toe Verdi—scum, if ever there was scum—we didn't come up with a single solid thing to nail the deaths of the old people on them. But I know their game. And this perp in New Camden is just the latest in the string of killers we've been after. The only difference is that this one made a mistake. She left us these e-mails. How generous of her."

His partner's hands went up in surrender. "Okay, okay. Lay off the lecture. It was just a friendly warning I gave you. Can't let your old man's troubles mess with your mind on a case. My future's in your hands."

J.Z. snorted. "Last time I looked, there was a line of ladies wanting to take it in theirs."

Dan winked. "A man's gotta do what a man's gotta do."

"This man's—" J.Z. tapped Dan's chest then glanced at the papers on the desk "—got a job to do. He can't be thinking about his next date, and do it right."

"You complaining about my work?"

"Warning you against dropping your guard."

"That's uncalled for," Dan countered, his voice tight.

"Just put your social life on ice while we're on this one." J.Z. knew he was out of line but couldn't back down. Dan's reminder of the skeletons in the Prophet family closet rankled. "It's clear Wellborn's got brains and more guts than most. Takes a cocky crook to send this kind of message out for the world to read."

"Weeeell…," Dan drawled, "e-mail's not exactly out there for everyone to read."

"We got copies, didn't we?"

"Sure, but it took Zelda—computer geek extraordinaire—days to track them down. It's not as if Wellborn posted them to a bulletin board or announced them in a chat room."

J.Z. rolled his eyes. "Don't give me that Internet junk. If we can get the stuff, anyone can. Maryanne-the-library-anne is one arrogant cookie. It's time to wrap up months of paper trails, bank- and account-hopping fortunes that then disappear without a trace, if you'll remember. We did interviews, surveillance and pored over autopsy reports that coughed up nothing concrete. We even planted an agent at the nursing home in New Jersey. The pattern's the same at Peaceful Meadows—cushy retirement home, dead seniors, buckets of money. Wellborn's in the thick of it, ordering hits, and I'm going to bring her down."

Paperwork in hand, he stood. "Come on. We have to get a judge to sign the permits so we can bug her office and tap her home phone. Then we can head out to New Camden."

"I'll have Zelda come with us—you know, for the computer stuff. We'll probably get more from that than the other."

J.Z. grimaced. "That Internet stuff is garbage. This is going to take the usual: surveillance, taping, interviewing witnesses. Not that e-mail business."

"Still an Internet-phobe, huh?"

"And proud of it."

"Have it your way, but I want Zelda's magic fingers on our side. From the looks of it, we're going to need all the help and evidence we can get."

J.Z. crossed to his office door. "Do whatever you want. Bottom line, I'm going to nail Wellborn. Who'd figure a librarian as a mobster, putting out hits on old people in a nursing home? And for money... As if her breed—mobsters, not librarians—doesn't have enough of the bloody kind already. Organized crime's the worst form of scum, but this woman's taken their usual a notch lower."

Dan's arm lay heavy on J.Z.'s shoulders. "Don't let it get personal, okay? I know this is about the Verdis, but the past is past, and your old man's locked up. He's going nowhere."

J.Z. shrugged off his partner's arm and ground his teeth. "*That* was uncalled for. I wasn't thinking of him. Wellborn's the one who's out there. In New Camden. With a bunch of seniors who can't help themselves. Just like the ones who couldn't help themselves and wound up dead. You know it, I know it, the department knows it. Disgusting scam."

"Let's go see what we can do."

They strode down the hall and into a large room full of cluttered metal desks, the hub of the FBI's Philadelphia organized-crime unit. On their way to the elevator, an unmistakable pair of high heels clicked toward them.

"Special Agent Prophet. In my office. Now."

J.Z. groaned. Once upon a time, Eliza Roberts had voiced his name in sweet, loving tones. Not anymore. He'd never felt the truth of the old chestnut about women scorned until he broke up with her after she demanded more than he was ready to offer.

He shook his head and caught the glee in Dan's brown eyes as he entered his superior officer's cubicle. Eliza had clawed her way up to the position he turned down just before their breakup. The way he figured, she did it to spite him. But it didn't bother him. He had turned it down first. Pushing papers appealed to him as much as a case of Montezuma's revenge during a worldwide Imodium shortage.

When Eliza closed her office door, J.Z. gave up hope of a neutral encounter. She was out for bear. He might as well have Smokey, Yogi or Boo-boo written across his chest.

He couldn't wait to get away. "What's up?"

Eliza rounded her desk then sat in her expensive and very new leather chair. The Bureau didn't provide that kind of luxury. She must have bought it to make it look as if she'd wormed the perk from the higher-ups. J.Z. was glad he'd noticed her less appealing attributes and cleared out of their relationship before he wound up with heel marks down his back—and heart.

"Well?" he prodded.

She handed him three pieces of paper. "Another nursing home hit."

Great. As he scanned the pages, a familiar name jumped out. "Carlo Papparelli? As in Laundromat Jr.? Mat, the mob moneyman?"

"The one and only."

"No way. The Gemmellis had him gunned down a week ago. The Philly P.D. got Joey-O behind bars for it, too. Didn't they?"

"Read 'em and weep."

He did—read the papers, that is—he'd never waste a tear on a mobster. "I don't get it. I heard the family'd shipped the body back to the old country for burial."

"Read on."

He did. And frowned. "What is this? Papparelli was only fifty or so. What was he doing in an old folks' home? Oh, who cares? What really went down?"

"That, J.Z., is the most intriguing detail." She pointed to the paper in his left hand. "There's Maryanne Wellborn's e-mail ordering the hit. In your right hand, you have his death certificate—but not for a week ago. He died day before yesterday. And the cause of death is a stroke, *not* the bullets we know about. No autopsy. The family refused."

"This clinches it. She's as dirty as they come. She's mixed up with either the Gemmellis or the Verdis and took out the Laundromat. But how'd Mat slither into the nursing home when he was supposed to be dead? How can this librarian get away with all this? Does she have doctors on the take? Is the coroner in on the kill-the-rich-old-folks-for-their-bucks scam, too?"

Eliza smirked. "Don't you think finding those answers is a field agent's job? Your much-loved field job. You know…what you're paid to do."

Something in her voice made him ask, "Do you doubt I can do it?"

She waved. "Of course not—ordinarily."

"Ordinarily?" His stomach plummeted. "What do you mean?"

The back of J.Z.'s neck prickled at the gleam in her blue eyes. When she pursed her lips and tapped her polished nails on the desktop, his gut churned. When she stood and leaned toward him over her desk, his survival instinct compelled him to run.

But he couldn't.

"There is one tiny thing, J.Z.," his Supervising Special Agent said. "You know that problem you have with rules?"

Since he'd yet to meet the rule he wouldn't get around for the sake of justice, J.Z. shrugged. He always got the job done. Nothing else mattered.

"Well," Eliza went on, "we're going to do things my way this time. This case will be investigated by the book. You got that?"

"What's that supposed to mean?"

"That since you recently went off like a half-cocked shotgun—*again*—and this case involves your preferred target—the mob—I will yank your badge and gun if you pull one of your stunts on my watch."

"Come again?"

Her eyes narrowed and her lips thinned. "I mean it, J.Z. You're off the case if you cross the line. And if you're half as smart as you like to think, you'll believe me. I have the power now."

Blood roared in his ears. She'd known just how to hit him.

How could he ever have found her attractive? These days, he only saw the spite in her glare; he only heard the gloating in her voice.

"So you want a pound of my flesh."

She looked away. "Something like that."

He turned and opened the door, his rage barely leashed. "I'd be careful if I were you. Blue-eyed redheads don't look good with pea-green skin."

Her voice, low and nasty, made him pause. "One toe over the line, J.Z., and you're out. Got it?"

"Loud and clear, *boss*."

He made for the bank of elevators where Dan slouched against the wall, busy charming the new girl from the secretarial pool.

J.Z. asked, "The permits?"

Dan patted his jacketed chest. "All set." He then arched an eyebrow. "Your mood took a different turn. It's safe to say you didn't kiss and make up with the dragon lady."

J.Z. ignored the comment. "Need to pack?"

Dan pushed the elevator call button. "You know I keep a bag in the trunk of my car."

"Let's go." J.Z. followed Dan into the elevator. As the silver doors closed out the disappointed young woman, Dan faced J.Z.

J.Z. held up a hand; with the other, he punched the button. "Don't say it."

"I did warn you before you started dating her. You can be as charming and kind as you want, but you can't get involved with coworkers. It'll smack you in the face sooner or later. Keep business and pleasure far, far apart, I say."

Exhaustion hit all of a sudden. "Just drop it."

Dan stepped out of the elevator. "It's just that when you make a mistake, Prophet, you really make a doozy."

J.Z. followed the younger man to the street. Dan's words continued to mock him. The Prophet family was known for their mistakes. And as Dan had put it, whenever they made one, it was of the doozy variety. J.Z. was determined to stop making mistakes.

He would have to take extra care this time, if for nothing else than to avoid Eliza's payback. Because, without a doubt, he was going to nail Maryanne Wellborn for the murders.

Even if it killed him. And it might. If Eliza grounded him, the failure would do him in.

"Happy Birthday, dear Stanley…Happy Birthday to you!"

As the residents of New Camden's Peaceful Meadows Residence and Nursing Center sang to her father, the guilt Maryanne Wellborn had carried for months began to lessen. Maybe Dad had been right to insist on the move into the multilevel care facility.

"I want to be where the action is, Cookie," he'd argued, roguish grin in full bloom. "All the—" he winked "—dudes and babes are there, the ones old enough to speak my language, that is."

Maryanne had wanted to care for her only surviving parent at home—his home. But Stan Wellborn's obstinacy rivaled a mule's, and he'd insisted on putting the family home up for sale. It had sold distressingly soon.

She'd known how much attention he needed. An insulin-dependent diabetic and recent amputee, his blood-sugar levels needed constant monitoring, as did his blood pressure and diet. Not to mention, his penchant for merriment and trouble. He'd been lonely and bored at home while Maryanne worked. Boredom had led to nutty amusements, which then mushroomed into mischief. Mischief had invited risk along, and both had courted danger.

She couldn't discount the friendships he'd made since he moved in. He wasn't bored anymore.

"Hey, Stan!" called a bald-headed fellow of her father's vintage. "Whatcha waiting for? Blow out them candles already. We want some of that cake."

Murmured agreement broke out.

Her dad winked. "I'm making my wish, don't you know?"

"Ha! What do you need more wishes for?" This gent leaned on a cane. "The ladies here have made them all come true since you moved in."

The birthday boy grinned, closed his eyes and then blew out the eight candles—seven fat ones for the decades and a thin one for his additional year—on the large blue-blossomed cake. "You're just jealous of my irresistible charm, Hughie."

The residents howled at the banter, no one louder than Maryanne's dad. For a moment, she wished her mother were still alive to share his pleasure. Then she realized how silly her wish was. Mother would have frowned upon the whole scenario. Quiet and unassuming, Martha Wellborn would have been mortified by her impulsive, happy-go-lucky husband's lack of restraint.

Propriety had been Mother's underpinning, and she'd drilled its need into her daughter's psyche from the moment Maryanne could understand.

What she never did understand was how two such disparate souls had made a match in the first place, but she'd never questioned her parents' love for each other. Martha's death two years ago had plunged Stan into a depression deeper than Maryanne had expected in such an upbeat man.

The depression vanished once he moved into the home.

She shook off her dark thoughts, stepped closer to her father and kissed his high forehead. "I brought you something."

His hazel eyes twinkled. "What are you waiting for?"

With a nod to the nursing home's activities coordinator, Maryanne smiled back. "Let me help Sherri bring it in."

The two women lugged in a stack of cartons and set up the stereo. Tears gleamed in his eyes.

"Oh, Cookie. I oughta say you shouldn't have, but I'm tickled you did."

Blinking her own mistiness away, Maryanne said, "I knew how much you missed your music, and your old record player was useless. Enjoy this one, okay?"

"You know I will. C'mere." He patted his blanketed thigh. "Let your old man give you a hug and kiss."

Maryanne perched on her dad's lap and hugged him tight. She loved the old scamp, and she meant to keep him as healthy and happy as possible for as long as she could.

"I love you, Dad."

"Love you always, baby."

"Harrumph!" offered the bald man. "You're getting too mushy for a party. Let's try out that stereo."

With a final pat to his daughter's back, Stan gave a whoop. "Go for it, Charlie. We need music to make this a real party."

Under cover of the hubbub, Maryanne said, "You're really happy here, aren't you?"

"Yes, Cookie, I really am." He winked. "Now it's your turn to find some action. Of the young, male, falling-in-love kind, that is. It's not God's plan for a beautiful young woman to spend her life buried in a library or visiting a bunch of geezers."

"You're not a geezer, and I love books."

"You need a…a—Oh, yeah! A *chunk* to show you what's what, girl."

Maryanne rose to hide her blush and stifle a nervous giggle. "I'm too busy, and I'd rather spend my free time with you."

Stan shook his finger and grinned. "Mark my words, girl. When that lovebug bites, you're gonna fall hard."

"Hey, I use bug spray by the gallon. It's my favorite fragrance. But I'd better go help Sherri—look at that mob of cake-starved partiers around her."

While she doled out cake, Maryanne watched her father from the vantage point of the activities hall stage. The stack of small gifts from his friends thrilled him. Then, after they'd finished eating, with his favorite Glenn Miller, Guy Lombardo and Jimmy Dorsey tunes on the new stereo, he drew each ambulatory lady near and twirled her around his wheelchair.

"I told you not to worry," Sherri Armstrong told Maryanne as she tied off another bag of trash. "He practically begged you to move him here."

"I know. But it was hard."

"He's busy, and he's happy. And he wants you to build a life for yourself. That's your next assignment, you understand?"

"Not you, too. First Dad, now you."

Sherri, happily married mother of two, nodded. "We know what we're talking about."

"We'll see." Maryanne gathered the empty punch bowl and headed for the kitchen. "Right now, we have a mess to clean."

No sooner did she enter the vast, equipment-filled white room, than Dean Ross, Peaceful Meadows' director, called her name. Her middle knotted. The busy man rarely found time to discuss the library cart she brought twice a week to the home. She doubted he'd come for the birthday party.

"How are you, Dean?"

He grimaced. "Same as always. You're going to have to cancel Audrey White's library privileges."

"Oh, no. I missed her at Dad's party and meant to stop by her room to see how she liked the last historical novel I suggested."

"The ambulance just took her to the hospital. She slipped into a coma a little while ago, and she won't be back."

"Are you sure?"

"As sure as I can be. You saw how weak she was when you brought her books."

"You're right. She couldn't even sit up when I came…was it day before yesterday? The day before, maybe. Rosie, Audrey's nurse, was getting the other bed in the room ready for a new patient. I helped her…I had to push the meds stand out of the way to get to Audrey's side of the room. And Audrey mentioned she was headed to another floor."

"She was. Intensive care. And the new patient did no better."

Maryanne winced. "Audrey didn't say a thing. Now… can't they do anything more?"

"Cancer at that stage is merciless. Morphine for the pain is the best we have. Nature helps and lets the patient enter a coma toward the end, but I'm afraid Audrey—"

"I understand," Maryanne said around the lump in her throat. "I'll take care of her library card."

"She's not the only one."

She bit her lip. "Who else?"

"I don't think you had a chance to meet him. Mr. Papparelli, the patient who moved into Audrey's old room. He passed on, too."

"You're right. I never did meet him." His death wouldn't hit her as hard as Audrey's decline. "I set up his privileges as soon as I got word he was coming—I never knew he was the one moving into the bed I helped make. Then day before yesterday Marlene in Admissions called to say he'd gone into cardiac arrest and wouldn't need books. He wasn't dead yet, but close. I terminated him right away."

Dean sighed. "It's never easy, you know."

Maryanne nodded and again tried to swallow the knot in her throat. "I know, and I'd better say good-night to Dad. I have to be at work early tomorrow."

She fought more tears—these hot and painful by comparison to her earlier tender ones—on her way back to the activities hall. As usual, a bevy of aged belles surrounded her father's wheelchair, smiling and chatting with the unrepentant flirt. Maryanne sighed in relief. It was foolish to need the reassurance just because a sweet woman she had befriended was near the end. And yet, she did.

She donned a bright smile and made her way through

his admirers. "I'm going home now, you party animal. Some of us have to work."

"You work too much," he countered. "But I won't keep you. You need your rest. Thanks for everything, Cookie. Just don't worry about me. I'm in my element."

Feminine laughter tittered around them. Maryanne swooped down for her good-night hug and kiss. Then, before she broke down and cried for real, she rushed from the building and into her car.

She was going to miss Audrey. Just as she missed Mary Margaret Muldoon and her love of mysteries, Helmut Rheinemann's armchair travels and Toby Matthias's penchant for art books. She loved to serve the nursing home residents. She felt called to bring the joy of books into their often lonely and frequently pain-filled days. If only she could learn the art of detachment. Each loss broke her heart.

Tomorrow she would order Audrey's termination. Then she would work surrounded by sadness. And she counted on the Lord to see her through the day she had to terminate her own dad.

Maryanne wiped her eyes with a tissue and then typed the curt e-mail first thing the next day. Terminate Audrey White. She expected a visit once Sandy Rodriguez, the card privilege clerk, downloaded that morning. The young man had learned that each message was written with a fresh batch of tears.

She clicked the Send icon and received the message sent confirmation. Before she signed off, however, the screen went blank. "Rats."

The system was down. Again. The glitch, no matter

how short-lived, would only make what had started out as a crummy day even worse. Since the county library system joined the information superhighway a couple of years earlier, it had become close to impossible to operate without the computers.

She set her sad thoughts aside and reached across the desk for her correspondence folder. She might as well wade through it while the equipment stayed down. Who knew how long it would take to get things up and humming again.

A short while later her door swung inward and two men in jeans, white shirts and navy ties, brass nameplates over their pocket, stepped in.

"Hi," said the shorter of the two, his brown eyes as warm as his smile. "We're from Uni-Comp. I'm Dan Maddox, and this—" he glared at his companion "—is J.Z. Prophet. We're here to fix the system and check the machines."

Surprised by that odd look, Maryanne took note of the names on the plates and stood. "Be my guests. I can't do a thing until you do yours."

Dan Maddox went right to her desk, but the other man, J.Z. Prophet, stayed in the doorway, his gray eyes fixed on her.

"Maryanne Wellborn?" he asked in a deep voice.

"Yes, and if you'll excuse me, I'll leave you to your work."

Maryanne stepped out to the hall. What an intense man. His eyes...so cold. She shivered. With a deep breath, she regained her composure.

But from the other side of the not-quite-closed door, she heard Maddox say, "I'm waiting for that modem card."

J.Z. muttered a response she didn't quite catch.

Maryanne's curiosity got the better of her and she pressed up against the door frame. Holding her breath, she peered through the crack into her office.

Long seconds crawled by, minutes...centuries. No one moved.

Maddox turned to his partner, who still stood, statue-like, by the equipment case. "Come on, J.Z. Before the librarian gets back."

Gray eyes speared to the door. Maryanne froze under the impact of that icy stare. She suddenly wanted to run, take cover.

J.Z. Prophet, a complete stranger, really, *really* didn't like her.

Why?

TWO

"Whatever you say, Trudy Talbot." Maryanne tucked her work-loosened brown-and-white gingham blouse into the waistband of her dirndl skirt. "But you should have seen the look in his eyes. So tell me. What would make a computer geek look so…so scary? So disgusted? So angry?"

The classy, prematurely gray director of the Children's Collection shrugged. "Beats me. Maybe his wife served him eggs for breakfast when he wanted Frootie Tooties instead. Or maybe his cat presented him with a dead mouse…just before he swallowed the eggs. The adult male is beyond my comprehension. That's why I stick to those under the age of twelve."

"Last time I checked, Ron Talbot was a quite adult thirty-five."

Trudy slicked on a coat of soft plum lip gloss and dropped the tube into her tailored black leather purse. "That doesn't mean my husband's any easier to understand than others of his kind."

Maryanne tucked her lip balm in the side pocket of her tote. "You don't fool me. You two have been married thirteen years, you share a mortgage, car and minivan, a dog, four cats and two kids. You must have figured him out at least a little."

"Three."

"Three? Three what?"

Trudy's fair skin bloomed a delicate rose. "Three kids."

"Huh?" Maryanne glanced at her friend's flat middle. "Oh! Really?"

Trudy's smile lit up the dingy bathroom in the basement of the New Camden Public Library. "Mm-hmm."

The two women hugged, then Maryanne held her friend at arm's length. "That's wonderful! And you look wonderful, too. When are you due?"

"Sometime in mid-November."

"A Thanksgiving baby—how perfect."

"It is a perfect time to give thanks for all my blessings." Trudy eyed Maryanne. "So much so that you ought to give it a try. Marriage and motherhood, that is."

"Are you crazy? You just finished telling me men are impossible to understand, and now you want me to hook up with one of them?"

"I said they're impossible to understand, not impossible to love and live with." Trudy hitched the strap of her purse onto her shoulder. "Come on. I have to get back. The Thursday story-hour kids are about to get here, and we don't want them on the loose."

"And I have to go see what those guys got done on my computer."

The two women went upstairs to the library's main level. Trudy gave Maryanne a sideways glance. "You know Uni-Comp's people are always great. You never know what's going on in people's lives. Maybe that one guy had a fight with his wife."

"Maybe…but he still gave me the creeps."

"How so?"

Cold gray eyes popped into Maryanne's mind. So did the flat slash of lips, the rigid line of shoulder, the direct and deliberate gait. "He made me feel like the deer in a hunter's crosshairs."

"That makes no sense. You don't know him, do you?"

"Trust me. I'd remember if I'd seen him before."

In the warm oak-paneled-and-floored lobby, Trudy placed gentle hands on Maryanne's shoulders and met her gaze. "Now don't get mad at me, okay?"

Maryanne went to speak, but Trudy shook her head.

"Listen. *Please.* Do you think maybe you imagined the guy's anger because your emotions were already in a tangle over your friend at the nursing home?"

Maryanne's urge to deny the possibility felt right, but because Trudy was so perceptive, she gave her earlier state of mind careful consideration. She thought back to when she first saw J.Z. Prophet, to that last look in his eyes, to the way he'd made her feel.

"There's always that chance," she said, "but I don't think so. I'd prayed through my tears by the time those two showed up. I'd come to peace by then, and was even bored since there's so little I can do while the system's down."

Trudy looked skeptical, but then, she hadn't seen the man. Maryanne hugged her massive tote bag and added, "I can't begin to imagine why someone would look at me with so much…oh, I don't know. I can't really describe what that Prophet guy gave off."

Another frown lined Trudy's brow. "This isn't good. Don't you think someone should do something about it? Someone official, that is."

"What do you want them to do? And who would you have me tell?"

"Maybe you should speak with Mr. Dougherty."

"Why? I don't think the library system's director knows much about Uni-Comp or its employees. The IT department handles that service contract."

"Well, then, talk to Morty. He runs IT."

"What do you want me to say? That a tech from Uni-Comp gave me a weird look? Sure, and then he can call the guys in the white suits to come get me."

Trudy bit her lower lip. "You're probably right. All you have is a funny feeling, and that's nothing to go on. Just be careful. Don't let the guy catch you alone in your office or anything, okay?"

"That won't happen. Not even if I have to spend the rest of the day in the bathroom downstairs. If worse comes to worst, I'll grab what little paperwork I have left and do just that."

"That's nuts. You don't have to go to extremes, you know. You can always head over to the staff lounge or hang out with me and my munchkins."

"Oh, right. I'll get a whole lot of work done then."

"Make up your mind, will you? You said you were bored earlier and didn't have much to do while the system was down. I can always use a hand with the incoming zoo inmates."

"Ha! Your Mark is in that crowd, isn't he?"

When Trudy blushed, Maryanne went on. "Figures. You just want me to watch your son so that you can be the serious librarian."

Trudy raised her hands in surrender. "Okay. You outed me. But do you blame me?"

"Who can forget his first story hour? You reminded me of *Make Way For Ducklings*. The seventeen of them looked awfully cute following you around and calling you Mrs. Mommy."

They chuckled, but then Maryanne squared her shoulders and smoothed a hand over the waist of her shin-length beige skirt. "I really do have to get back to my office—if for no other reason than to see if the Uni-Comps finished their shtick, and my computer's up again."

"I still think your imagination ran away with you, but please be careful. You never know what kind of kooks are on the loose."

"If you get a chance, keep me in your prayers."

"You know I'll do that."

Maryanne approached her glorified cubicle at the rear of the Research Department with apprehension. Were the two men still there?

At her office door, she paused and studied her name in gold letters on the black plaque. If that Prophet man wanted to hurt her he not only knew where she worked, but he also knew her name. With so many search sites on the Web, he'd have her address in no time. Then again, maybe he and his wife had argued earlier in the day. But Maryanne couldn't imagine a woman who'd put up with him.

"Oh, Lord, help me, please," she prayed then turned the knob.

The room was empty. A couple of pages covered with computer test gobbledygook in her trash can gave the only testimony of the men's earlier presence. Maryanne experienced a momentary letdown.

Weird, since she hadn't wanted to face his—*was* it anger?—again.

To be honest, she had to admit that the puzzling J.Z.

Prophet had sparked her interest—in a crazy, scary sort of way. He'd kicked up her curiosity, and he'd even revved something inside her. Excitement? Maybe. Inquisitiveness? Definitely.

Maryanne sat behind her desk and braced her forehead on the heels of her hands. "Argh!"

She had to be partway to certifiable. No sane woman would be interested in some stranger who'd looked at her funny. A sane woman wouldn't try to figure out why he'd done it.

It didn't make sense—*she* didn't make sense.

So was Trudy right? Had she imagined J.Z.'s instant dislike?

Now that the Uni-Comp men had left and she was alone, Maryanne began to question her earlier take on the incident. A stranger would have no reason for anger, not toward her.

Oh, well. Trudy probably was right. It wouldn't be the first time Maryanne let her imagination run wild.

After all, J.Z. Prophet was an attractive man, of the rugged, dark and brooding sort. He would catch her eye, no matter what—any woman's at that. But of course he wasn't the kind of man she'd want to get to know. He was not her type at all. Still, no seeing woman would call him nondescript.

Steel-colored eyes above angular cheekbones pierced deep. And the dark hair that tumbled over his forehead revealed a lack of self-absorption. Although J.Z. Prophet's hair shone with health and cleanliness, as did his pristine white shirt and faded jeans, he wasn't the blow-dried, manicured, crease-pressed new-jean type, a trend she found disconcerting.

If he hadn't fixed those stormy eyes on her, she might have been attracted to him.

"Good grief, Maryanne," she muttered as her computer booted up. "There you go again. No sooner do you decide the guy couldn't possibly have given you an angry look, than you make a U-turn and think the opposite one more time."

She sighed. It was time to get back to work. Time to put the enigmatic J.Z. Prophet out of her mind.

The next two hours proved productive. At around three o'clock, when Maryanne felt the urge for her usual cup of tea, she stood, walked around her desk and crossed the room.

At the doorway, she stopped.

A weird feeling crept up her back—hair-raising was the only way to describe it. Someone was watching her.

Maryanne looked up and down the hall, but saw no one, found nothing unusual. Then the door across the hall came to a complete close with a soft, automatic *swish*.

She stared. The men's room. *Had* someone been watching her?

Had that someone—the one she was sure had watched her—just gone in there?

Had J.Z. Prophet spooked her so much that she saw boogeymen all around? Had some innocent guy done nothing more than walk by her office door to use the restroom instead? And she'd let herself freak out.

Or had *he* been watching *her?*

J.Z.'s face materialized in her mind. Why? Why would he want to watch her?

Maryanne's knees gave. She fell back against her office door. She began to shiver, but refused to give in to fear. She closed her eyes and turned to God.

Why, why, *why* was she so shaken?

"Your strength is sufficient for me," she prayed. Over and over again, she whispered the words until the tremors subsided.

But no matter how long she prayed, and no matter how hard she worked, Maryanne failed to erase the memory of J.Z.'s stare.

Trudy was right about at least one thing. Should Maryanne ever see him again, she wouldn't hesitate to call the cops. Although she preferred to avoid clichés, she felt she was living one right then.

If looks could kill....

The rest of the afternoon crawled by in a blur of stress. By the time five o'clock rolled around, Maryanne's shoulders had frozen rigid and her temples pounded a vicious beat. She'd accomplished precious little in that time, since no matter how hard she tried, the image of J.Z. Prophet slammed into her thoughts every few minutes.

She couldn't concentrate on anything she read, and hadn't been able to type up her notes for the report due next Tuesday. Her fingers shook like leaves in a gale. Even simple filing became a challenge of inordinate proportion.

Ibuprofen did nothing to alleviate her headache—she doubted anything would until the memory of J.Z. Prophet's intensity melted away on its own. She hoped she never had to set eyes on him again.

In the library parking lot, she waved goodbye to Trudy and Sarah Myers, who worked with the rare collections. Then, because she'd fed Shakespeare the last of his food and the kitty litter was also running low, she drove straight to the grocery store. The ride served to soothe her raw nerves. Her favorite radio station had on a Darlene Zschech special. Maryanne liked the Aussie's contemporary style of worship music.

At the store, she grabbed feline supplies, romaine lettuce, fresh chicken breasts and an Idaho potato the size of the state where it grew. Dinner would be a simple matter of shredding greens and nuking stuff—about all she could face today.

At the register, Joe Moore, a retiree who augmented his social security with part-time cashier duty, smiled when he saw her. "How's old Stan doing these days?"

Maryanne arched an eyebrow. "Old? Dad's two years younger than you."

The scanner beeped as Joe ran her purchases before the screen. "Age is just a matter of the mind, honey bun."

"Oh, and Dad's matured beyond his mischievous adolescent mental age in the last twenty-four hours?"

"A man can always hope."

They shared a good-natured chuckle, and the pounding in Maryanne's head began to ease.

"How's Amelia?" she asked.

"Sore and crotchety, but the doc says the hip replacement went even better than he'd expected—thank the Lord."

"You two have been married how long?"

Joe puffed out his chest. "Fifty-three years and still going strong, honey bun. You oughta try it, you know."

Maryanne grabbed the bag of groceries and made for the door. "Don't you get started. It's bad enough with Dad and Trudy and a couple of others badgering me right and left. You know how I feel. If God's got a man for me, well then, it's up to Him to find me the guy."

"And how're you going to see this gift from heaven if

all you do is hide behind books at the library or hang out with the oldsters at the retirement home?"

"I'm not hiding," Maryanne said, her chin tipped a hair higher. "I'm serving where the Lord's planted me. I'm sure He'll lead me where He wants me if He wants me to go elsewhere."

"Whoa, girl! That's a mouthful there." Joe shook his head and scanned his next customer's laundry detergent. "Strikes me you're a mite defensive on the subject. I suggest you pray a little on it, and see if I'm not right."

Maryanne sighed. As if she didn't already pray her way through each and every day. "I'll do that, Joe. Give my love to Amelia, will you?"

"Of course, honey bun. And you tell that crazy daddy of yours to stay out of trouble at that country club place where he lives nowadays."

"I will. Why don't you stop by and see him sometime soon? He'll get a kick out of it."

With a nod and a wink, Joe turned his full attention to the young mother of three little girls under the age of six. Maryanne left the store, and then popped open her Escort's trunk. She balanced the groceries against the bag of sand she always stored there for just in case. When she shut the trunk, a car crawled down the row behind her.

Her neck prickled as it had earlier that day.

She spun, but saw nothing other than the mom and her three girls walk away from the store's automatic door—and the unremarkable gray car braked ten cars down beyond her. Although she couldn't make out the driver's facial features, something about him slammed fear right back into her gut.

She felt just as she had when J.Z. Prophet had glared at her.

A chill ran through her and she shivered. If the stormy computer tech was at the wheel, then she wanted to get as far from him as fast as she could. And if he wasn't, then she also wanted to leave that parking lot just as fast. Just because.

Frustrated by her shaky hand's failure to get the button on her automatic keychain to work, Maryanne took a deep breath, clenched her fist around the plastic rectangle, and then prayed a blunt "Help!"

She unfurled her fingers and with deliberation, aimed the gadget straight at the lock. It popped. She slid behind the wheel, flicked the locks back on, and then started the car. As she pulled out, she kept the gray car in sight out the corner of her eye. She sighed in relief when it took the spot she'd vacated.

The adrenaline drain left her even shakier than before, and she had no idea how she drove home without hitting anything on the way. She had to get her imagination under much better control. She couldn't freak out at even the tiniest thing. That driver had just wanted her parking space.

Later that evening, she watched her favorite home-decorating show before she decided an early bedtime would work wonders on her frazzled nerves. Tomorrow would be a better day—it had to be.

She hoped.

And Friday was better. By noon, she'd settled back into her normal routine. With a clear head, she ate a sandwich for lunch at her desk, determined to make up for yesterday's lack of productivity. By five, she'd caught up and only had the report to do. She'd finish it tomorrow afternoon on her home computer.

Trudy stuck her head in the office.

"Come on in," Maryanne said.

"No, I'm on my way home. Are you still coming tonight?"

Maryanne logged out of her word processing program and shut down her machine. "It's my turn with the youth group's sixth graders this month. I wouldn't miss the scavenger hunt for the world. I had a blast when I helped out last year."

"Good. David's been looking forward to special attention from his honorary aunt."

She slung the sturdy straps of her large tote bag over one shoulder, flicked off the lights and closed the office door. "He'd better rethink that plan. I'm not about to show your darling son any favoritism. I'm just there to count noses and make sure no one gets left behind in a store at the mall."

"That's what I told him," Trudy said with a chuckle. "Somehow, though, I think you're going to have to work hard to avoid his charm. That boy's going places…someday."

Maryanne nodded. "It's a good thing you and Ron have channeled that energy and appeal in positive directions. Otherwise, who knows where he'd end up?"

"Thanks. Your opinion means a great deal. And you're right. David is a handful. It's hard to walk that fine line between guiding and stifling a child."

"You and Ron are terrific parents, Trudy. You teach by example, and I think that's the best thing for kids." Maryanne thought back on her earlier years. "Mother and Dad were great, even though they had such different personalities."

"I miss your mom, you know?"

"How could I not? You and I grew up in each other's homes. Besides, Mother pretty much liked you better than she liked me."

Trudy pushed on the massive, revolving library door. "You know that's not true—even though you did give her some pretty good headaches now and then."

On the sidewalk, Maryanne paused and sighed. "It's that goofy side of me, the Dad part, that always got me in trouble. But Mother did have a point. When I finally surrendered and did things her way, my life went much smoother. As it has ever since."

Trudy studied Maryanne. "Maybe it's been easier, but I wonder if it hasn't been a lot more boring, too."

She jolted as if Trudy had pricked her with a pin. "My life's not boring. Not at all. It's full and rich and satisfying. I have a great job—a career. And I love my church family. My calendar's full of wonderful activities, and I even have a fabulous cat. I love my life just the way it is."

Trudy resumed the walk to the parking lot. "When's the last time you did something on the spur of the moment? Something unexpected and fun?"

Maryanne scoffed. "That's what I mean. Mother taught me well. Dad's nuttiness creates chaos, and I don't want that in my life. Well thought-out choices and prudent decisions up front make much more sense than to struggle to fix things after you've made a mess of them."

Trudy shook her head and her silver bob swung in a smooth arc. "That's boring."

"No way. I don't want to climb a rock face, travel to strange places where I'll wind up with malaria or put myself in situations where I might meet people who could do me harm. Even you warned me against the computer clown yesterday."

Trudy reached the driver's side of her cherry-red

Sunbird parked alongside Maryanne's tan Escort. She looked over the roof and said, "Read my lips: booooooor-ing!"

As she unlocked her car, Maryanne gave her friend one last disgusted look. "Nope. Not at all. Just safe, secure, familiar and comfortable. See you later at church."

She started the ignition and shook her head. She'd had her fill of spur-of-the-moment living, thanks to Dad. What kind of woman would want a steady diet of madness?

J.Z. snapped his cell phone shut. "Joey-O's not talking."

Dan looked up from the file folder he'd just picked up. "Did you think he would?"

"His kind usually does—to point the finger at someone else, of course. Especially if it means they can save their sorry skin."

"Is he denying that he killed Mat? Or has he just zipped his lip?"

"David says no one can get a word out of him."

Dan's gaze turned thoughtful. "Latham's good at getting perps to talk. So if Joey's not talking, then he's more scared of what might come his way from the outside than by staying in for…oh, say a hundred years or so."

"I want to know how Joey got word to Wellborn so she could finish the job. He's been in the slammer since minutes after he emptied his gun into the Laundromat."

"I'm telling you, you're barking up the wrong tree with the librarian, J.Z. There's nothing, *nothing* here—" Dan waved the papers from the file "—that even hints at her involvement. Even her bank records are clean—you've read it in black-and-white, same as I have. Look at them again."

Dan held the pages out to J.Z., but J.Z. did know what they said…and didn't say. He shook his head.

His partner wasn't ready to quit. "Not a dollar goes into her account that doesn't come from her paycheck, J.Z. So what would she have to gain? Why would she kill for the mob? What's her motive?"

"Remember the e-mails. They're pretty clear. *Terminate Carlo Papparelli.*" J.Z. ran a hand through his hair. He felt the answers he needed were just on the other side of his grasp. "She's got to keep her stash somewhere. Maybe Mat did the laundering for her dollars, and didn't want to cough them back up. We just have to dig deeper than we have."

"It doesn't fit," Dan argued. "She's clean if you ignore those e-mails. So where's the connection? A librarian doesn't just hook up with the mob out of the blue."

J.Z. shrugged. "That retirement home's an awfully cushy place for a librarian's salary to afford. Maybe she saw the chance to get the dough that'd keep her dad there."

"Sure, but how would she turn to the mob?"

"That's what you and I are going to find out."

Dan stared straight at J.Z. A wriggle of discomfort wound through him. "I think there's nothing for us to find. And there's a lot of valuable time to waste, time we can't afford to waste. Your personal bias against the mob in general and the Verdis in particular might just cost us six long months' worth of work."

The image of his father's stony face at the defendant's table came back to haunt J.Z. "The good ones always look that clean. Only a fool will let himself get caught up in their smokescreen. I fell for my father's lies when I was too young to know better. I won't do it again."

"Just make sure you don't lose yourself in a fun-house

mirror and leave reality behind. Don't miss the obvious for looking so hard through the filter of your past."

J.Z. gritted his teeth. He knew what was what.

Maryanne Wellborn's days as a free woman were numbered.

She was going down.

Maryanne gasped. Her heart began to pound and her stomach twisted.

That same, creepy someone's-looking-at-me feeling hit her again. She looked around, and she went cold.

A familiar male figure was walking in the direction opposite from where she stood in the mall's food court. Something about the dark hair, the set of wide shoulders, the taut fluid walk…

Could it be?

But she could only see the man from the back. She couldn't be sure it was—or wasn't—J.Z. Prophet.

Coincidence?

She doubted it. Mother always said she only believed in God-incidence. But if that was the case, then what did God have to do with the computer tech? His anger wasn't the kind of emotion the Lord encouraged. It certainly didn't dispose her to approach the man. Besides, she couldn't see herself as a missionary to crazy computer techs.

She'd thought herself safe by going straight to church, joining in the potluck supper then taking her charges on their scavenger hunt. She'd sat at a table in the food court and made sure the teams understood they had to check in with her every thirty minutes—church rules.

The kids were great. And she enjoyed the time their

pursuit gave her to work on her needlepoint project. At least, she had until a couple of seconds ago.

That itchy discomfort that seemed to strike so often since she'd met J.Z. Prophet had crept up the back of her neck again. When she turned in the direction of the lingerie store across the way, she'd spotted the dark-haired man propped against a pillar. But because his face had been hidden by shadows, she couldn't be sure it was J.Z.

If it was him, what could he possibly want?

She didn't know, but she did know one thing: she'd never felt like a hunted animal until he showed up at her work. She crammed her needlework into the tapestry sewing bag, grabbed that bag together with her tote bag and then slung the handles of both over her shoulder. A quick glance at her watch told her the kids should be back any moment now.

She'd have to get them out of the mall before that madman decided to hurt her, much less them.

"There you are," Trudy said at her side.

Maryanne yelped. "Don't you ever skulk up like that again! You just cost me ten years of my life."

Her friend gaped. "What is wrong with you? I've never heard you speak like that before."

Maryanne's tremors grew so great that she collapsed back into her chair. The bags slid down her arm and fell to the floor.

"I think he's here," she whispered.

"Who's here?"

She saw concern in Trudy's eyes. "The Uni-Comp tech with the icy-cold eyes—that J.Z. Prophet guy."

"You really think so?"

Maryanne nodded, unable to say more.

"Where did you see him? Did you call security? What are you going to do?"

"I don't know what I'm going to do. I can't even think straight. And of course I didn't get a chance to call security. I just saw him a moment ago, right before you came up."

"Show me. Where is he?"

With her eyes shut tight, Maryanne pointed in the direction of the lingerie store, reluctant to again feel J.Z. Prophet's anger. But when Trudy didn't say a thing, Maryanne looked up at her friend.

With worried brown eyes, Trudy looked from the lingerie store to Maryanne and back again. "Are you sure you're okay?" she asked. "I've never known you to be so paranoid."

"Aside from that guy scaring me half out of my wits, of course, I'm fine."

Trudy kept silent for long moments. Maryanne looked up at her friend. A frown on her forehead, Trudy said, "There's no one there."

Maryanne stood, used the table for support and slowly turned to look across the expanse. As Trudy had said, no one stood by the window draped in frivolous, pastel-lace frills; no one leaned in that distinctive way against the pillar at its side; no one glared at her right then.

"He's gone," she said, not reassured. "For now."

"What do you mean?"

Maryanne met her friend's worried gaze. "Everywhere I go, I feel someone watching me. I can't shake the feeling. And somehow, I'm sure I'm going to see him again. I just don't know when or where. Or why."

THREE

"You're nuts," Dan told J.Z.

"Why? Because I know she's pulling a fast one?"

"No. Because, man, you've taken a long walk down the diving board and gone off the deep end this time. You've let something personal get in the way of your work. Will you just look at her? I doubt she's ever even killed a fly."

J.Z. looked at Maryanne Wellborn as she smiled at and hugged other worshippers on her way down the church steps.

"That," he said to his partner, "is what she wants us to believe. I'll admit she's good—very good."

When J.Z. had first seen the librarian, she'd worn a boring baggy tan skirt and brown-and-white checked shirt. The next time, she'd sported garments in a gloomy shade of gray. Today, for Sunday School and the worship service, she had on a dingy-taupe dress that hung to about an inch above her ankles. A narrow brown belt caught the shapeless thing at her waist.

"Even if you can't," he added, "I can see right through her."

Dan tapped J.Z.'s shoulder with a fist. "Then you must have X-ray vision. I don't think there's anything here. I've a feeling she's just what she looks like, a serious librarian with more on her mind than the latest fashions."

After a pause, Dan went on. "Don't take it wrong, okay? I'm worried about you. You're not yourself. I mean, you almost blew it at the library, and then at the mall. All that after you promised you'd be careful."

J.Z. went to argue, but Dan held up a hand.

"She's not dumb, you know. You shouldn't have talked Zelda into letting you take her place. You have to keep a professional distance."

"You forget I'm the senior agent here."

"But you're acting like a rookie with a bone to pick. Unless you want to blow a case we've worked for months, you'd better get a hold of yourself."

"So what do you have to say about the lab findings? Those were her fingerprints on Laundromat's IV-fluids stand. They match the ones we lifted from her desk."

Dan shrugged. "She's in and out of that nursing home with her library cart and to visit her father all the time. Who knows when she might have touched the thing? For an innocent reason, I mean."

J.Z. snorted. "They have sick people there, Dan. All that equipment is cleaned and disinfected and sanitized—all the time. It'd be pretty hard for fingerprints to survive that kind of scouring."

"Hey, there's always a first time for everything."

So as not to continue the argument, J.Z. ground his teeth. He followed Maryanne's progress toward her plain little Ford, and took note of how she patted the tight bun at the back of her neck.

He didn't buy the story she was selling. No woman would choose to hide her hair like that without a reason.

Many years ago, his father had mastered the art of the innocuous appearance. The plain black suits, black ties, white shirts and black shoes he'd worn were the male equivalent of Maryanne's dowdy wardrobe. Her bun was the perfect counterpart to Obadiah's unremarkable barbershop cut.

He had to give the devil his, or in this case her, due— Maryanne Wellborn had her cover down pat, just like his father had. But J.Z. wasn't about to let the illusion of respectability get in the way of his mission. He hadn't gone over the edge; he just knew the difference between a trick and reality.

Everywhere the librarian went he'd be sure to follow. He would keep the pressure on her until she cracked. Sooner or later, she'd talk. And then he'd bust her, Olive Oyl disguise notwithstanding.

Maryanne ran into her father's suite, out of breath. "I'm so sorry I'm late. The Sunday School Council meeting after the service dragged on forever."

"Gimme a hug," Stan said. "And in about an hour I'll be the one griping about endless meetings. The Residents' Senate has an agenda fatter than the Federal budget for today's meeting."

"Oh." She plopped onto his bed. "Well, then, I guess I'd better be going. I'll come back later…maybe after dinner."

Stan caught her fingers. "Don't you dare leave me to the mercy of that bunch of geezers."

"Dad! How can you call them something so ugly? Besides, you're one of them, aren't you?"

"Yup. And that's why I can call us anything I please. We're geezers, all right. Just you come and listen to us. I know you'll agree before the pecking party's over."

Since her father rarely asked of anything, Maryanne

didn't have the heart to turn him down. "Okay. I'll stay. But only if you promise I won't fall asleep during this senate thing."

Stan winked and pushed the forward button on his wheelchair. "I can promise you fireworks, Cookie. Besides, I still have some of my birthday cake in the fridge. Come back here with me after the shoot-out's over, and we can make a serious dent in it."

Maryanne frowned. "How's your blood sugar?"

"Bah!" Stan waved and rolled ahead. "I'm sick and tired of all that poking and bleeding. Can't a man have himself a piece of cake without it turning into a big deal?"

"Oh, Daddy." She hated the part of party pooper. "I wish I could tell you it's no big deal, but you're in that wheelchair because of the diabetes. The amputation was no joke, and we have to take care of your heart."

Irritation flared in Stan Wellborn's blue eyes, but he stifled it almost as soon as she saw it. "Don't mind me, Cookie. I just get testy when I can't have my way. I know the Lord's blessed me with a bunch more days to hang around this side of life, and I can't dishonor His gift by misbehaving. But I won't deny I'd sure like to every once in a while."

Before she could respond, he opened the apartment door, and waited for her to join him. He locked up, then propelled his wheelchair toward the elevator at the end of the long interior balcony that served as a hall.

They made their way down in silence, consumed by private thoughts. Once the elevator pinged at the mezzanine level, they waited for the doors to open. Maryanne followed her father to the activities hall. His friends greeted her with affection, a fondness she returned. Soon, however, petite Mitzi Steinbrom tottered on her stiletto heels to the podium.

"Yikes!" Maryanne leaned closer to Stan. "Has Mrs. Steinbrom ever fallen from those spikes?"

"Alls I know is that she says they give her a regal bearing. I guess if you translate from Mitzish to English, that means she feels a need to make up for her lack of height."

Maryanne glanced forward again, but the plucky widow had disappeared. "Where—"

"Watch," her father answered. "She had maintenance build her a set of steps. Otherwise, we'd never see her over that dumb stand she insists she needs to run these goofy gatherings. She likes to follow Roberts' Rules, but no one else here's willing to waste time on those kinds of things."

Sure enough, the tangerine curls popped up over the lectern and Mrs. Steinbrom tapped the microphone. The woodpecker beat self-destructed into a wicked screech. From the control room at the back of the hall, a man hollered, "Sorry about that."

Mrs. Steinbrom smiled magnanimously. "We're used to it, Reggie. We'll wait until you've fixed it."

"Hey, Mitzi!" A bald gentleman waved a cane from the far right bank of chairs. "We heard Reggie, so it's fixed. Get on with your dog-and-pony show. I want to catch my before-dinner nap."

An eleven-type fold appeared between Mitzi's penciled-in brown brows. She smiled, clearly comfortable with the noblesse oblige she felt the position of chairwoman required.

"Very well, Roger. We'll bring this meeting to order."

"Ah…give it a rest, will ya, Mitz?" another man called out, this one seated near the back door and garbed in a blue polo and pants. "Just get on with the stuff you wanna talk about and forget all this other junk. We're all too old to sit around and wait."

Mitzi pursed her orange-coated lips. "It's best if we do things properly, Charlie. Have some patience."

"It's best," Maryanne's father offered, "if we're efficient, Mitzi, so why don't you start with number one?"

The chairwoman's cheeks blazed red. "Fine," she said in a curt voice. "What do we think about cats?"

"Litterbox stink!" a lady Maryanne didn't know yelped.

That one's neighbor to the left added, "They yowl."

"Are you going to pick up my garbage when they go dig for stuff?" the impatient Charlie asked, his jaw in a pugnacious jut.

Someone up front offered, "I'm allergic…."

"Those claws…they scratch everything," came from the right.

A frail wisp of a woman stood with difficulty, aided by her aluminum walker. "They're a great comfort when one's all alone."

The room silenced at the dignified tone.

"Eloise has a point," Maryanne's dad said. "None of us has too much company at night. It's worth giving that some thought."

Eloise nodded, and abundant waves of white hair rippled at her temples. "I think we can tolerate some inconvenience if a pet helps another of us during a time of need. I vote for the cats."

"But no dogs!" Charlie bellowed, arms crossed.

Mitzi smiled in what looked like relief. "Let's discuss the canines, then."

Roger stood. "See this cane?"

Everyone nodded.

"It means," he went on, "that I can't walk so good anymore. How'm I gonna stay on my feet when a mutt jumps all over me?"

"Obedience classes," suggested a woman who didn't look old enough to meet the community's fifty-five-year minimum-age requirement. "Those are fun. My late husband and I had a wonderful time training our dogs."

Charlie snorted. "More work. I retired for a reason—I'm tired and old."

The young-looking senior arched a brow. "No one says you have to own or train a dog, Charlie."

An uncomfortable silence descended. Then Mitzi gave a smart crack of the gavel against the lectern. "I think we've reached an agreement. Cats will be allowed, but dogs won't. Sorry, Connie."

The woman who'd suggested the obedience classes stood. "I don't think anyone's agreed to anything about the dogs—at least not yet. We need to discuss it some more."

"Okay," Charlie ventured. "Let's talk. I don't want to step on any when I go for my walks every morning."

A portly blonde in the front row turned to glare at Charlie. "Everyone must clean up for him or herself," she said. "It's only reasonable that those who want dogs take care of it."

"What's your plan?" Charlie asked. "Have management hand out official pooper-scoopers with our lease agreements?"

Maryanne swallowed a laugh. She could just envision the scene…a battalion of geriatrics armed with long-handled double shovels and baggies, all leashed to members of a motley crew of canines.

"That would work," the blonde said.

"Baloney," Charlie countered.

Mitzi banged again. Her compatriots ignored her and clamored over each other's comments.

"They shed all over, and then there's the drool."

"Petting one's been proven to reduce blood pressure…."

"They can be rambunctious. That's dangerous—"

"Seizure dogs are true lifesavers."

"Leashes can cause accidents…."

"They'd have puppies—"

"They bite!"

"Fleas—"

"When are we going to get to the liver?" Charlie demanded.

Eloise smashed her walker against the metal chair in front of her. The residents turned toward the source of the din, and when they spotted her, fell into a stunned stupor.

"I didn't think when I moved here my address would be the Tower of Babel," the slight woman said, her voice distinct and determined. "But this bickering certainly sounds like it."

Maryanne noticed more than one red face in the group.

"It also strikes me," Eloise went on, "that a fair amount of selfishness has taken root among us. I want no part of that. The Lord created animals and left them in our trust. He also urged us to do unto others as we would others do unto us. So I'd like to see us show some forbearance in our small community."

A chair squealed in the back of the room. Clothes rustled to Maryanne's left. Someone cleared his throat to her far right.

No one ventured a remark.

Eloise stepped her walker forward. "We can determine a safe size for dogs—say about twenty pounds and under. Of course, we'll enact leash laws. And Connie's right. The owner must be responsible for the pet's…ah…production."

A nervous chuckle began near the side door and soon gathered strength. Before long, everyone was laughing, even Roger and Charlie. Everyone but Mitzi.

Her elevenses deepened and furrows lined her lily-white forehead. She pursed her bright lips and looked ready to stomp and cry at her loss of control—and her lost battle against dogs.

"Silence!" the diminutive chairwoman yelled.

No one listened.

She banged her gavel to no avail, so she banged some more, and banged yet again, this time, however, with a bit too much force. The gavel broke.

"Oooh!" she cried. "Just look what you made me do!"

Her wail penetrated the good-natured chatter. Everyone faced forward, and more than one chuckle had to be smothered.

"Come on, Mitzi," Maryanne's father called out. "We're done. The place has gone to the dogs, and I want to go home."

"But…but we haven't discussed the liver," she said with a shuffle of paper. "Or the steamed spinach. I can't abide them."

"Hear, hear," Charlie cheered.

Roger stood. "Aw, give it up. It's nap time."

Mitzi ran her fingers through her bright hair, spiking it into a ridge of exclamation marks. "Oh, and we haven't even touched on the fountain outside. It's an absolute disgrace. Who ever's heard of pink flamingos in Pennsylvania?"

"That's it!" Stan Wellborn said as he spun his wheel-chair toward the rear of the room. "I'm gone. Those fla-mingos are just about the funniest thing around here. Go rent a sense of humor, Mitzi."

Maryanne hurried to open the door for him.

"They stay," he said. "They stay, and they stay pink."

As they waited for the elevator, Maryanne kept quiet. Behind them, other residents poured out of the common area. Each voiced an opinion. At her side, her dad tapped his fingers on the wheelchair's control panel, a sure sign of annoyance.

The elevator doors opened. Father and daughter stepped inside. No one else joined them, and the conveyance soon glided upward. Just before they reached the sixth floor, Stan chuckled.

"What did I tell you, Cookie?" he said. "Fireworks, right?"

She gave him a wary look. "Were you just fanning the flames?"

"Nah. Mitzi's gone too far with her chairwoman thing. Those who want cats should have their cats, and those who want dogs should have them, too. Just don't mess with my liver and onions, and leave my pink flamingos alone."

When the elevator stopped, he flashed her a grin and winked. "Welcome to the loony bin, Cookie. And thanks for listening to me. I'm right where I belong."

Just like that, Maryanne's last qualms about her father's move to Peaceful Meadows vanished. Stan Wellborn had found a home.

Her guilt lifted, she relaxed and the afternoon went by fast, full of laughter, good conversation, a killer game of checkers and a serving of her dad's birthday cake.

All in all, it was a perfect Sunday afternoon.

* * *

"Good night, Cookie."

"Good night, Dad."

She hadn't meant to stay so late, but Maryanne hadn't wanted to leave her father. She'd had a great time, even though liver and onions was not her favorite dish. Dad had wanted her company at dinner, and since all that awaited her back home was an uppity cat and the report she'd written yesterday afternoon, she'd stayed. She could proofread the whole thing in no time once she got home.

The rain started around sunset, typical for a late spring evening in South Central Pennsylvania. Now, on her way out, she lowered her head, covered it with her tote bag, and ran into the night. In her hurry to reach the car, she didn't watch her step, and her shoe hit a puddle. She slipped, yelped and dropped.

Muscular arms broke her fall.

"Thanks," she said and then looked up. "NO!"

She froze in the circle of J.Z. Prophet's clasp, tight against his chest, close to his warmth and clean scent. Not the smartest thing to do, but until she could breathe again, she couldn't move. To gather her wits, she tried to think of something—anything—other than those intense gray eyes.

"You should be more careful," he said, his voice deep.

She fought for breath, and this time, gulped in a lungful of fresh-washed air. "What are you doing here?"

"Taking care of business."

His tone spoke volumes, but she didn't understand a thing. Still, she had no intention of carrying on a conversation with the miserable creature. Certainly not while she remained in such a vulnerable position—at his mercy.

She shoved against his chest, and to her surprise, he let her go. She almost fell again, but she summoned her strength and stood upright. She tugged down her belt from where it had slid way up on her ribs; she straightened her skirt; she ignored the rain.

"I don't know what you think you're doing," she said. For good measure, she tipped up her chin. "But I do want to know why you've been following me."

Something sparked in his eyes, but he still didn't speak.

"Fine." She stepped toward her car. "You can play Mount Rushmore all you want, especially in the rain. Just remember, if I see you again where you don't belong but I do, I'll call the cops."

"Go ahead."

The rain sluiced over his dark hair, plastered it to his head like a robber's skullcap. It did nothing to endear him to her.

"If you want to convince me the law doesn't bother you, then try something new. Quit following me and really mind your business. No sane man would dog an ordinary woman. There's nothing interesting about me. I'm a librarian with an elderly, disabled dad."

He shrugged, that incomprehensible intensity as always in his eyes. "I am minding my business, and I'm good at it."

A shiver racked Maryanne. It had nothing to do with the rain and everything with the man. "Stalking's a crime, you know," she said, steps from her Escort...and safety. "They can lock you up for a long time, so quit before they do."

She fumbled with her keychain, but to her dismay, she dropped it. With the last of her courage, she said, "Go crawl back under the rock from whence you came."

As she went for her keys, his hand shot out and grabbed

them. Fear churned her gut, and she prayed he wasn't like a dog, able to scent it on her.

With a click, he unlocked her car door then handed her the keys. In silence, he strode into the dark. Maryanne collapsed against the fender and just stood there, drenched in rain and sweat. For long moments she just breathed and shook, thankful she could still do both.

"Lord God, thank you for…for…whatever. Just help me."

When she could move again, she opened the door and sat. Long minutes later, she turned on the ignition. The drive home was a numb haze—another mindless drive under her belt. If she kept this up, she'd soon qualify as a homing pigeon, functioning on some instinctual plane.

That, and she'd have a couple of centuries of thanks and praise to offer her Lord.

In the garage, Maryanne sat back and tried to relax her shoulder muscles. She failed. Miserably.

The memory of J.Z. Prophet returned with the vengeance of hurricane-spurred ocean waves. What did the man want with her?

Because, without a shadow of a doubt, Maryanne knew J.Z. had come to Peaceful Meadows to keep tabs on her. What she didn't know was why?

And she'd better figure it out soon…before it was too late. For her.

At ten the next morning, Maryanne called the cell phone rep Trudy had recommended. In a few minutes' time, she'd agreed to stop by the kiosk at the mall and sign a contract for a year's worth of service. Next time J.Z. Prophet showed his face, she'd be ready. Her new phone came with preprogrammable automatic dialing.

The first number she'd record would be 911.

The day went by in the same kind of blur as when she drove home last night. By five, she didn't remember much of what she'd done. Well, she turned in the report, but other than that...mush.

Determined to regain some semblance of sanity if not control, she concentrated on the drive to the mall. She even sang along with Rebecca St. James's latest on the radio. She parked, locked the car, ran through the ongoing rain to the food-court entrance and made a beeline for the cell phone and safety.

The young man had the papers ready for her. All Maryanne had to do was sign her name and give him a check. After a handful of directions, she felt confident enough to head home with the gadget and its instruction manual. On her way back to the car, she detoured by the frozen yogurt counter. She didn't often indulge, but today she ordered a swirl cone. She didn't want to choose between chocolate and vanilla.

Because of the rain, she opted to finish her treat at one of the food court's small tables. Then, on her way to the great outdoors and the deluge, she tossed away her napkin and saw the man watching her from the sandwich shop line. She came to a halt.

J.Z. Prophet wasn't besting her again.

Maryanne marched up to him. "I told you I'd call the cops the next time I saw you." She pulled out her phone. "Watch me."

He covered the gadget and her hand with his much larger one, his clasp gentler than she would have imagined. "It won't do you any good. I know what you are—"

"What are you doing, J.Z.?" asked the other Uni-Comp

clown, a bag redolent of corned beef in his hand. "You're worse than a kid. You can't leave well enough alone, can you? Do you want Eliza to charge out here and tear a strip off your hide—"

He stopped just when things were about to get interesting, when Maryanne might have learned something about the probably psychotic J.Z. But the two men glared at each other, and if it weren't for the minor matter of her captured hand, she would have taken her leave. Instead, she looked from one to the other, only too aware of J.Z.'s warm clasp.

"Ahem," she said.

The men turned.

"Would one of you please tell me which episode of the *Twilight Zone* you're rerunning here?"

"Let her go," J.Z.'s partner said.

J.Z. captured her gaze just as firmly as he held her hand.

"Who are you guys?" Maryanne's fear fired up again. "What do you want with me? And don't even mention computers. I know you've been following me."

"Come on, J.Z. Let's go."

Maryanne smiled her gratitude at the blond man who didn't work for Uni-Comp—she wasn't dumb.

"Yes, J.Z. Let me go. I'll go my way and you can go yours, and never the twain shall meet. Okay?"

"Let her go," her pal—Don? Dan? Yeah, Dan Something—repeated.

J.Z. acceded, but a strange look she couldn't read, not the anger she'd seen, maybe frustration, filled his eyes. "Watch yourself," he said. "One mistake, and I'll make my move."

"Who are you?" she asked yet again.

"Tell her, J.Z. You've blown this out of the water, so you may as well tell her now."

Maryanne's eyes ping-ponged from one man to the other.

Dan muttered something else, this time nothing Maryanne could make out. He thrust his sandwich bag at J.Z. and rummaged in his back pocket. But instead of the wallet she'd expected, he extended a small leather card case toward her.

"What…?"

"Open it," he said gently.

She did. Four words jumped out at her: Federal Bureau of Investigations.

Her head spun. Ice replaced her blood. The world tipped under her feet. "Why?"

"You're under investigation," J.Z. said in clipped tones. "You're good, but I'm better. I'm going to get you and your mob pals, so say goodbye to freedom, your frozen yogurt and your little phone."

Everything went black.

FOUR

"Are you satisfied now?" Dan glared up at J.Z.

J.Z. frowned down at the woman sprawled flat on the mall's food-court floor. "Come on, lady. We aren't playing games here—"

"Take her pulse, will ya?"

Dan's expression gave him no alternative, so J.Z. went down on one knee, took the librarian's wrist in his hand, and pressed to check for her heartbeat. To his surprise, it was weak and unsteady—just what one expected in a person who'd fainted.

He shook his head. "I told you she was good. I've never known someone who could faint on demand. I guess there's always a first time for everything."

Dan's look of disgust hit him like a slap.

"Your compassion underwhelms me," his partner said. "If you won't help her, then at least give me a hand and keep this mob from crushing us."

Only then did J.Z. notice the crowd that had gathered around them. Two sandwich-shop employees flapped their aprons in an obvious attempt to circulate air around Mary-anne. A quartet of mall-walkers, senior citizens who exercised in the shelter of the covered mall, whispered among themselves, curiosity and pity in their lined faces. A maintenance guy stood to their right, both hands clasped around the mop's wooden handle, the bucket-on-wheels contraption where it sat in danger of rolling and leaving him without support.

Heat rushed up J.Z.'s cheeks. "Okay, folks. We have it under control. Please move on so that we can take care of her."

The onlookers dispersed, their backward glances full of reluctance, his sudden relief at their departure surprisingly strong. Did Dan have a point? Was he overreacting to *everything* about this woman?

"Think those weird guys there are some of them white slavers in the news?" asked a white-haired lady in lime-green sweats, her voice scissors-sharp as she resumed her laps around the shopping center.

J.Z. groaned. "That's all we need."

"What? For someone to report you for manhandling a helpless female? That's probably what it looked like you were doing."

"Look. I'm not going to drop the pressure on her. Sooner or later she'll crack—"

"Either that, or she'll crack up from your intimidation. Chill, man. You don't even know she's involved."

He snorted. "Did you bother to read the profile we got last month? I'm telling you, the description fits her perfectly."

"It also fits about fifty percent of the female population. That doesn't mean they're all mobsters, does it?"

"Don't give me that. That fifty percent doesn't have her kind of access to an old folks' home where a bunch of seniors died after one of that fifty percent ordered their termination. And don't forget the Laundromat's demise."

Maryanne's eyelids gave a twitch. Good. She was coming to. But before he could say anything, Dan spoke.

"I'll admit those e-mails look pretty bad, but any hacker can get into her account to cast suspicion on her."

"Fine. Let's assume that's what happened." J.Z. ran a hand through his hair. "Where's the hacker who fits the profile? Who else has access? Who else is the typical 'neighbor-next-door' type who won't raise suspicion? Who else does the dowdy, harmless librarian routine as well as Maryanne Wellborn?"

Dan's ministrations were having results on Maryanne. Color seeped into her cheeks. With a split-second glance at J.Z., he asked, "Have you bothered to stake out the place?"

"Why would I need to?" J.Z. let his breath out in a gust. "We have the e-mails, the wealthy, dead seniors, the very dead—*this* time—Laundromat, and finally, her fingerprints on the IV stand. And she's there, all the time, in and out to see her dad—or so she says. Doesn't that stink rotten to you?"

"I'm going to tell you one more time," Dan said through gritted teeth. "Appearances can be deceiving. There's a reason why clichés become clichés. They have a bunch of truth to them, and her appearance, because it reminds you of your past, may be deceiving you."

"So you want me to believe even the fingerprints are a coincidence."

Dan shrugged, his attention on the librarian. "She could have moved the stand for a nurse…for Mat, himself. You can't be sure what happened. You weren't there."

J.Z. belabored his point. "Give me a break. What are the chances all these deaths—especially a mobster's—are unrelated and unconnected to the librarian who sends killer e-mails?"

Maryanne blinked.

J.Z. crossed his arms. "Well?"

Dan muttered, "Not now."

"It's as good a time as any," J.Z countered. "There's no such thing as coincidence. If something stinks like a skunk, looks like a skunk and skulks like a skunk, then more than likely it's a skunk."

When Dan ignored him, J.Z. bulldozed ahead. "That phony librarian look doesn't fool me. I've spent my entire adult life smoking out mob scum. I'm going to bust her."

Almost more for him than for his partner, he added, "Just because my father chose a life of crime doesn't mean I'm going to ignore what's staring me in the face. I've chosen to sop up crime, and that's what I'm going to do. I'm going to bring her in."

Maryanne blinked. Male voices caught her attention.

"…skunk…mob…crime…"

What was going on? And why was she lying down?

"…I'm going to bring her in…."

Her head swam. Her stomach lurched. She had no idea where she was— Wait! She'd gone to the mall to pick up her phone, and there she'd found—

"You!" she cried when her eyes focused on the maniac who stood, Mr. Clean-style, over her. "What did you do to me?"

The boy-next-door blond one who hung around with the nutcase wrapped an arm around her shoulders and helped her sit.

"He didn't do anything to you," Dan said with a lethal

glare for J.Z. Prophet. "That is, he didn't do anything to hurt you. He has been pretty busy acting like an idiot, though, so I can see where you'd think he had."

Maryanne shook off his arm. "Thank you, but I can get up on my own."

She stood, and again the height difference between her five foot five and J.Z.'s six foot something threatened to intimidate her. As did the memory of Dan's FBI badge.

Everything rushed back. "Okay. Let's say you guys really are Feds and not some loony fakes."

J.Z.'s scowl deepened. Maryanne ignored the urge to step back. She tried again. "Let's just say you're what you say you are. Why are you wasting your time on me? What real, live G-man would try to make a case out of a librarian, so-called mob pals, frozen yogurt and a new cell phone?"

"Great," J.Z. said. "She's even got the diversionary tactics down pat." He met her gaze. "Playing dumb and going for the funny bone won't get you anywhere."

Maryanne gave him a pointed up-and-down look. "I see you speak from experience. You wouldn't know funny if it ran up and bit you, plus you do a great dumb."

"Look lady. We have evidence. And we have the corpses to go with it."

Maryanne squinched her eyes shut. She shook her head to try and clear it, to try to make sense of what he'd said. She blinked a couple of times, looked from J.Z. to the mortified Dan and back at J.Z. again. She shook her head one more time.

It still made no sense. "Could you explain the corpses part a little better?"

He ran a hand through his dark hair, a gesture she'd seen

him do on a couple of occasions, like when he'd stared at the box of computer stuff in total frustration.

"Fine," he said after long minutes. "I guess you're pretty good at dumb, too. Do the names Helmut Rheinemann, Toby Matthias, Muriel Harper, Audrey White, Carlo Papparelli and others ring a bell?"

With each name, Maryanne's queasiness grew. A momentary sadness swept over her, but she couldn't afford to let emotions cloud her thoughts. She had to keep a clear head.

"Yes, of course, the names ring a bell. They were all patients at the same nursing and retirement community where my father lives, and you know it, too. They…they all passed away recently. But why would you come after me?"

Maryanne let her words die. All of a sudden everything clicked. "You morons think I killed them!"

Dan shot J.Z. a stern look that didn't escape Maryanne's notice. Maybe one of the two wasn't totally out of his mind.

"Miss Wellborn," he said in a kind voice, "you have to agree that there have been a number of sudden deaths at the home recently."

"It's a place for the elderly," she replied, determined to stay calm. "Especially the elderly who are ill. As sad as it is, it's not sudden or surprising when they do pass away. I mean…emphysema, heart attacks, liver failure…all these things are killers, not me."

Dan gave a vague wave. "I understand. The problem is that a series of…*questionable* e-mails has been traced back to you."

"Questionable?"

"Incriminating might be a better word."

Her head spun and her stomach dove. "Look. None of

this makes sense, and I'm still a little shaky. Could we sit down? Please?"

"By all means," Dan answered, his hand a gentle brace under her elbow. "Here's a table where we can talk things through."

As she went to take a step, J.Z. took hold of her other arm. Warmth radiated from his hand. Although he looked and sounded formidable, his clasp felt even gentler than Dan's.

She glanced up. That strange expression she first spotted under the rain the other night crossed his face again. Her steps faltered, but the support he offered kept her upright.

"Thank you." She sat in the nearest chair and waited until the two men were seated across her. Then she continued. "I spend very little time online, so I have a hard time putting myself in the picture you just painted. Tell me about those e-mails."

J.Z. rapped his short nails against the tabletop in a nerve-racking rhythm. "I'm sure you remember them," he said. "They're the ones you used to order someone to terminate those people."

He seemed more outraged at the thought of murderous e-mail than at the deaths themselves. She looked at him in disbelief. "Is that it? Is that why you've come to haunt me? Is that what's got you all lathered up?"

"Pardon my skepticism," he said, sarcasm in his words, "but your try at innocence doesn't change a thing. We have a bunch of dead old people—*wealthy* old people—and your e-mails putting out contracts on them. And a mobster. We can't forget him. Those are the facts."

Before she could stop herself, Maryanne burst out

laughing. True, it was nervous, almost hysterical laughter, but she couldn't escape the absurdity of her situation. The more she laughed, however, the more menace darkened J.Z.'s expression and the more frustrated Dan looked.

When, at length, she regained control, she wiped her eyes and shook her head. "You're really, really crazy, you know that?"

Silence met her ears.

"No, really. I send e-mails to the library's membership department when I get word that a patient's become too ill to make any more use of library privileges. I operate the library's Cart O'Books program at the nursing home. Those specific e-mails you mentioned went to the membership clerk so that he would *terminate* their library cards."

The men traded glances.

Something in Dan's expression, or maybe it was his sudden relaxation, told her she'd gotten her point across. But everything about J.Z. blared out his cynicism.

His nails beat a new syncopation on the food court's minuscule table. Maryanne felt it in every corner of her throbbing head.

"Maybe," he said without a hint of graciousness, "maybe you could talk your way out of the first few deaths, but how do you explain the Laundromat?"

Could he really be that dumb? "Easy. I explain it the same way everyone else does. The laundromat's a place where you take your dirty clothes to get them clean. That is, if you don't have your own washer and dryer."

His stare grew harder—if possible. "Okay. If that's the way you want to play it, then that's how we'll play." He sat up straighter in his plastic-and-steel chair. "Even though we all know that Carlo Papparelli's nickname is Laundromat for the obvious reason—"

"No," Maryanne said. "This part of *we*—" she thumbed her chest "—doesn't know anything about nicknames. This part of *we* didn't even get to meet Mr. Papparelli. I got an e-mail from the residence's business office the day he arrived, and I sent e-mail to start the process that sets up library privileges. That's what I do for every new resident at Peaceful Meadows. But Mr. Papparelli had a stroke four days later. He never regained consciousness after that. So when I got e-mail notification of his death, I sent Sandy the e-mail to terminate his privileges. And I *don't* know that his nickname's Laundromat or Carwash or even Drive-Through-Fast-Food for that matter."

J.Z.'s response to her words gave Maryanne a clear image of the true meaning of the word *seethe*. If a human could spontaneously combust, then the maybe-Fed was on the verge of doing just that.

His jaw grew rock hard and his eyes narrowed. "How did you do it?"

"Do what?"

"Give him a stroke."

Maryanne stood. "I've had enough. The man had a stroke. That's all I know about him. Nothing more. Nada. Zilch. Zippo. Zero. I don't even think you can 'give' someone a stroke."

He surged to his feet. "Someone snuck the bullet-filled guy we were told had died two weeks ago into that nursing home. The family let everyone think he was a goner. They even shipped a casket to Sicily. But now it's clear he lived long enough to fall into your clutches. We know he lost a ton of blood at the scene. That's what we were told was the cause of death. So how'd you get a blood clot to kill him?"

"I don't know how a blood clot killed him. I didn't do it, so since you think you have the answers, why don't *you* tell *me?*"

"While you're at it," he continued as though she hadn't spoken, "why don't you tell us how you got autopsies that showed emphysema, liver failure and other diseases to cover your crimes?"

A sense of futility filled her. "I'll tell you again—in simple words, now. I am a librarian. I visit my father at his nursing home. All the residents there will eventually die—*everyone* does. I know nothing about Laundromats, bullet wounds, strokes, caskets to Sicily or slow boats to China. And now that we cleared it all up, I'm going home. I have a cat that will more than likely have clawed the place to shreds since I have yet to present him with dinner."

Before she got more than a step away, J.Z. blocked her path. "I know what you've done. What I don't know is how you did it. But you're not going to get away with it. Not even the hit on Papparelli."

"I didn't hear you," Maryanne said in a singsong voice. She darted to her right.

He bobbed in front of her.

She tried again. "You're just a figment of my imagination." And what a figment…thundercloud was more like it. Tall, dark, rugged and dangerous described J.Z. Prophet to a T.

Maryanne zagged to her left.

He zigged.

"You can run all you want," he said, his voice low and steely, "but you won't get far. I'm going to be right behind you all the way. As nasty a character as Laundromat was, no one has the right to have him killed. And you sank too low when you did in those old folks. You people make me sick. Don't you get enough dough from your crooked deals? How about the profit from Laundromat's money games? Why'd you kill the seniors? They didn't have long to live anyway—oh, *that's* right. It's all about the money."

His look of disgust made Maryanne wince. But he hadn't finished yet.

"Tell me." He repeated his earlier question. "Don't you get enough dough from your crooked deals? How about the profit from Laundromat's money games?"

Maryanne drew a long, ragged breath. "I have nothing more to say to you. You'll hear from my lawyer very soon. Harassment was still illegal last time I checked."

"So are murder and dealings with the mob. You've two strikes against you, and I'm not going to let you get to three."

"I didn't strike or kill—"

"Children, children," Dan said in a patently fake conciliatory tone.

Maryanne included him in her glare. "Unless you're ready to arrest me, and I doubt you are, since I'm sure Mr. Leap-to-Ridiculous-Conclusions here would have done so if he'd had even a shred of the evidence he says he has, I'm going home. I suggest you both crawl back under your dank, wormy rock again."

As she walked toward the mall exit, J.Z. spoke, presumably to Dan. "She has her cover down pat, all right. But I'm not Obadiah Prophet's son for nothing. No fun-house-mirror illusion's going to get the better of me. She's busted."

* * *

Maryanne tried out her brand-spanking-new cell phone less than two minutes later. "You are *not* going to believe this."

"What am I not going to believe now?" Trudy said.

"Remember the freaky Uni-Comp guys from the other day?"

"You think I'd forget?"

"Good. I'm glad, and I hope you actually remember everything I told you—*everything*, Trudy. It could be a matter of life or death. My life or death."

"Are you all right? I've never known you to be so dramatic."

Maryanne checked her watch. It was past six o'clock. "Is Ron home yet?"

"Ron? What does he have to do with all this?"

"I need a lawyer. Your husband's the only one I know."

"Oh, brother. What'd you do to the Uni-Comp guys?"

"Is. Ron. Home?"

Trudy's exasperated sigh came right through the down-payment-to-a-phone at her ear. "Yes, Maryanne. My husband arrived about…nine and a half minutes ago."

"Excellent. I'll be over in less than that."

She clapped the phone shut, and cut off Trudy's squawks. Maryanne didn't have the emotional energy to explain the insane, inexplicable mess she was in more than once. With a long-distance plea to Shakespeare for forgiveness, she got into the Escort and drove to the Talbots' in record time.

Thank goodness no cop caught her on the way there.

By the same token, however, she didn't lose her G-man tail either. Not that she tried. She had nothing to hide.

At the Talbots', she parked in the long driveway of their beautiful 1920s brick home, and despite her better judgment, gave in to her inner imp. She turned, made sure both Dan and J.Z. were watching, then gave them a sweet smile and waved.

The sound of spinning tires was like music to her ears.

Once inside, she let her friend's mothering take over.

"Before you say one word," Trudy murmured, an arm around Maryanne's shoulders, "you have to come in here, sit and have a cup of tea. Take a break. I think you've been doing too much lately."

No amount of arguing budged Trudy's conviction. Maryanne gave up when she'd said that a job and the weekly book run to Peaceful Meadows didn't exactly paint a Type-A lifestyle for about the fifth time.

The strong, Irish breakfast–style tea was good, though.

Finally, when she placed the antique English transferware cup back in its saucer and returned both to the 1800s leather trunk Trudy used as a coffee table, Ron Talbot came into the beautiful living room.

"Hey, there, Maryanne. How's it going?"

Ron looked more like a high school wrestling coach— which he was—than a high-powered attorney—which he also was. His decrepit burgundy T-shirt, with its New Camden High School Bulldogs lettering faded from gold to a bilious yellow, was as far removed from the fine, tailored business suits he wore to court as any two garments could get. And the gym shorts with the label Coach on his right thigh matched the shirt to perfection.

"Oh!" she cried. "Am I keeping you from practice?"

"No. Because of the crazy demand for the gym, my team's scheduled for seven-to-nine practice. That's the only reason I can coach. Court's usually done by then on any given day."

Trudy's husband exuded a calm confidence that immediately made Maryanne feel better. "I think I'm in trouble, Ron. And I haven't even done anything."

Husband and wife traded glances. Then Ron faced Maryanne. "Why don't you start from the beginning, and tell me everything you can remember. Tell me even how you've felt, and any ideas, no matter how crazy, that may come to you."

Maryanne went over the events of the past few days, thankful for her good memory. Although none of it made sense, and Ron's occasional frowns echoed her own bewildered frustration, she laid everything out as clearly as she could remember.

"And I made sure they were both watching when I waved to them from your front walk. J.Z. was in the driver's seat, and I feel confident you'll find burnt rubber on the street from how fast he peeled out."

Ron leaned forward, pressed his elbows into his thighs and stared at his clasped hands between his knees. After a couple of minutes that felt like centuries to Maryanne, he looked up.

"You're right about three things," he said. "You've done nothing to bring this on yourself. You're also in a whole lot of trouble. And what's worse, none of it makes sense."

"Great. So where does that leave me?"

"In my living room while I make a couple of phone calls," the lawyer answered. Ron's persona virtually morphed right before her eyes. The ratty clothes looked more incongruous than before.

Despite his obvious confidence, though, she felt no better.

Trudy knew her well enough to bypass any attempt at small talk. The two friends sat in silence, each consumed by her thoughts, Maryanne's very real dilemma a third, if ominous, presence in the room.

Finally, exhausted by her convoluted thoughts, Maryanne turned to prayer. *Lord. You know what's real and what isn't. Please, please keep the fear from warping how I perceive reality. Help me see this mess as You do. I need Your wisdom.*

"Well," Ron said, breaking into Maryanne's prayers. "At least I can assure you that Prophet and Maddox are who they say they are."

"They really are FBI agents?"

"They're with the Philadelphia organized-crime team. So that much is clear. What still makes no sense is why they think you've killed the patients at Peaceful Meadows."

"All I know for certain is that J.Z. Prophet has it in for me. He doesn't have to put it into words, but I know he's convinced I'm a killer. He even thinks I ordered a…what do they call it? A hit?…on a Philly mob family's money launderer."

Ron merely nodded.

"Can you believe they call the guy 'Laundromat'?"

Trudy's nervous giggle made Maryanne feel better. "I couldn't keep myself from laughing at the mall earlier. It's so stupid. All I did was ask Sandy to terminate the reading privileges of those poor, poor dying folks."

"When you put it that way," Ron said, "and knowing you as we do, then it does sound ridiculous. But those e-mails coincide with the deaths and the fingerprints. To an outsider predisposed to suspect everything, it can all look incriminating."

Maryanne stood and shrugged. "J.Z. is determined to pin those deaths on me. But I'm innocent, and I'm Dad's only living relative. He needs me even though—or maybe *because*—he's living at Peaceful Meadows now. It costs a bundle to keep him there, but he gets excellent care, and that's how I want it."

"I'll do everything I can to help you keep it that way— to keep you where you belong," Ron said. "You know, at the library, at home and with your dad."

At the front door, Trudy hugged her tight. Maryanne appreciated the affection. "Thanks. You guys are the best friends a woman could ever have."

"Oh, I'd wait until I clear this up before making such a broad statement," Ron countered with a mischievous wink.

Maryanne stepped outside. "I don't have to wait. I know I can trust you."

And God, she thought on her way to her car. She turned the key in the ignition, and only then noticed the G-men in their bland-gray car across the street.

At this rate, she was going to bore them into accepting the truth.

"Who cares?" she murmured. She stepped on the gas, and started the drive home.

The only thing she cared about was to honor her earthly father as her heavenly Father called her to do.

And she wasn't completely helpless. She knew what she had to do to take matters into her own hands. She was going to prove her innocence.

She was going to show J.Z. how crazy his accusations were.

FIVE

It felt really weird to go places and know two grown men were trailing along behind her. More than once Maryanne thought of Trudy and her story group kids, not to mention *Make Way For Ducklings*.

But J.Z. Prophet looked nothing like a duck.

He was an odd duck, though—an attractive odd duck. But his good looks did nothing to endear him to her. Maryanne couldn't figure out what made the guy tick. Something about his vehemence scared her; nobody was that passionate about a job. Not without a good reason. She just had to figure out his.

She got a kick out of watching him waste his day at the library. As much as she loved books, she would have gone nuts after three days of nothing but watching her office door and pretending to read. At one point, she even caught him holding a car magazine upside down.

He didn't like her friendly little waves when she got to her destination. Like today after work. He no longer bothered to speed away, though. He just parked his gray car, glared at her and Dan and settled in to watch her condo complex.

Maryanne hurried inside, glad for the air-conditioning.

The humidity in her part of Pennsylvania reached sticky heights this time of year. She changed into an ancient and well-worn denim skirt and a sleeveless blouse, made a sandwich and doled out Shakespeare's favorite can of salmon and sardines, then hurried to her desk. She booted up her laptop as she munched away at her ham and cheese.

The phone rang as she scrolled down an enlightening page.

"Anything new?" Trudy asked.

"Depends. All this mob stuff is new to me, but that Papparelli Laundromat guy's crimes go way, way back."

"What was he into?"

"Just about everything crooked." Maryanne peered at a grainy picture of the late money launderer in younger days. He looked tough as old boots and meaner than the average hungry shark. "Hiding drug traffic profits took up a big chunk of his time, and from what I can read between the lines, he had something going that involved ladies…er…of the night."

"Yuck!"

"You got it." She scanned on down. Another picture caught her attention. "Wow! Look at that!"

"I can't see! Just tell me."

"Looks like he got himself a trophy wife about six years ago. She's gorgeous, blond, and looks young enough to be his daughter."

"What are you looking at?"

"I'm online reading old newspapers. This article's all about the lavish nuptials. Wonder how a woman like her winds up married to a creep like him."

"If you can go by what you read, a lot of those mob marriages are arranged. They're more business alliances than anything else."

It was Maryanne's turn to say "Yuck."

"Amen, sister. I wouldn't want anyone to decide who's going to share my life besides me and the Lord."

"I couldn't agree more." Then she remembered something from her earlier research. "Hang on a minute, Trudy. Let me look at something more recent again. I think I'm getting an idea."

She clicked on a couple of different links, and seconds later wound up at the most recent press piece about Carlo Papparelli. "Here we go. Listen to this. J.Z. said something about bullets and the Laundromat bleeding to death. When I first read this article, I only paid attention to the stuff about the shooting and the police's possible suspects. But now…"

She reread the particular paragraph, and as she did, her idea gelled. She smiled. "I've got it! I know what I have to do."

"What? Will you tell me already?"

"Poor Trudy. I have been pretty disjointed." She clicked out of the Web site, signed off from her ISP and shut down the computer. "The widow's the key. I'm sure of it."

"What do you mean?"

"Sure. Just think about it. She was there when someone pumped Papparelli full of bullets. She saw everything. When the cops got there, she was holding his head in her lap. They questioned her, but these articles don't say anything about what she might have seen."

"Do you think she knows who shot him?"

"Maybe."

"Don't you think she would have told the cops? I'm sure they interviewed her to within an inch of her life."

"I'm not so sure she would have. I've got the feeling she

knows she's next in line for a bullet if she talks, so she probably kept her mouth zipped around the cops. And there's my problem. I have to find a way to reach her conscience, to get her to see that if she doesn't help me, she'll be responsible for a whole lot of grief, maybe even a death—mine."

"You're being melodramatic again—"

"No way. If I'm tried for this, it'll be a capital punishment case. J.Z.'s trying to prove I killed three or four patients at Peaceful Meadows as well as this Laundromat guy. Cold-blooded hit men generally get the electric chair or a shot of some nasty stuff to put them to sleep—for good."

Trudy's silence spoke volumes.

Maryanne sighed. "Well, at least now I know what I have to do next."

"And that would be…?"

"I'm heading for Philly first thing Saturday morning. I'm going to find Carlotta Papparelli—"

"Carlotta? Married to Carlo? You've got to be kidding."

"Trust me, Trudy. I'm not about to kid about this. I don't particularly want to wind up like a chunk of Swiss cheese, and I can't leave Dad all alone."

She stood, squared her shoulders and walked to her front window. There, she took note of the ever-present gray car. "Don't worry. I can be mighty persuasive when I want to be. Carlotta Papparelli doesn't stand a chance. She's going to sing like the proverbial canary."

"Ah…Maryanne?"

"Yes?"

"Have you noticed that you've started to talk like some gun moll in a bad black-and-white movie from the forties?"

"What are you trying to tell me, Trudy?"

"Just make sure you don't get caught up in some crazy game of make-believe. Keep your eyes on the truth."

"Why would you say that? I know I'm not playing make-believe. I'm doing what I have to do to keep that nutcase from locking me up...or worse. I know what's real and what's not. And as far as the rest goes, I'm keeping my eyes right where they belong, on God. He'll help me through this whole stupid mess."

"Good luck."

The lack of conviction in Trudy's words stung Maryanne. "Thanks," she muttered. "Thanks a whole bunch."

Her sarcasm met with silence, then Trudy added, "I'll be praying for you. You're going to need all the prayers you can get. You and that J.Z. Prophet guy, too."

That she could accept. "Okay, Trudy. I'll keep you updated as I go. Don't worry. I'll be fine."

When she hung up, Maryanne couldn't help the niggling sensation that she'd actually spoken for her own benefit rather than her friend's.

"Help me, Lord. I can't do this all alone."

On Thursday after work, Maryanne ransacked her closet. When not an item remained on its hanger and every dresser drawer was empty, she gave in to the inevitable. She didn't own a thread she could wear on her detecting-run day after tomorrow. She'd have to go shopping.

Blech! She hated the whole mall/store/fitting-room/twisting/turning/embarrassment/disgust deal. But she'd have to put up with it. Otherwise, she might have to put up with a fitting for a gross, one-piece orange jumpsuit.

Orange wasn't her color.

Laughing a bit hysterically, she began to restore some

order to her room. "You've got it made, Shakespeare. You don't have to go shopping, and your coat's always the height of style. Even the PETA folks can't hit you up for cruelty to critters."

The cat twitched an ear, but never paused in his grooming routine. "Yeah, yeah. Quit whining and get with it, Maryanne. I know, I know."

Once she had the chaos back under control, she gathered her Bible and curled up on the nest of fluffy pillows at the head of her bed. She knew all the answers she'd ever need could be found here in the pages of this blessed Book. And it also offered infinite comfort. Time with her Lord was just what she needed right then.

Instead of heading for the mall, Maryanne decided Wal-Mart made more sense. She didn't want to invest a lot of money in detective garb, since she would probably never wear it again once she accomplished her mission. Besides, she'd be less conspicuous in the crowded discount retailer than in a more upscale and less populated mall store. After all, very few women went shopping with a thundercloud of a man at their heels—one that wasn't their spouse, that is.

Just because, and as a result of her more mischievous side, Maryanne made a beeline for the lingerie department. True, it was right next to the sportswear she was really after, but a glance over her shoulder confirmed what she'd expected.

A ruddy glow spread over J.Z.'s lean cheeks, and a mortified expression replaced his usual ferocity. He slunk away.

With a grin, she made for the slacks.

After six unsuccessful treks from the racks to the fitting room and back again, she came to the conclusion that those who designed women's clothing had torture rather than decently clad females in mind. She'd tried on thirteen pairs of pants, all in the same size, mind you, but none of them had fit. And not for the same reason.

"These didn't work, either?" asked the patient lady at the desk just outside the fitting rooms.

Maryanne gave a tight shake of her head. "These were too long."

"And the last ones were too short, the ones before that too tight, and the others too loose or too something or other."

"That sums it up pretty well."

The gray bun on the top of the woman's head bounced with her nod. Then she eyed Maryanne with shrewd blue eyes. "Why don't you try a pair of jeans? If they're a little big, you can always wash them in hot water and stick them in the dryer. They'll shrink up just right. That's what we used to do when I was a teen."

"Jeans? I don't wear jeans." Maryanne glanced toward the rack of denim. "I mean, I have an old denim skirt I love, but…jeans?"

"Give them a shot." The attendant slapped her generous, jeans-clad thigh. "They're really comfortable, otherwise they wouldn't have lasted this long and people wouldn't wear them all the time."

Maryanne was so otherwise discouraged that she trudged over to the jeans. She found two different styles in her size, then marched back to the fitting room.

She didn't see any sign of J.Z., but she knew she wasn't so fortunate as to have lost her unwanted shadow. Still, it felt good to pretend she was alone.

In the fitting room, she found that both pairs fit. Surprise, surprise. They weren't expensive, and it made sense to buy both. Who knew what her investigation would lead to or how long it would last? It never hurt to be prepared.

"An ounce of prevention is worth a ton of repair."

Her mother's voice echoed from her memories, and Maryanne figured that a woman as sensible as Martha Wellborn would have planned for any unexpected… um…clothing disaster. What she would have thought of her daughter in the jeans she so despised was another thing altogether.

A rainbow of cotton knit tops later, Maryanne headed for the shoe department, her cart full of assorted foreign outfits. She'd always liked to play dress-up as a child, so the drastic, temporary change didn't intimidate her. Besides, it was all for a good cause.

No self-respecting snoop did her thing in tailored twill skirts and button-down dress shirts.

Running shoes made sense—especially if she got into trouble. Her sensible loafers were functional for the library, but they wouldn't give her any traction if she had to outrun a mobster. Or a G-man.

On her way to the cash register, she passed a rack of sunglasses, and on impulse snagged a large, dark pair. A few feet farther up, a khaki billed cap, just a notch above a baseball hat, beckoned. It wasn't much of a disguise, but at least it would keep the sun's glare from her eyes.

Maryanne paid for her purchases, and once everything was stuffed into the blue plastic bags, she headed toward the exit. That's when she spotted her tail again…not six feet away.

"Here," she said, thrusting her purchases at J.Z.'s middle. "Since you're sticking to me like used bubble gum to my shoes, you can make yourself useful. Carry these to my car, please."

She left him, arms full of bags, jaw agape, and went to buy a soft pretzel and an icy drink. That first bite of salty, mustard-daubed chewy bread was so good that she closed her eyes to savor the sharp flavors. Then, as she swallowed, someone barreled into her back, shoved her to the ground and knocked the wind right out of her. As she fought for air, she heard a harsh whisper.

"Payback time."

The blue-vested greeter, an older gentleman with a friendly smile, hurried over. "What happened?" He helped her sit. "Was the floor wet? 'Cause if it was, then I gotta get maintenance out here to fix it. Can't be having customers falling all over the place."

She shook her head. "Someone bumped me from the back and I fell. I'm fine now. But my drink spilled. You'll want someone to clean that up."

After she reassured Clyde, as his nametag said, and sent him for the cleanup crew, Maryanne shuddered then stood. Her back was sore and she still needed big gulps of air, but otherwise she was fine. Who had bumped into her?

She looked around, but the store was crowded and a mob was in line at the pretzel stand. Anyone could have stumbled into her.

A group of teenaged boys and girls in front of the pretzel vendor, laughed and pushed each other out of the line. She sighed. One of them must have hit her instead of his intended victim.

The pretzel and drink no longer held any appeal.

Outside, J.Z. hadn't budged. Except for his jaw, that

is. It was even more squared than usual. And that was saying plenty.

He followed her in silence, but then again, he didn't need to speak. She was that aware of his presence.

At the car, she opened her trunk and he dumped her purchases inside. "So how'd I do?" she asked.

He blinked. "What do you mean?"

"Aren't you going to hunt down a reporter and give him the scoop? Since you've been so good at making up a life of crime for me, why don't you clue me in on tomorrow's headlines?"

J.Z.'s frown deepened.

Maryanne crossed her right arm over her chest, tipped her head and pressed her left index finger to her cheek. "Hmm…I can just read the headlines. Mobster Goes Wal-Mart. She tapped her nose then pointed at him. "No, that has a wimpy ring to it. C'mon, J.Z. Tell me what heinous crime I committed today."

For a moment, Maryanne couldn't believe she'd just spoken like that to a Federal agent. Was she nuts? Had J.Z. infected her with his kind of lunacy?

Then she remembered all he thought she'd done. And what he wanted for her future. Yes, she was acting way out of character, but then again, this was the first time she found herself the subject of an FBI investigation. Still…

She took a deep breath. "At some point you're going to owe me an apology. But I'd rather not wait until then to ask forgiveness for my sarcasm. I'm sorry. It's been tough having you just a step behind me, especially since I know I haven't done a thing to warrant your suspicion. Still, that's no excuse. And I am sorry."

He couldn't hide his surprise. "No need to apologize."

"Just for the record, I'm on my way home now, no detours, no shoot-'em-ups on the way there. I won't even stop when I pass Go."

He reverted to his stony silence.

Oh, well. She'd tried. It was time to head home and get ready for tomorrow. She figured it'd be a big day.

One way or another, Maryanne was about to meet Carlotta Papparelli, the woman who, once and for all, would put an end to J.Z.'s insane suspicion.

She hoped.

The next morning, Maryanne took longer than usual to get ready. The jeans were comfortable, but they felt strange, very much like a costume. Something about them, though, made her feel good. Free somehow. The soft green T-shirt she chose made her hair take on a rich glow, something kinda-close-but-not-quite-there-yet to the auburn family. And the sneakers gave her an odd sense of invincibility; she could almost see herself as bouncy, capable and yes, free.

Just what she felt freed from, she didn't know. But she did know a bubble of excitement rose from her middle as she locked the door behind her. Shakespeare wasn't happy, even though she'd left him ample food.

The drive to Philly took almost two hours. The Feds never left the middle of her rearview mirror as the MapQuest directions led her to the Papparelli residence. And then—

Well, then she parked and sat. Just sat. And waited. Waited some more. What next? Should she walk up and ring the doorbell?

The structure the Papparellis called home was daunting.

It resembled a cross between a Mediterranean villa and a medieval fortress—in suburban Philly—and Maryanne's gumption didn't want to carry her across the figurative moat of sidewalk in front.

After a while, Dan Maddox left the gray car and took a walk.

Her legs were cramped, too.

Then a European sportscar drove up and honked its horn. One half of the ornate mahogany doors to Castle Papparelli opened, and her quarry came out. Carlotta was even more beautiful than her newspaper photos made her out to be. Model-thin and model-gorgeous, she was blessed with a thick mane of streaky blond hair, elegant, high cheekbones, and huge, dark brown eyes. She was also young, maybe a couple of years older than Maryanne, no more than thirty or so.

The widow ran down the wide front steps and opened the yellow car's door. A woman inside called out. "Hey, Carlie. Vittorio says he has a fresh pot of your favorite raspberry-flavored coffee ready."

"Great!" the widow said. "I'm going to need it. You have no idea what this week's been like—"

The door slammed and the yellow car zipped away. Maryanne's trusty Escort followed, and the gray car…well, it just trundled along behind her all the way.

Vittorio probably owned the very glamorous Santino's Day Spa in front of which the yellow car parked. The women went inside the brownstone with the huge sign, but it took Maryanne a good ten minutes to find a parking spot. Then again, she didn't have to worry. A visit to a salon took longer than that to achieve the kind of results Carlie Papparelli was obviously used to.

After she finally squeezed in between a Bimmer and a Jaguar, Maryanne raced back toward the salon, her every step accompanied by prayer.

"Lord," she said between gasps. "I'm as out of my element here as…tuna casserole at a White House dinner. Please help me…don't let me make a fool of myself…or not too much, okay?"

With a deep breath for courage, she opened the door. The lush scent of potpourri and the classical sound of Verdi enveloped her, but underneath the fragrance she caught the tang of chemical concoctions.

"May I help you?" asked the vision in caramel-and-cream behind the sage-green reception desk. She was of indeterminate age, wore heavy gold at ears, throat, wrists and fingers, and her honey-colored hair enhanced her tawny tan and burnt sugar-brown eyes.

Maryanne winced at the thought of her sneakers and jeans. "Doubt it," she blurted out before she could stop herself. She winced again. "I'm sorry. That didn't come out right."

The elegant lady allowed herself a small smile. "Let's try it this way: What can we do for you?"

Way more than I can afford. At least this time, she kept her words in her head. "Ah…my hair can use a trim."

Perfectly arched brows rose. "A…trim…. *Just* a trim?"

She could stand to ditch her split ends. "Uh-huh."

"O-*kay.*" Vittorio's glamorous receptionist stepped out from behind her green counter. "Follow me. I think Sissy's just about done with her last client."

Maryanne made herself put foot in front of foot, even though she had the sneaking suspicion that she'd be better off if she ran the other way. What had she been thinking?

Women swathed in the same muted verdant hue as the

reception area filled leather and steel chairs. Their heads bristled with an arsenal of torturous beauty. A couple had shrieking fuchsia stuff smeared on their faces, and at least four had their feet in tubs of foamy water.

What was she doing here, for goodness' sake? She was a quiet librarian from little old New Camden, PA, and not some society creature in need of constant maintenance. Just when she'd decided to give an excuse and flee, she caught sight of Carlie Papparelli no more than ten feet away.

As luck would have it, the receptionist invited Maryanne to sit at the shampoo station next to the one occupied by the Widow Papparelli.

"Thank You, Lord," she whispered and took her seat.

In seconds, she became the hub of frenetic activity. Sissy, an attractive thirty-something with spiky black hair, turned Maryanne's face from side to side, her expression critical as she evaluated what she had to work with. Maryanne got the impression she offered meager raw material. Sissy then pulled pins from Maryanne's bun and let the entire length cascade down her back. She ran long fingers through Maryanne's hair, sifting it as if to measure its worth.

At the same time, a teen introduced as Minerva Maude brought Maryanne a cup of the most incredible coffee she'd ever tasted. It was fragranced with raspberries and who knew what else.

Maryanne sipped, and Sissy clanked through a drawer of metal tools. Minerva Maude disappeared and returned with another of the green cloaks, with which she covered Maryanne. Finally, when her new sneakers were removed and a pair of—yes, green, too—comfy slippers put in their place, Sissy gave her the verdict.

"It's gotta go, dear."

"Huh?" *That was eloquent.* "What do you mean?"

"All that hair, girl. It does less than nothing for you."

Maryanne didn't know whether to howl at the insult or to ask for more details. But her indecision took a backseat when Carlie lifted her suds-covered head from the bowl and grinned.

"You've never been here before, have you?"

Maryanne shook her head.

"Get used to it," the widow said in a friendly voice. "They don't take no for an answer, so if Sissy says your hair's gotta go, then it's gotta go. Trust me, you won't regret it. Whatever she does will look a million times better than the best you might imagine. By the way, I'm Carlie. Who're you?"

The woman's friendliness surprised Maryanne. She wouldn't have thought the wife, now widow, of a crime boss would be so open. She'd always imagined that kind of people would keep a low profile so they could pass under the radar.

"I'm Maryanne Wellborn, and I'm not sure I should be here in the first place."

Carlie frowned. "Then why'd you come, if you don't want to be here?"

"It's not that I don't want to be here, it's that I have to— I mean, I'm not sure why I decided to come in. I'm not sure I want a change."

Carlie eyed her then gave another of her bright grins. "You've never had your hair done—really done, have you? You probably only get the ends chopped off when they get too ragged and messy."

Maryanne blushed. "Something like that."

The mob widow's stare went on for a few seconds longer than Maryanne would have liked. "You must have a secret wish to change," Carlie said, "otherwise you wouldn't have come here. Are you sure you're not ready to let the secret you out of hiding?"

Was there a secret Maryanne? If her mother had been right, then that Maryanne would only get her into trouble. Did she really want to risk that?

If she up and left, however, she'd never get another go at Carlie. Here she was, right next to her quarry, both of them stripped of outward differences. Something about a hairdresser's cape and a headful of shampoo foam made equals of all women.

Instead of answering, and perfectly aware that Sissy awaited permission to go to town on her almost waist-length locks, Maryanne asked, "What are you having done?"

Carlie looked upward, as if to look at her hairline. "My roots need a touch-up, but I'm not sure I want to keep this color. Vittorio's going to take a look at it, and we'll decide what to do then." The widow looked at Sissy. "Have mercy on her, will you? Don't even think of doing choppy or spiky things to her innocent hair. Ease her into the wild, wild world of Vittorio Santino hair."

Maryanne looked from one to the other, her heart pounding, grateful for Carlie's words. "Ah…what did you have in mind?"

Sissy grinned. "There's a redhead trying to come out of you, you know. And how about some curls?"

"Red? *Curls?*"

"Yeah, curls. Let's cut and give you a perm, and dig out the redhead you really are."

"Redhead…." She felt faint. *Lord! What am I doing*

here? Help me, please! "How about we just start with the…the c-cut, and then we can decide what to do next?"

Carlie laughed. "Nah! If you're going to do anything, do it all. Take a chance on yourself. Who knows who's waiting underneath that hair for Sissy to find?"

"Yeah," Maryanne said, all of a sudden queasy. "Who knows who's been hiding in me…?"

Sissy rubbed her hands in glee. "Oooh, yeah. Let's get a shampoo and go find out."

SIX

"How much longer do you think she'll be in there?" J.Z. asked Dan.

Dan chuckled. "There's no question you don't have sisters. In a place like that? She could spend the rest of the day there."

"Are you serious? Why?"

"Because all the things they do take a whole lot of time."

"Hey, we're talking Maryanne-the-library-anne, here. I don't think our Olive Oyl needs a whole lot of beauty treatments to ball up her hair in a little bun-thing."

Dan shrugged and went back to the card game on his Palm Pilot. "Why don't you go buy yourself a book or a magazine? I saw a convenience store about a block away."

J.Z. checked his watch for the sixth time and sighed. "I guess I can. This surveillance is the strangest I've ever done. Who knows how long it'll take to get the goods on her."

"I'm going to remind you again, J.Z. She could be innocent."

He glared at Dan then got out of the car. The chances of Maryanne Wellborn being innocent were less than those of a steak dinner's survival around an unsupervised dog.

J.Z. hurried to the convenience store, scanned the selection of popular fiction, moved on to the magazines, chose one on vintage cars and then grabbed a crossword puzzle volume just in case. He wasn't a big fan of word games, but he might need something more time-consuming than a magazine, since Maryanne was proving such a hard case to crack.

On his way back to the car, he scanned the magazine cover, his attention snagged by the teasers for some of the articles inside.

"Oh!" a woman exclaimed as they collided. "I'm sorry—"

"Excuse me—"

The apology froze in his throat. He squinted, blinked a couple of times, then plain-old stared. "Maryanne?"

She stared back, her brow furrowed with obvious irritation. "Of course, Maryanne. You don't let me out of your sight for longer than overnight in my apartment. And then, you still watch the garage door."

This time he had let her out his sight and she hadn't been sleeping at all. If he hadn't seen her up close, he wouldn't have recognized her. Before, Maryanne had worn dowdy, serviceable clothes, but this woman had on well-fitting, attractive jeans and a soft-green knit top that did nice things for her skin color. He peered at her some more, and noticed the faint and subtle shades of well-applied eye makeup and a hint of warm color on her cheekbones. A soft, peachy sheen brightened her lips and made her look like the twenty-six-year-old woman Maryanne Wellborn was.

But those changes were minuscule when compared to her crowning glory. Gone was the Olive Oyl bun at the

nape of her neck. In its place, warm-brown curls rioted and
bounced every which way with each move she made. The
sun caught a reddish sparkle in the masses of wild hair and
gave the illusion of a halo.

She was beautiful.

But the halo had nothing to do with her, with Maryanne
Wellborn, hit woman for the mob. "You should've checked
to see if we were still here before you left your fairy god-
mother's lair. You might have pulled it off. But now, the
disguise won't get you anywhere."

"Pulled what off? What disguise?"

He waved toward her head, and then down at her jeans.
"Give me a break. This is *not* what you've been wearing
the past few days. And that hair? Is it a wig?"

She sputtered like an overheated radiator, then slammed
her fists on her hips, an indignant expression on her really,
really pretty face. "Let me tell you," she said as she
grabbed an auburn corkscrew and pulled it out straight, "a
wig would've been a whole lot cheaper than this!"

Before he could catch himself, he laughed. She didn't
like his laughter, so she scowled. That only made him
laugh harder.

She spun and started toward her car. "Men!"

He watched her, still smiling. Reluctant admiration
began to grow in him. He had to give her credit. When she
did something, she went all out. This was not the dowdy
woman he'd first met. This was the woman he'd been sure
she'd stifled under the dismal clothes and blah hair.

This was a woman who'd appeal to any man.

And he had to be careful. He couldn't let this change-
ling throw him off guard with this kind of diversionary
tactics. He couldn't forget that the changes in Maryanne

were nothing more than an illusion Santino's Day Spa had created in a handful of hours' worth of work.

He loped back to the car. "Get going," he told Dan. "She's going to lose us if you don't step on the gas."

"What are you talking about? The librarian hasn't come out of the salon yet."

"Ha! Shows you how good she is. See? She's getting into her car."

Dan looked at the beige Escort. "That's not Maryanne Wellborn."

"Oh, yes, that is. That's the kind of stuff they do in that snooty place she went to."

"No way! That woman's stealing the librarian's car. Call 911, will you?"

J.Z. laughed, but this time there was no humor in his laughter. "I told you Maryanne Wellborn was good. *That,* my friend, is the new and improved librarian from New Camden, PA. And I'm sure it's her because I bumped into her—literally. I got up close and personal, and the change is incredible, but that's our hit woman under the mop of curls."

"Wow!" Dan said, admiration all over his face. "She looks great. Wonder what took her so long to get herself one of those makeovers women like so much."

J.Z. scoffed. "Give me a break, Dan. We're tailing the woman, she's under suspicion for a bunch of murders, we're about to bring her in and you wonder why she got herself a disguise? Maybe what we're seeing is the real Maryanne Wellborn. Maybe she's just now thrown off her disguise."

Dan clicked the turn signal on, then shot J.Z. a glance. "Are you sure either one's a disguise? This is a pretty public place. You'd think if she was trying to hide, she'd have someone come to her and do their magic where no one, especially us, could see the results and bust her."

"I don't know why this woman does any of the things she does, but it'll take a lot more than a pair of new jeans and a bunch of in-your-face curls to fool me. She's not about to distract me from my case."

Dan said nothing for about ten miles. Then, when J.Z. was nearly lulled into a nap, his partner spoke again. "You've made this case way too personal. I really think it's pushed you over the edge."

J.Z. took a deep breath. "I won't deny that I hate organized crime, and that any chance I get to lock up one of those scumbags, I'm going to do everything I can to do it. But—and that's a big but here—I haven't gone off the deep end. The idea that this woman killed those old people gets to me. And the way she plays the Goody-Two-shoes so well… You really have to watch out for those too-too perfect ones. They're too good to be true—literally."

Dan switched lanes to let a truck full of chickens at the end of the ramp onto the freeway. "Okay, so what kind of clear, solid evidence do you have against her? You're going to have a hard time convincing a jury that a bunch of e-mails to cancel senior citizens' library privileges and a good-looking hairstyle are proof of her guilt."

"I beg to differ with you. We have more than the demands for the hits and her disguise. We not only have the dead seniors, each one of them the subject of one her e-mails, but we also have an e-mail-mentioned dead mobster and her prints on his IV stand. All this happened in her territory."

"Circumstantial at best, J.Z. You're going to need more than that to lock her up, much less go for the death penalty."

"You call fingerprints circumstantial?"

"We went over this already. The e-mails can be explained in the context of library privileges, as Maryanne has done, and you can't assure me she didn't just move the IV thing out of her way at some point."

"You forget that nursing homes clean their medical equipment thoroughly and often."

Dan shrugged. "They might have missed that stand, or the spot on the stand. Perfection doesn't exist. Not even for you, J.Z."

"I'm not looking for perfection, just evidence. And it's my job to get that evidence. One way or another, I'll get it."

Dan fell silent again. After a while, J.Z. sighed in relief. He didn't like to argue with his partner. It could make for all kinds of trouble during an investigation.

Twenty-five minutes later, they took the Lancaster exit off the turnpike, and, as they waited for the cars ahead of them to pay their tolls, Dan gave him another one of *those* looks.

"What is it this time?" he asked.

Dan frowned. "I sure hope you aren't about to cook up any of your 'great ideas' on this case. Remember Eliza's threat. If you really want to pursue this one all the way to the end, then you'd better stay away from your loose-cannon stunts. You don't want her to pull your badge."

The memory of the meeting with his former flame set off a burn in his gut that had nothing to do with heartburn. "Don't worry about me. I'm not about to give Eliza the pleasure. I know how to do my job, and like I told you earlier, I'll do everything possible to purge my territory of organized crime. Even when the criminal looks like a granny in the making or a red-haired spitfire beauty."

Dan hit the brakes hard and the car jolted. He turned and gave J.Z. a piercing look. "A red-haired spitfire beauty, huh?"

"Well, what else would you call the woman Vittorio's Spa spit back out today?"

Dan nodded slowly. "Yeah, I guess that sorta says it all."

Because J.Z. knew the man at his side quite well, he was certain that Dan hadn't said all he had on his mind. He figured he'd wait his partner out, but if Dan hadn't spilled his thoughts by the time they reached wherever Maryanne was headed, then J.Z. would have to find some way to dig it out of him.

Even though he wasn't going to like it one bit.

Sure enough, Maryanne turned into the driveway of her condo complex and drove through the entrance to the underground parking garage. Dan pulled into an open space on the street, turned off the car and sat back with a yawn.

"Okay," J.Z. said a moment later. "I've given you plenty of time to tell me what you really think. So go for it. Talk, and don't hold any punches."

Dan turned sideways, hooked his right arm around the headrest on his seat. "I gotta tell you, man. There's something happening here between you and the librarian. You're just a little too hot under the collar, even more since you actually met her."

"What are you, nuts?"

"Just listen to me. You asked me what I thought, and I'm gonna tell you. Every time the two of you are in the same room, you set off some kind of weird storm. You're like a pair of weather fronts that smash together and make lightning bolts. I'm not so sure it's all about the mob and the dead seniors, either."

J.Z. gaped. Dan didn't mean what J.Z. thought he meant. Did he?

"Go ahead," his partner said, a crooked smile on his choirboy face. "You can close your mouth. This thing with Maryanne reminds me of those few crazy months when you and Eliza thought the sun and the moon hung on each other. Consider this just a friendly reminder. Job-related romances can be deadly—if not physically, then to a career, for sure."

J.Z. shook his head. "I can't believe you said that." He stared at his partner for a moment longer, then took a deep breath. "Tell you what. I'm going to do you a favor. I'm going to forget the last few minutes happened and that you came up with the dumbest stuff I've ever heard."

"You'd show your smarts if you didn't forget them…or the so-called dumbest stuff you ever heard. After all, I'm not the one who called Maryanne Wellborn a red-haired spitfire beauty, okay?"

J.Z. sucked in a sharp breath. There wasn't much he could say to that. He had called Maryanne a beauty. He couldn't take back his words. He couldn't deny how much she'd piqued his interest from the very start.

He also didn't want Dan to know the librarian's new look had nothing to do with it. Something about Maryanne got to him. He'd never been in a situation like this before.

It put him at a greater risk than dating Eliza Roberts ever had.

The next morning, Maryanne knew regret. "Why did I ever think this perm might be a good idea?"

Shakespeare lifted his head from the paw he'd been grooming, and graced her with a feline stare. Then, without further ado, he went back to his morning toilette.

"Great help you are." The corkscrew curls resisted her hairbrush's attack, but she refused to show up at church looking like a latter-day brunette Shirley Temple. No one would understand.

She wasn't sure she did, either, so she couldn't expect it of anyone else. She'd given up impulsive behavior a long time ago, and yet, yesterday at Vittorio's, she'd cast aside years of control and gone with the flow.

"Argh!"

After expending an excessive amount of patience, and monumental brush-to-kinks combat, she subdued the mop enough to pin it into a ghost of her former chignon. At least she'd made Sissy leave the hair long enough to tie back.

Still, certain determined wisps defied brush, gel and even hairspray. They bounced at her temples and at the nape of her neck in a very soft, feminine way. They looked unprofessional, but if she were honest with herself, she had to confess that she liked them. They made her look pretty.

She grabbed a serviceable gray skirt and a black-and-white striped blouse, slid into her black loafers and hurried to the car. She didn't want to walk into church after the choir had started the morning's hymns.

Mercifully, no one stopped her as she went straight to her usual pew. She did, however, notice a handful of curious looks. In an effort to return to pre-J.Z. Prophet normalcy, she put on her horn-rimmed reading glasses, even though she didn't need to read right then.

Maryanne gave herself up to worship and praise, and as usual, paid close attention to the sermon. Pastor Craig was new to their congregation, but she'd learned from the first service he conducted that he was a gifted teacher. She appreciated his wisdom and the clear way he presented Bible truths.

Then the final blessing dismissed the congregation. That's when Maryanne's ordeal began. At the hands of Trudy Talbot, of course.

"What did you do to your hair?"

"I got a trim."

"Since when do trims turn stick-straight hair into sweet little wispy curls?" She came a step closer. "And there's something else that's different. Did you color it, too?"

The shock in her friend's voice matched Maryanne's own surprise. "A very determined hairdresser caught me at a weak moment. What can I say?"

"It's nice. The red makes your eyes look almost gold, and now your skin has the prettiest peach tone. Is it permanent?"

"As permanent as a colored henna treatment is."

"Too bad. I think you should go all the way with it. When this fades, have that smart hairdresser dye it this same shade."

Maryanne couldn't believe that Trudy had hit on the same faint urge she'd tried so hard to deny. "I don't know. It's frivolous, expensive and doesn't go well with the professional look I prefer."

"You mean the Olive Oyl disguise, don't you?" J.Z. Prophet said from behind Maryanne.

She spun. "What do you mean, disguise? And why are you here? I doubt you came to worship."

His steely eyes raked her from head to toe. "I came to do my job. I intend to keep you under surveillance at all times."

"Why? Do you think I'm going to take out a fellow congregant? I don't think you're that stupid."

"No, but your contacts might be posing as congregants here—like you. A church makes for a great cover. Trust me, I know."

The bitterness in his last words caught Maryanne by surprise. She was used to his anger, and yesterday, his laughter had surprised her—a pleasant surprise, at that. But this? She wondered what lay behind the resentment.

"I wouldn't desecrate the Lord's home like that. I take my heavenly Father seriously, and I only want to honor Him, here and everywhere else I go."

"Such piety," he taunted.

"Excuse me." Trudy's cheeks blazed and her nostrils flared. "You have no right to judge Maryanne's faith. Only God knows a person's heart. We can only witness the fruit their faith produces, and Maryanne's is nothing but—"

"Ah, yes. The fruit." J.Z.'s jaw looked rock-hard. "That would be her actions. Interesting you should bring them up. I'd say a string of dead seniors paints a vivid picture of rotten fruit."

Ron strolled up and held out a hand. His smile didn't temper the reproach in his gaze. "I don't believe we've met. I'm Ron Talbot. Trudy's my lovely wife and she's also Maryanne's best friend. I'm Maryanne's attorney. You would be…?"

Instead of shaking, J.Z. reached into his back pocket and withdrew a black leather card case like the one Dan showed Maryanne at the mall. "Special Agent Prophet with the FBI's Philadelphia organized-crime unit. As I'm sure you already know."

Ron took the ID, examined it then closed the case and handed it back. "I did know J.Z. Prophet was hot on Mary-anne's trail, but I've never met you nor did I bother to look for a photo. I knew I'd have a hard time digging one up. Special agents tend to keep a low profile."

J.Z. returned his badge to his pocket. "Part of the job. I'm sure you understand, counselor."

Ron looked Maryanne's tormentor up and down, much the same way said tormentor had sized her up moments earlier. He then laid an arm around her shoulders. At the same time, Trudy took her left hand.

"I understand more than you think." Ron's voice came laced with as much determination as J.Z.'s jaw displayed. "I understand you're harassing an innocent woman, that you've falsely accused her of crimes she hasn't committed and that you might be on a personal vendetta."

Maryanne gasped. Ron warned her with a look. She closed her eyes and prayed.

Ron spoke again. "You're on shaky ground, Agent Prophet. Not only could you lose your job, but you could also wind up in jail. Maryanne Wellborn is no killer. The woman you see here is just who she says she is."

Through slitted eyes, Maryanne saw red stain J.Z.'s cheeks.

"The woman I see," he said in a taut voice, "is actually two women. One is the too pious, Goody Two-shoes librarian that she shows friends and neighbors. The other one—" a dangerous smile lit his dark features with something Maryanne didn't want to identify "—is the amoral criminal who kills old people for their dough. She's the one who pals around with a mobster's widow. In fact, that woman—the real Maryanne Wellborn, if that's even her name—is a hit woman for the mob."

"Watch your words, Agent Prophet."

"I am watching my words. Just as I'm watching her." J.Z.'s gaze speared to her. Maryanne couldn't turn away.

He went on. "Even if her disguise fools everyone else, I know my way around the fun-house illusions the mob's so good at. Life's taught me to see beyond the smoke and mirrors they use to hide and do their dirty deeds."

Tears burned the back of Maryanne's lids. "I haven't done a thing—"

"Why don't you let your hair down, Maryanne-the-library-anne?" he taunted. "Where's the pretty woman with the makeup and the jeans? What'd you do to those sassy red curls? And where's your friend Carlie Papparelli this fine day?"

"Makeup?" Trudy whispered. "Jeans?"

"*You* know Carlotta Papparelli?" Ron asked.

J.Z. spread his legs shoulder-width apart and crossed his arms, his smug smirk a challenge Maryanne dared not take.

She couldn't deny anything he'd said. He'd seen the change she underwent yesterday. She had befriended Carlie Papparelli, and at that moment, even had the widow's phone number keyed into her cell phone—after they'd spent the morning at Vittorio's chatting, they'd agreed to stay in touch. Maryanne had called her a number of times, and Carlie had returned the gesture.

And, true, she'd chosen to revert back to her normal appearance this morning, reluctant to face the stares and questions of those who knew the "old" her. Even she could see where someone prepared to doubt her would have his suspicions bolstered by what she'd done.

She had nothing to say.

"Watch yourself." J.Z.'s voice came out soft and deadly. "'Cause you can count on me watching you."

SEVEN

Ron and Trudy tried to reassure Maryanne after J.Z. swaggered away, but nothing would do that until J.Z. himself conceded his mistake. She spent most of the afternoon either crying or shaking, and sometimes both.

What had Dan Maddox said back at her office? Oh, yeah. He'd warned J.Z. not to make another of his "doozy-sized" mistakes. So J.Z. was prone to big blunders. Interesting.

She called Dad to warn him she'd be late for their usual Sunday visit. She couldn't let him see her in this state. So she took time to eat a sandwich, and then, Bible in hand, to seek the comfort and guidance God never failed to provide.

At a quarter to four, she drove to Peaceful Meadows, finally at peace herself. A smile on her face, she went straight to the activities hall, where she knew Dad and his friends would be gathered in front of the large-screen TV to watch the last eighteen holes of that weekend's golf tournament.

Partway down the long corridor to the hall, she saw the frail woman who'd stood up for pet ownership at the nutty senate meeting she'd attended. If she remembered right, Eloise was her name. The lady would have a hard time at the heavy glass door, hampered as she was by the aluminum walker, so Maryanne hurried to catch up.

"I don't believe we've met," she said. "I'm Maryanne Wellborn, Stan's daughter."

Beautiful violet eyes held her gaze. "It's a pleasure to finally do so. Your father talks of little else but you. I'm Eloise Thurman, and one of the veterans here. This is my thirteenth year at Peaceful Meadows. And I will confess that I'm not a reader. That's why we've never met."

Since discretion was the greater part of valor, Maryanne chose her next words accordingly. "Wow, I'm impressed. Thirteen years. You must like it here."

"Our staff is excellent, the doctors top-notch and the chef's from the Cordon Bleu School of Cooking in France, so the food's great."

More confirmation that she'd done the right thing for her dad. "That's what I hear." She held the door for Eloise. "Dad seems to have settled in well, too. I guess those of you who've been here a while are kind and welcome newcomers."

The violet eyes told Maryanne her gesture hadn't gone unnoticed. She blushed.

"Well, dear," Eloise said, "there's welcoming and then there's *welcoming*. Some consider newcomers nothing more than recruits for their cause."

Mitzi Steinbrom *click-click-clicked* up on her stiletto heels. "Oh. Stan's daughter. The pigheaded lothario's over there with the rest of his chums." She waved toward a corner of the room then tottered off down the hall.

Although her father wasn't and never had been a lady's man, Maryanne couldn't deny his stubborn streak. She fought to stifle a grin.

"Go ahead, honey," Eloise said with a sweet smile. "Laugh all you want. Mitzi's a caution, and your daddy's as obstinate as can be. Those two disagree on almost everything."

"I want to know where she gets the balance to march around on those spiked heels."

Eloise glanced down at her own feet then shook her head. "Hard to believe I used to do the same. We all did back then. My darling Herbert—Mr. Thurman, you understand—used to say I had the best legs east of Hollywood."

The poignancy in Eloise's voice brought a knot to Maryanne's throat. Although it was a blessing that the widow had memories to keep her company, her longing and loneliness saddened Maryanne.

"You're still a lovely woman, so you must have been beautiful then."

A wise gaze took Maryanne's measure. "I think you really meant that, dear. It's rare to find a youngster who isn't given to flattery or condescension around an old woman like me."

Maryanne gathered the quilted wrap that lay across the back of the caramel-colored armchair Eloise chose. She also held the walker while the older woman took her time to settle in.

"There's no reason for flattery," she said as she collapsed the walker then leaned it against the chair. "In the long run, the truth's always better. And as far as condescension…that's just plain nasty."

Eloise chuckled. "I'm glad Stan did so well at something as important as raising a daughter. And I understand he didn't do it alone. But your mother went home to the Lord not too long ago, didn't she? I think your father truly misses her."

"We both do. They were the two most different people you can imagine, but they loved each other very much. It's been hard on Dad, and especially with his surgery. He didn't have her support when he most would have wanted it."

"I know how that is, dear. It's life." Eloise spread the quilt over her weak legs despite the warmth of the day. Maryanne tucked the folds around the precious lady's feet.

"Those of us who know the Lord," Eloise added, "recognize He's always at our side. I don't know how unbelievers do it. Life is livable only by His grace."

"Amen." Maryanne caught a glimpse of her father's happy face. "And with the help of the loved ones He puts in our path."

"Amen and amen." Eloise took hold of Maryanne's hand. "You've been a dear to help me, and I'm grateful to you and to the Father for bringing you today. But go on. Stan will worry if you dawdle with me much longer and he doesn't see you soon."

On impulse, Maryanne bent down and pressed a gentle kiss on Eloise's cheek. "You've blessed me more than you can know. Our chat has meant a great deal to me. You've reminded me of what really matters. Thank you, Eloise."

Tears glimmered in Eloise's eyes. "As you have also blessed me." She gave Maryanne's hand a final pat. "Now go. Go give your daddy a hug, and stop by and see me next time you come by."

"A-ha! The invitation I needed. I'll make a reader of you yet."

Eloise chuckled. "I'm ninety-eight, Maryanne, and set in my ways. I doubt you'll change me at this late stage."

"You just wait! We'll see what you say when I find the right read for you."

With a lighter heart than when she first arrived, Maryanne headed for the corner where her dad sat with a group of men around a table. It appeared that he and three of the other five were deep into a game of Scrabble. The remaining two were self-appointed cheerleaders. Scrabble was Dad's favorite board game.

Mitzi's unmistakable high-heel clatter came back into the room. Maryanne glanced over her shoulder and saw a familiar face at Mitzi's side. He, however, wore unfamiliar clothes. Mitzi clung limpet-like to his strong arm.

"Look what I found, ladies!" the chairwoman of the residents' senate cooed. She patted the arm covered in uniform-white. "I'd like you to meet Jerry, our new part-time orderly."

New orderly? *Jerry?*

It took all of Maryanne's will to keep from howling. Not only had she heard J.Z. tell Dan Maddox not to call him by his full name, Jeremiah Zephaniah, but now, by the expression on his face, she gathered he hated nicknames, as well.

The wretch deserved Mitzi.

Although the resident females crowded around the chairwoman and her attractive find, J.Z.'s gaze never wavered from Maryanne's face. But this time, she took it in stride. She went to her dad, hugged and kissed him, pointed out a high-point word he could make with his jumbled tiles and then met the G-man's gray gaze.

"Hi, *Jerry.* I hope you like working here. I understand it's a great place."

Predictably, J.Z. scowled. "I'm sure the new job'll be fine."

Maryanne grinned. "And I'm sure Mrs. Steinbrom will do everything to help you feel welcome."

He extricated his arm from the sassy senior's grasp.

"No need to go to any trouble. I'm used to working all kinds of jobs."

No doubt. "So you have trouble *keeping* a job."

"Not exactly. I…ah…have just had the opportunity to try many things, wear many hats, so to speak."

"Hmm…trouble with focus, then. Or maybe a case of misguided tunnel vision, which among other things, can sometimes lead to problems at work."

"You know there's nothing wrong with my focus," he said just inches from her ear. "And I don't suffer from tunnel vision. I'm just here to prevent any more unnaturally 'natural' deaths. That's my real job. Remember, wherever you go, I go."

"Talk about a disguise, J.Z. You've got me beat." She gave him a hard look. "And now you tell me I'm Mary and you're my blind-follower lamb."

"This isn't a game, Maryanne. Every one of the seniors you killed left a pile of dough to this place. I'm here to keep an eye on that money, help track down who should have it instead, and make sure you don't 'terminate' any more patients."

Her lack of fear came as a surprise. "Fine with me, if that's what the government pays you to do with your time." Something occurred to her. "You know? I think I do want you to hang around. That way you can see I know nothing about any money, that all I do around here is bring books for the residents and visit my dad."

He tilted his head, narrowed his eyes and stared.

Maryanne turned back to the table where her father had just trounced his fellow players. "Way to go, Dad!"

She checked over her shoulder. J.Z. hadn't budged. She winked. "See ya, Shadow."

Feeling lighter than she had since the first time she saw J.Z. Prophet, Maryanne spent a great afternoon and evening with her dad. Her heart sang with the certainty that the Lord was at her side. Any difficult moments that came her way would be tolerable—survivable—by God's abundant grace.

The Lord would lead her through this mess.

Maryanne Wellborn was a bundle of contradictions. On the one hand, J.Z. had her killer e-mails, the dead seniors and their lavish bequests. On the other, he had a woman who took time to help a fragile lady settle in to a chair almost too large for her shrunken frame.

Maryanne's tenderness seemed genuine. As did the love she showed her father. The latter, he didn't question—even the most heartless animal could love family and friends. But the former, the tenderness and friendship she offered the elderly people who stopped to visit with her and her dad, that did make him wonder.

"Whoa!" she cried out.

J.Z. looked her way. She dipped down and picked up a gentleman's cane. But instead of handing it over right away, she checked out the end. And frowned.

"Mr. Corbin, the rubber tip's almost all gone." She crooked an elbow, and then led Mr. Corbin to her father's side on the teal-blue sofa. "This is dangerous. Let me see if I can get one of the nurses to find you a new one. We can't have you slipping and sliding away, you know."

Stan Wellborn grinned at his new neighbor. "Isn't she something?"

"You're a lucky fella," Corbin said. "My kids are spread out all over the place. One's in Alaska, another's in

Chicago and the youngest is an archaeologist digging up bones in Peru, if you can imagine that."

"Yep. My Maryanne's a treasure. Can't wait to meet the lucky man who'll talk her into marrying him. Better yet, I want to see her with a bunch of babies who'll drive her nuts."

"Those grandbabies make getting old almost worth the while."

An image formed in J.Z.'s mind, vivid and clear. Maryanne with an infant in her arms, sweet tenderness directed toward the fortunate child, joy and peace on her pretty face.

Then the efficient librarian returned with the cane. The picture vanished.

"Here, Mr. Corbin," she said. "Your walking stick's all fixed. I'm so glad I was here and could take care of it right away for you. Let me know the next time that rubber thingy starts to go." She leaned closer to the charmed older man, made a big deal of looking both ways, then winked and added, "I know their secrets now. I found the stash of rubber tips."

Who *was* Maryanne Wellborn? Other than the prime suspect in a major organized-crime case, of course. In spite of the evidence against her, and despite his belief in her guilt, he did have to wonder.

In spite of everything, Maryanne intrigued him.

He had good reason to worry.

As the week went by, J.Z.'s worries grew. Either Maryanne Wellborn was an Oscar-worthy thespian, or—

No. He wasn't ready to consider *that*. Not yet. He still had too many questions for and about her.

Dan took back to Philly chunks of computer stuff

from Maryanne's office machine. He insisted that Zelda would extract answers from the data—if any were there to be found.

J.Z. had his doubts about all the Internet junk.

Maryanne must have decided to lay low for a while, because instead of meeting the Laundromat's widow again, on Saturday she went to the grocery store, the dry cleaner's and, of all places, to a bookstore where she bought two huge bags of books. Nevermind that the woman worked at a library with stacks and stacks of books—she still bought more on her time off.

He wondered if there was something about the specific books she'd bought that might keep her from checking out copies from her place of work. He'd have to get a good look at her bookshelves when and if he ever had the chance to check out her home. He'd let Dan go over the apartment. He was responsible for tailing her.

After she left the bookstore, Maryanne stopped at a designer coffee shop and picked up an overpriced creamy something-or-other, then went by a bakery for what looked like a pie. Finally she headed home, where she didn't stay long. At around a quarter to six, she pulled out of the underground garage and drove straight to church. There she parked under the floodlight closest to the door of the adjacent barn-like structure, and hurried in.

J.Z. watched members of the congregation arrive with covered dishes of all sizes. The pie; now he knew why she—a single woman—had bought a whole one.

The potluck supper brought back long-forgotten memories. He remembered the feasts where, as a boy, he faced so many choices he couldn't begin to make even the first. His mother had always insisted he take a small spoonful of every dish, determined that he try them all. J.Z. believed that was the reason for his eclectic tastes in food.

Suddenly, the drive-through burger and fries sitting on his lap paled in comparison to the memories.

At ten o'clock, Maryanne came back out, got into her boring little beige car, and drove back to the condo complex. The lights went on in her apartment but they didn't stay that way for long. Either she took a flashlight and one of those many books to bed with her, or Maryanne went to sleep before eleven o'clock.

He knew what to expect from her the next day, but even so, he was glad when Dan came to relieve him in the middle of the night. He needed a nap.

"Anything?" his partner asked.

"Not yet. How about you?"

"The same. Zelda's still messing with the disks, but so far all she's found is legitimate library stuff. You have to wonder, J.Z. I'm of the opinion that Maryanne's exactly who she says she is. I think we're wasting our time here."

J.Z. turned the key. "I'm not ready to give up yet. But right now, I need sleep. See you later."

Although he dozed off right away, J.Z.'s vivid dreams woke him up a number of times. Once, he even found himself reaching out for...*her.* The maternal image he'd conjured the week before at Peaceful Meadows of Maryanne with a child in her arms returned to his dreams over and over again. It stirred something in him, something he didn't want to examine or acknowledge. So he turned on his side each time it returned, and fell back asleep.

By eight o'clock, he gave up hope of any other dream. He took a shower and went to meet Dan. At nine-fifteen, Maryanne would head for church. She'd stay there for the rest of the morning; Sunday School went until ten-thirty, and then the worship service lasted until noon.

"Go to bed," he told Dan. "I don't think she'll get in too much trouble in church."

"I keep my cell phone on the nightstand. Call if you need me."

J.Z. again watched the congregation arrive. A strange urge overtook him, one he didn't examine any more than he did his dreams, and he followed them inside…for the first time since his father's arrest.

"He's here again," Trudy whispered as Maryanne followed her friend outside after the service.

"You mean J.Z.?"

At Trudy's nod, Maryanne smiled. "I know. I think I'd start to worry if he didn't show up everywhere I went. I'm kind of used to him now."

"Are you serious? How could you be?"

"There's nothing I can do about him—I can't chase him away, and I can't convince him he's wrong. I decided to hand him over to the Lord."

"That easy?"

"Well, it wasn't easy. And I didn't get to that place all by myself. A beautiful old lady at Peaceful Meadows said a couple of things that brought this whole mess into perspective."

She sensed a presence at her right. Without looking, she said, "Hi, Shadow."

"Care to share that old lady's words of wisdom?" J.Z. said. "I'd also like to know what kind of perspective you now have on things."

"You remember Trudy Talbot, don't you?"

He glanced sideways. "The lawyer's wife."

Trudy stared him up and down. Her expression left no illusions about her opinion. "Yes, I am Ron's wife. And if you'll excuse me, I'll go find him and our two sons."

Mischief bubbled up in Maryanne. "Wow! What a terrific effect you have on others."

"It's a gift."

She blinked. Had he cracked a joke?

"You can smile," he said with a smile of his own.

The expression looked strange on his face, kind of rusty, as if it was one he didn't often use—which Maryanne already knew. She smiled back.

"I see you came inside today. What did you think of the sermon?"

J.Z.'s smile disappeared and ice glossed his gaze again. She hadn't expected such a strong reaction.

"It brought back memories that are best forgotten."

Something had happened to him. In spite of all he'd put her through, and all he still intended to put her through, Maryanne's compassion grew.

"I'm sorry." She placed a hand on his forearm. "I'll pray for you."

He stepped away. "Don't bother. I saw through the faith sham years ago."

She drew in a sharp breath at the pain behind his words. "My faith is real, J.Z. I love the Lord and I trust Him. I even trust Him to get me out of the mess you've cooked up for me."

"You'd do better if you confessed. We can probably get you a pretty good deal with the D.A. Especially if you turn state's evidence."

"The only sin I have to confess is my resentment toward you when you first showed up. I already confessed to God, and I even turned you over to Him. I'm confessing to you now. Just so you know, I'm not really angry anymore—even though sometimes you drive me right up a wall."

"I'll take myself back from your God. He never did me any favors."

"God doesn't deal in favors. He mostly works blessings through His children's actions. He is faithful, you know, and generous, too. Why don't you give Him another chance?"

"I gave Him more than one. He failed every time."

"Are you sure God failed? Maybe it was the people around you who failed instead."

"Same difference. If what you said is true, that God works through people, then that means He fails through them, too."

"Not really. He's not a puppeteer who pulls strings. People can and often do choose to turn away from Him. That's when things get nasty down here."

"I'll say they get nasty."

Maryanne took a long look at the hurting man before her, the man who she was sure would deny the hurt with his last breath. "You sound as though you once believed, but something happened and you let bitterness grow between you and the Lord."

He shrugged again.

"He's still there, J.Z. Right at your side."

"I don't think so." He slanted her a look. "From where I'm standing, you're the only one here with me."

"If you give Him a chance, if you join me in prayer, right here, right now, God will join us, just as He promises to do."

He might have meant that cynical grimace as a smile. "You mean…'when two or more are gathered together in My name' and all that?"

It was her turn to shrug. "I take Him at His word. He's never let me down."

"You want me to believe you've never been hurt? Never been disappointed?"

"Of course not. I've had my knocks, and losing my mother was the most painful thing I've lived through. But just because her health failed and her body couldn't continue to sustain her, it doesn't necessarily follow that God let me down. He comforted me through the sadness and the loss. He even saw me through my father's surgery a few months ago. Dad lost his leg. That was rough."

Her words must have struck a chord in him, because a softness she'd never seen before appeared in his eyes. "You miss your mother, don't you?"

"Of course."

"I know how that goes."

"Your mother's gone, too, then."

"For years now."

"And you muscled through it on your own."

"She died because God didn't come through for us." The bitterness was back. "*She's* not the one who should have died."

The depth of J.Z.'s pain surprised Maryanne. She'd seen a hint of it moments earlier, but now he'd made clear that he had seen tragedy and still hung on to it to a certain degree. She didn't know what to say, so she prayed for the right words.

But before she found them, J.Z. went on. "You could say my mother's the one who led me here, to you."

"You'll have to explain that one to me. I thought a bunch of my e-mails and your stupid suspicions brought you here."

"What my mother suffered made me choose a career in

law enforcement. I learned back then that things aren't often as they seem."

Maryanne met his gaze. The steely determination she'd come to know had replaced the pain. "Maybe you should take things as they come, without looking for the bad in everyone you meet."

"Too late. I learned how worthless and rotten people can be a long, long time ago. Especially those who work hard to keep an innocent face."

She again reached out and touched his arm. "I think you've let your loss blind you to the truth. You need to see things as God does."

He jerked away. "You want to know how I see things? How your God—if He's really there—has to see what's behind the covers and the pretty fronts?"

For a moment, the fear she'd felt when she first met him struck again. But then, just as quickly, a deeper, greater emotion took its place. Her compassion of only moments earlier gave her the courage to speak. "Yes, please. Tell me how you see things. Tell me about the covers and the pretty fronts. I want to know what you see behind all that."

He squared his shoulders, looked around the empty parking lot, cast a bitter glare at the church itself. "I see a pseudo-pious man, greedy and power hungry, who cared only for himself. I see a man who made an unholy pact with the mob. A man who always looked the meek, mild and innocent Bible-sales rep he posed as, even during his nightmare of a trial."

Tears welled in Maryanne's eyes. "I'm sorry."

J.Z. didn't seem to hear. "You see, Maryanne. Good ol' Dad, Obadiah Micah Prophet—or whatever his real name might be—is a hit man doing life for his sins. He's the reason I can see beyond your dull clothes and your frumpy hair. Your quick-change-artist switches tell a lot. I'm not one to buy an illusion, at least not more than once."

Tears rolled down her cheeks. "I'm so, so sorry. But just because your father let you down, just because he did those awful things that got him sent to jail, doesn't mean that I'm like him. I'm me and no one else."

"It didn't take me long to learn that there are two of you, Maryanne. I'm going to bring in the one responsible—"

"You need help, J.Z. The kind of help only God can give." She took a deep breath, asked the Lord for strength, then plunged ahead. "I dare you to take God up on His offer of help, of love, of support and forgiveness and joy and peace. Especially peace. I challenge you to ask the Lord to bless you with the wisdom to discern, once and for all, the truth. But I wonder if you have the courage to take Him up on that offer?"

He flinched as though her words had been a blow.

Maryanne walked to her car, a prayer on her lips and grief in her heart. J.Z. Prophet wasn't a man to fear. Instead, he was a lonely soul who'd shut himself off from everything God had to offer. She wondered if he'd take her challenge.

"Father God, don't wait too long to bring him help."

EIGHT

Maryanne walked into the children's section just before she headed home after work on Monday. "I wanted you to hear it from me rather than from Mr. Dougherty."

Trudy put down the winter catalog from a children's book publisher. "What are you up to now?"

Maryanne led them into the otherwise empty staff lounge then closed the door. "I told our fearless director that I have to take my vacation now, starting tomorrow."

"What? I thought you'd made plans to go to England and visit the Bard's stomping grounds in the fall."

"I had, but this whole mob thing, the FBI mess, all that's more important in the long run. If I can't prove I had nothing to do with those deaths, then I'll never have a chance to visit England. On the other hand, once everything's cleared up, I can finish the plans for my trip."

Trudy placed her hands on Maryanne's shoulders. "I think you're serious."

"Of course I'm serious. Don't you think I should be?"

"I don't know what to think."

"Tell you what." Maryanne patted Trudy's not yet rounded belly. "Don't think so much about me when you have to plan the Thanksgiving welcome you're going to give that sweet baby on the way."

"Care to tell me what you have in mind?"

"It's better if you don't know."

"No way. Someone has to know what you're up to in case something goes wrong. Think of me as a human Saint Bernard. I'll lead the monks—in this case, the cops—to rescue you from the snows of disaster on whatever loony peak you decide to perch."

The last thing Maryanne wanted was her pregnant friend worried or ready to chase after her. "I can be reasonable. I'll check in with you once a day."

"Not good enough. What are you planning to do?"

"I refuse to involve you. Ron would skin me alive, and I may still need him to represent me, no matter what I find out." When Trudy went to argue some more, Maryanne stopped her. "I'm serious. I will take care of myself, but I'll give you a hint. I'm going to Philly."

Trudy waved her arms in disgust. "I knew it! You've been talking with that mob widow. She and her hairdresser did more to your head than just color and curl your hair. Not that anyone would know it, since you slicked it straight back into that plain old bun."

Maryanne shrugged. She was guilty as charged. She'd spent hours on the phone, cultivating an odd but nonetheless real friendship with Carlie, and the auburn curls didn't go with the professional image her mother had taught her to prefer.

When she didn't respond, Trudy went on. "I can't believe this is you, the woman who always says she wants a drab, dull and boring life. Now you're telling me you're about to walk into a viper's nest of mobsters. What's going on? Why won't you let the Feds take care of this?"

"You've heard my very own Fed. He just wants to lock me up."

"Give them time. Even J.Z. isn't so dumb that he won't eventually figure out what really happened."

"That's the whole point, Trudy. I don't have that kind of time. I can't go to jail. I have to take care of Dad. I can't wait for J.Z. to stumble onto the truth while he does everything he can to lock me up."

"I can't talk you out of it, can I?"

Maryanne shook her head, a riot of dive-bombing buzzards rather than butterflies in her gut. "I have to do it."

"What are you going to tell your dad?"

"That I'm going out of town on business. He knows I take all kinds of courses at various times of the year. He won't question it. And I will be taking care of business— *my* personal business."

Lines marked Trudy's forehead. "Here I thought you and J.Z. had finally come to some kind of agreement. Instead, you spring this on me now. I'm really worried."

"Just keep me in your prayers." Maryanne said a quick one of her own before she added, "J.Z., too. He really needs help, even more than I do. And the Lord's the only one who can help. I've been praying for him."

Trudy's eyebrow arched. "Is there something you want to tell me?"

Maryanne turned toward the door to hide the blush. "No, not really. There's nothing more to tell. Just pray, and wait for my calls in the evening. I'll let you know if I need help. Oh! And have the kids take care of Shakespeare for me."

"Of course we'll watch your cat. But be careful, Maryanne. This isn't a game."

Trudy's words, the same ones J.Z. had used, echoed in her thoughts. Still, Maryanne walked out of the library, drove home and made another call to Philly.

"Hi, Carlie. It's me, Maryanne. I wondered if your offer still stands."

Carlie's friendliness came through over the phone. "Of course it does. I meant what I said last night. Come on over. We're going to have so much fun, and I really need that right now. I've told you how things have been pretty grim around here since my husband died."

After another lengthy chat, Maryanne hung up and went to her room to pack. There wasn't much to do; it didn't make sense to take one's old stuff when one was headed toward a complete and utter overhaul of one's old self.

Who'd have thought she'd someday live out her own weird and warped version of *My Fair Lady* with a mobster's widow as her very own *Pygmalion?* Truth was, against all odds, she really liked Carlie Papparelli. What had begun as a means to prove Maryanne's innocence had led to an unexpected friendship. Long-distance and over the phone, true, but she felt the two of them had established a great bond.

As far as her makeover went? Was there more to her willingness to undergo such a transformation than just the opportunity to persuade Carlie to help her out?

Had she actually liked the difference the jeans and Sissy's efforts had made? Or did the fact that J.Z. had called her pretty have something to do with it, too?

Maryanne didn't know, and she didn't have the time to find out. Not right then. Later, once she'd put his suspicions to rest, she'd look inside, examine herself and her motives and face the truth.

It seemed she and J.Z. actually did have something in common. They both needed the Lord's help to see what was what. But not right away. Not yet. Definitely not. Maryanne now knew why Scarlett O'Hara had so often put off thinking to another day.

After his conversation with Maryanne in the church parking lot, J.Z. fought the urge to kick himself—more than once. He deserved more than one kick.

What was it about Maryanne that brought out the worst in him? He couldn't believe he'd let her see so much, straight to his greatest weakness. Was he nuts?

Maryanne was a suspect, a mob hit woman. And now she knew how to whip up his emotions and divert his focus away from the case and onto his private demons. She could really go in for the kill now. He'd have to be more alert than ever.

She was good, as he'd told Dan many times. All her faith talk had sounded sincere. She'd even squeezed out a couple of tears. Had they been real? Or had she called them up for his benefit?

At the worship service earlier that day, she'd listened to the pastor with fervent intensity. She'd even jotted down a note or two. And when the congregation stood and joined the choir in worship, the joy on Maryanne's face had moved him.

He'd thought he'd caught a glimpse of her private self. But could he trust that it was real?

In spite of his bitterness and cynicism, J.Z. hoped it was. Something about Maryanne-the-library-anne reached out to him and stirred feelings he'd shut down a long time ago.

At first, he'd tried to stifle them all over again. But now…now he had to wonder.

But not for long.

After her usual Sunday afternoon visit with her father, Maryanne got back in her little beige car and, instead of driving home, she turned onto the freeway on-ramp, rolled down her window to give him a playful wave, and took the Pennsylvania Turnpike toward the City of Brotherly Love.

He hated to use his cell phone while driving, but this was a desperate time. "Dan. J.Z. here. She's on her way to Philly. I don't need to tell you she's on her way to meet the weeping widow."

"Stay on her. Don't lose her."

"Ha! She has no intention of losing me. She waved when she got on the road."

Dan laughed. "You gotta admit, she's got style."

"Right now, she's got trouble on her trail. Call the office and let them know what's up."

"Will do. And be careful, man. I'll catch up with you in a few."

Partway to Philadelphia, Maryanne pulled into a rest area. She got out of the car, stretched and went inside the facility. J.Z. followed after Dan had called to tell him where to meet them.

Just as she was about to go into the ladies' room, she turned and winked. "Mother, may I?"

While J.Z. cooled his heels, Dan arrived.

"Anything interesting happen?" his partner asked.

"Nah. She's a careful, defensive driver, and she's making a pit stop."

"I gotta tell you. I'm surprised."

"I'm not. Remember how chummy we heard she's got with Laundromat's widow."

"Do you even know that's where she's headed?"

"Not for sure, but she's wearing the jeans and sneakers again, and her hair's bouncing all over the place."

"Too bad," Dan said. "I kind of like her."

"You like all women."

"She's different. I think she'd make a great friend."

Friend? "You must see something I don't."

Dan's grin quirked up on one side. "How unusual."

J.Z.'s cell phone rang. He pointed to the ladies' room. Dan nodded. He answered then fought a heartfelt groan.

"Hello, Eliza. Does Zelda have something for us?"

"No, but we have reason to think Wellborn's in danger. I've decided to take you off the investigation—leave that to Dan. I'm putting you on protective custody instead."

"What? You want me to look out for her?"

"Don't you want to prosecute her?"

"Yeah, but—"

"She has to live long enough to face trial. That's where you come in. Our informant says she's made some people very unhappy—she did kill Laundromat. They want to take care of her, if you get my drift."

His stomach lurched. He kept his voice neutral. "Okay. If you insist. But I don't see that it makes a difference. I've been tailing her all along."

"Don't just tail her. Stay closer than her shadow, you understand? Your job is to keep her alive until we get the goods on her. I really want this one."

Something in Eliza's voice gave J.Z. pause. He'd never known her to care much about a case or a witness—other than how it would affect her career. And Dan thought *he'd* gone over the edge.

"*Shadow,* huh?" Funny how Eliza had chosen that word, the same thing Maryanne had called him. He had been doing his job, after all. "Will do."

He slipped his phone into the sheath on his belt then saw Dan walk out of the building with Maryanne. She laughed at something he said. Her laughter rang out in the sunny afternoon, and J.Z. realized how much he liked it. He, on the other hand, made her cry instead.

Dan went toward his car and Maryanne to hers. As she crossed the parking lot, J.Z. heard the squeal of tires. A navy Mercedes swerved right at her.

"Look out!" he screamed. The car rushed on.

She turned. The Mercedes missed her and sped away. J.Z.'s heart pounded as he ran toward her.

"Don't you watch where you're going?" he asked. "You're in a parking lot, not a park."

Then he got a good look at her. The color had drained from her face. The shadows under her eyes looked like bruises. The auburn curls framed her features, incongruously cheerful. Her hazel eyes, often hidden by her horn-rimmed reading glasses, now looked like haunted crevices.

He cupped her chin in his palm. "Are you all right? From what I saw, the car didn't hit you. Did it?"

She sucked in a rough breath and gave a sharp nod.

Her chin quivered in his hand. And then he did something he'd never done before. At least, not on a case, and not with a suspect. He put his arms around Maryanne to draw her close.

Silent tears wet his shirt. Her shudders shook them both. He didn't know how long they stayed like that in the parking lot, but he suspected it was quite a while. When Maryanne finally took another deep breath, this one long and somewhat calmer, he looked around.

A crowd had gathered. Dan stood about twenty yards away, talking to a State Police officer. Moments later, the cop approached them.

"Your partner gave me most of your information," the officer said. "But I'll need a statement from the two of you, as well. What happened? What did you see?"

J.Z. looked down at Maryanne, who chose that moment to step away. He almost stopped her.

Almost.

But sanity returned.

"I caught a glimpse of a navy Mercedes," J.Z. said. "I'd been on the phone and wasn't looking at anything in particular."

Well, he had been looking at Maryanne, but not for any particular reason or with any degree of intensity. That's when the car veered toward her.

"I think the driver lost control," he said. "He might have been distracted, since the tires only squealed at the last minute. I don't think he hit the brakes until then."

The officer nodded. "We photographed the marks. Anything else?"

"No. Not really."

"Ma'am? How about you?"

Maryanne squared her shoulders and looked the officer in the eye. "I only saw something dark blue come at me. I heard the engine. Then J.Z. yelled. I heard the squeal, too. But that's about it."

"Too bad," the officer said. "No one got a good look at

the car, so I don't even have a partial license plate number to go on. I'd like to get this one."

J.Z. glanced at Maryanne, and her still-pale, ghostly look brought something hot and angry to life. He ground out his response. "So would I."

She met his gaze. Her gratitude was more than he deserved. J.Z. should have watched her more carefully. Actually, he should have been watching out for her. Eliza had just warned him.

He didn't think it wise to give the State Police any details just then. It could have been some idiot switching radio stations or on the phone with his girlfriend. It could have been.

His gut begged to differ.

When the officer left, Maryanne said, "Thanks, J.Z. You were very kind."

"Forget it. Are you really okay?"

"I think so. But I am running late. I was on my way to meet someone in Philly. I'd better give her a call so she doesn't think I've stood her up."

Reality crashed back in. "I doubt Carlotta Papparelli's waiting for you with bated breath. Unless, that is, she's waiting to either give you orders or to receive whatever you're bringing her."

Maryanne closed her eyes. "Not now, J.Z. I don't have the strength or desire to argue with you. I'm meeting Carlie because she offered to walk me through a makeover. We made plans for dinner, and now I'm going to be late."

"Need another disguise, do you?"

"I don't have a disguise. I have my regular clothes, and I bought some jeans and T-shirts to do some sleuthing on my own. I don't think tailored skirts are the right outfit for a P.I."

"When did you get your license?"

"I don't have one, and you know it. I just can't afford a real P.I., so I have to do it myself. I've done pretty well, if you ask me."

"Sure. And nearly got run over in the process."

"That was an accident. Someone's foot must have slipped off the brake pedal."

"Yeah, right. And the sky's really made of window-cleaning fluid. When it falls down, it corrodes brains. That's what must've happened to yours."

"Lame, J.Z." She shook her head. "I guess that guy really did scare you."

"I'd hate to have my prime suspect turned to roadkill by one of her pals."

"One of my pals! What are you talking about?"

"Yeah, J.Z.," Dan said. "What *are* you talking about?"

He ran a hand through his hair. He hadn't wanted to tell Maryanne about his new assignment, but circumstances had changed. "That phone call I took?"

Dan nodded.

"It was Eliza. Seems an informant says there's a contract out on Maryanne. Somehow, some way, Laundromat's pals learned about Maryanne—her e-mails, the finger-prints on the IV stand. They know we're investigating her, and there's been some rumbling about her part in his death. To put it in plain English, his 'family' isn't happy she took Papparelli out. So Eliza's pulled me off the investigation itself. She wants me to keep Maryanne under wraps."

Maryanne gasped. "Do you mean what I think you mean?"

"Yeah. Your mob pals aren't so happy with you. There's word that they want to take you out. For good, not on a date."

"I don't have mob pals—unless you think Carlie's in on

her late husband's deals. But from what I've read, the mob's really a man's thing. They're awfully chauvinistic and tend to keep women out of the loop."

So that's what those books she'd bought were about. "And you're indignant about it."

Her gaze bored right into him. "Discrimination is discrimination. It should tell you something."

"Good golly, Miss Molly. Lookee what we got us here. An equal-opportunity gun moll on a suffrage campaign. How special!"

The color came back to Maryanne's face. "You really are crazy," she said, her natural spark back in full flame. "You're the one who is absolutely, positively certain I'm some kind of hit woman. And now you're making fun of me because I pointed out another reason why I can't be the person you think I am."

"Okay. So you're not on a crusade for equal rights for gangsters." It was the best he could do to cover his surprise. She did have a point. The mob suffered from a gender gap.

"Goodbye, J.Z." She turned toward her car. "Thanks for the hug. You almost had me fooled. For a minute there I thought you might be human after all."

"Hang on!" He reached out and caught her hand. "Not so fast. Remember when you called me Shadow?"

She stared at their joined hands.

He let go.

"Thank you," she said, her voice icy cold. "Yes, I remember."

"I'm now your official shadow. So…that being said, you're stuck with me. And we can give the environment a break if we only take one car."

"You have got to be kidding."

"I've never been more serious in my life."

"You're tagging along on my *Pygmalion* adventure?"

"*Pygmalion*'s kind of outdated. 'The rain in Spain falls—"

"'Mainly on the plain.' *My Fair Lady*'s one of my favorite movies, but you're no Rex Harrison."

"And you're no—"

J.Z. stopped short. He couldn't say she was no Audrey Hepburn because he suddenly realized that behind the bulky glasses and dowdy clothes, Maryanne bore a vague resemblance to the late actress. How come he'd never noticed before?

Had she done that good a job with her Olive Oyl disguise? Had it fooled him at least in that regard? He, who was so certain he could see through smoke and mirrors?

He squared his shoulders. "Since there's no point for you to keep a new disguise from me, I see no reason, other than that you might bore me to sleep, why I can't go along with you and Carlotta Papparelli on that shopping spree. I can always carry packages. That should make it worth your while to put up with me. Especially now that someone tried to kill you."

"What do you mean, now that someone tried to kill me?"

"Just that I don't think the blue Mercedes materialized out of thin air. I don't think it was an accident."

"You are the most paranoid crackpot—"

"You don't know what you're playing with—"

"Someone should lock you up—"

"We've got to get you off the streets—"

"Enough!" Dan yelled. "Both of you should be locked up. Together."

"What?"

"Together?"

"Sure." Dan grinned. "The way I see it, one of two things would happen if we locked you up in a padded cell. You'd either fight to the death or you'd come out to the sound of wedding bells."

J.Z. turned to Maryanne, shocked.

She faced him, just as stunned.

They stared for long, silent moments. The tension grew tight and crackly. Then he remembered her tenderness toward the seniors at Peaceful Meadows. He remembered his dreams where she held a child near her heart. He remembered her tears when he told her about his father. He remembered how she'd felt in his arms...warm, delicate, vulnerable, scared.

He couldn't deny that he felt more alive when he faced off with her than he did at any other time.

"This is stupid," he said. "We can't just stand here and talk about padded cells and wedding bells. We have a mob widow waiting for us. Let's get going."

Moments later, after they'd arranged for an agent from Philly to come get his car and after he threw his duffel into hers, J.Z. and Maryanne got into the boring beige Escort and all three took off again.

But something had changed. J.Z. felt it in the car, in the silence around them. And it scared him even more than when that car took aim on Maryanne.

She'd begun to mess with his head.

But it was worse than that.

He now had to fear for the safety of the thumping organ in his chest.

* * *

Okay. So she did find him attractive. And he made her feel things she'd never felt before. But, come on. This was J.Z.

Why had she felt something shift inside her when Dan brought up those wedding bells?

She and J.Z. had nothing in common. Not even the most important thing—they didn't share the same faith. True, at one time he had believed, but he no longer did.

Did the man whose job it was to protect her pose a greater danger than a bunch of mobsters? She couldn't afford to feel so much for a man like J.Z. She wanted a quiet, simple life. One where she knew her routines, and where upheavals like the one she'd undergone when he first walked into her office didn't happen. He was not the peaceful, comfortable kind.

She had more to fear from J.Z. than from anything else.

"Explain to me one more time why you're meeting Carlotta Papparelli," the dangerous G-man in the passenger seat asked.

Maryanne prayed for guidance, for the Father to give her the right words, for the Lord's protection in the next few days.

"I'm convinced that Carlie can vouch for me. I read the accounts of the murder, and I'm sure she saw whoever killed her husband."

"Are you saying you think she's going to just trot into our offices and finger the killer, someone other than you?"

"I think she knows who wanted her husband dead. That might not be the person who pulled the trigger, but she had to have seen something. She was right there when it happened."

"Don't you think we spent hours with her, asked her every conceivable question about the shooting? About her husband and his contacts? Or don't you think we know a thing or two about interrogations?" He shook his head in obvious disgust. "Do you think she'd still be alive if she could prove who did it? Don't you think the hit man's pals would have finished her off if she knew?"

"I think that's why she *is* alive. Because she's kept her mouth shut. But I've come to know her a little since we first met. I think she's a pretty decent person. I think that once she knows my situation, she'll help me in whatever way she can. We've become friends."

"Lady, you're crazy. Either you're the most naive or the craftiest person alive. No one who's lived with the mob's going to do *you* any favors. I know better than that. You can't tell me you trust a mobster's wife. Unless the two of you have cooked up some scheme for your own dirty little purpose."

"Widow," Maryanne said. "And while I think she'll help me once I tell her about my situation, I don't trust Carlie any more than I trust you. My trust is in the Lord. He'll see me through this. I have nothing to fear when I walk through even this valley."

"Not a good idea, Maryanne. I came to faith in Christ as a boy. I was a child of God, a true believer when He let my world cave in on me. I was only in my teens. I'd never been in trouble and had always served the Lord."

J.Z. watched her drive in silence. And then he realized she'd started to pray again.

In spite of everything life had taught him, he couldn't help his grudging admiration. He wasn't sure he believed a word she'd said, but so far, he hadn't seen her do anything contrary to her faith. She'd even offered to pray for him, and she knew he intended to arrest and then prosecute her to the full extent of the law. Maybe…maybe she was the lone exception to what he'd come to know as truth.

Something about her got to him. Before he could stop himself, he said, "I can promise you one thing."

"What's that?"

"I promise I'll keep you alive. I won't let anyone hurt you."

"Thanks, but I'll still trust the Lord."

Unable to stop, even though he knew he was treading on dangerous territory, he took a deep breath. "Actually, there's another promise I can make."

"And that would be?"

"That while any question remains about your guilt, I'll do everything I can to keep you out of jail. Before anyone locks you up, I'll make sure they can prove you're guilty beyond a shadow of a doubt. You can count on me."

NINE

There had to be an easier way to prove she hadn't done what she didn't do. Trying to explain her shadow, her very own, private one-hundred-eighty-pound gorilla, to a mobster's widow had to rate among the weirdest things a woman would ever have to do.

The look on Carlie Papparelli's face when Maryanne introduced J.Z. as her friend was priceless.

Carlie's eyes widened. Then she frowned, her eyes narrowed to slits. "Let me get this straight," she said. "Your friend's car isn't available right now, so you offered him the use of yours while you're here in town. Is that right so far?"

Maryanne's cheeks sizzled. "So far."

"Okay. And he drove you here—" Carlie gestured toward the toga-clad valet outside the insistently Greek, lavishly columned restaurant where they'd agreed to meet "—so that we could have dinner."

She glared at J.Z. "Mm-hmm."

"But you're still going to stay at my place for the week."

Maryanne wanted to throttle the gorilla. She'd never been so mortified in her life. She could read between the lines to what Carlie really thought. How could she tell her new friend that she'd never had…never been involved *that* way with a man? Without coming right out and saying it, of course.

She couldn't. "That's right. That's the plan. J.Z. is going to use my car. Oh, and he might come shopping with us once or twice."

Carlie's eyebrows shot straight up her forehead. She pinned J.Z. with a ferocious stare. "What's up with that? I've never known a guy who'd go shopping with a woman—two, this time—without being either bribed or threatened within an inch of his life."

She watched him struggle with that one. Especially since a threat was part of the problem. "Maryanne had a minor accident this afternoon," he said. "Nothing serious, but I don't want her to strain herself carrying packages. I might come in handy."

The mobster's widow rolled her eyes. "Oh, brother. Does he ever have it bad for you, Maryanne."

"Oh, no! No, no, Carlie." Maryanne's blush kicked up a notch. "It's not like that at all. I mean, we're not dating or anything. I've only known J.Z. for a short time. He's just trying to look out for me. In his overzealous sort of way."

Maryanne refused to lie, and dancing around the truth like she'd just done came too close for comfort. She wished he'd just go away. But he wasn't easy to shake.

After a stern, caution-filled look at Maryanne, he told Carlie, "A guy can always tell when he's not wanted. I'll leave you to your dinner, and go take care of business." He turned to Maryanne one more time. "You know how to reach me. Remember, I won't be far."

"Yes, J.Z. Your number's programmed on my cell phone. We'll be fine."

Maryanne sighed when he drove off. She told Carlie, "I'm starving. Let's eat."

They ordered right away, and as soon as the waiter left, Carlie nodded toward the restaurant's entrance. "Are you sure he's housebroken? He seems a little wild to me."

Maryanne chuckled. "J.Z.'s different all right, but you get used to him after a while."

"I don't know. Shopping with him's going to be a whole new experience."

Maryanne remembered her trip to Wal-Mart. "Oh, yeah. The last time, he didn't look too happy when I asked him to hold a bunch of bags while I went to buy a pretzel and a drink...."

She let her words fade as another memory, one she'd almost forgotten, crashed back into her thoughts. Just as someone had crashed into her back.

Payback time. She hadn't given those words a thought. She did now.

Could that accident be related to today's near miss? If J.Z. was right, it could be. She'd never told him about it, and now she wondered what he would think. No, she didn't. She knew he'd insist the two were connected.

"Yoo-hoo!" Carlie called. "Earth to Maryanne! Looks like tall, dark and volcanic's got a bigger hold on you than you think. Just don't try and tell me he's some kind of kitty cat in disguise."

That word, the *D* word she'd come to despise since J.Z. started to fling it around, brought her right back to the present. She had a mission to accomplish.

She was careful with her words. "Well, he is concerned. I've had two accidents recently." Carlie didn't need to know that J.Z. had never heard of the first one. "He seems to have an overprotection complex or something."

"What kind of accidents?"

"Oh, nothing major, really. I fell while shopping at Wal-Mart, and a car almost hit me in a parking lot today. I was a little shaky after that one."

Concern softened Carlie's expression. "Are you sure you're up to a couple days' assault on Philadelphia's finest stores?"

Maryanne had wondered a time or two, but she couldn't back out now. "Uh…I think so. That's why I took you up on your offer."

Among various reasons.

"But that's enough about me. You mentioned you'd recently lost your husband. Are *you* sure you're ready for a shopping blitz?"

Carlie's smile looked strained. "I'm a strong supporter of shopping therapy. I'm ready for anything but more about Mat."

"Matt? Your husband's name was Matthew?"

Carlie sighed. "No. It was Carlo, but imagine the confusion Carlo and Carlie could create."

"So where did the Matt come from?"

"You won't believe this. It was short for Laundromat, of all things. He refused to let me in on what it meant. I think it embarrassed him. I always thought it had something to do with some crazy teenage thing."

That didn't sound right. And Carlie didn't look or sound a whole lot like a grieving widow. Maryanne had to prod more information out of her friend. "Was it recent? His death, I mean."

"A couple of weeks ago."

"You must miss him a lot."

Carlie looked down at the cream-colored tablecloth. "Please don't think I'm a monster, but I don't miss him at all. Mat was twenty years older than me, and he was…" She lifted a shoulder. "It wasn't a great marriage. From the time I was thirteen, I knew my parents expected me to marry him. His first wife died a couple of months after their third anniversary. Mom and Dad took five years to plan my wedding. I just played along."

It had been an arranged marriage. Blech! "I don't understand."

"The parties and the dress and the excitement of a wedding can dazzle an eighteen-year-old. Then when the parties were over, I was married. It was weird."

"That sounds like it came right out of a movie. So Mat was a family friend."

"More like my father's business associate."

"Something like a corporate merger."

"That's it."

Maryanne met Carlie's gaze. "What kind of business was it?"

To her amazement, Carlie gave an indifferent shrug. "I don't know for sure. Papa never, ever talked about his work at home. And I never thought to ask. Then, I started college right after Mat and I married. I never did ask him, either."

"Weren't you curious? Not knowing would've made me nuts."

"Like I said, Mat and I didn't have a great marriage. We weren't friends. And when I never got pregnant, he let his disappointment come between us."

Maryanne shuddered. "How sad."

And tragic.

If true.

She felt terrible about her need to pry, but she had no choice. She had to ask at least one more question; she couldn't wait. "Did you find out what he did for a living once his will was read? You were his wife. You must have inherited."

"Not the business. I got the house, a solid bank account and a check a month for the rest of my life. Everything else was divided between my oldest brother, Tony, and Mat's nephew Joey."

"And you don't know where the money for your house and the account and checks comes from."

"I might as well tell you everything, since you'll either read or hear all about it soon enough. It's been smeared over every newspaper and on every newscast here in Philly." Carlie took a deep breath. "They all insist that Mat was a mobster, that he was involved in money laundering for organized crime."

"What do you think?"

"I don't know what to think." She drew circles on the tablecloth with her well-manicured nail. "There were years of silence. Then that horrible shooting—I still hear the shots in my dreams. And the blood…there was so much of it. I thought he'd died then. That's what I was told, what the newspapers printed. It was horrible."

Carlie shuddered, and Maryanne felt a surge of sympathy. Then the young widow continued. "There was also some business about a coffin shipped to Sicily. It was supposed to have his body in it, but it didn't, since Mat turned up dead all over again in some little town near Lancaster. Weird—*creepy*—you know? None of it makes a whole lot of sense to me. All I know is that I've had enough of cops, FBI agents and reporters to last me for a hundred lifetimes."

The waiter rolled a large steel cart next to their table. In the middle, a skewer held a massive slab of roast lamb upright. With a wicked-looking carving knife, he peeled away thin strips of luscious, fragrant meat and piled them on their plates. Maryanne's mouth watered.

"That smells wonderful," she murmured.

"Just wait," Carlie said, her voice lighter. "It tastes even— Watch out!"

Maryanne turned as the carving knife hewed the tabletop right where her arm had rested a second earlier. The cart tottered and the meat fell, as did the waiter, who screamed, tangled with the tablecloth and brought everything else crashing down.

Carlie ran to Maryanne's side. "Did it hit you?"

Maryanne couldn't look away from the gleaming stainless blade. The knife still quivered from the momentum with which it fell. Had Carlie not warned her, she would have lost her right arm.

She whispered, "Thank you, Jesus." Then, in a louder voice, shaky, but still clear, she added, "It missed me. Thanks for the warning."

The maître d' rushed up, pale and with a sweat-beaded brow. "I saw what happened, Miss. The ambulance is on its way."

"I don't need an ambulance," Maryanne said. "But your waiter might. I think he's in a lot of pain."

The man held his thigh with both hands, and his face painted a picture of agony. Maryanne knelt at his side. "What happened?"

"Someone stumbled into me from behind," he said past tight lips. "I'm so sorry, Miss. I ruined your dinner."

"Oh, for goodness' sake, don't apologize. I'm fine and you're hurt. What's wrong with your leg?"

"Hot drippings spilled on me. I think the burn's pretty bad."

"You need cool water, then." She looked around. Carlie held out a glass, and Maryanne poured the chilled liquid on the man's leg.

He winced, but said, "Thank you."

Then the ambulance arrived. It whisked the waiter to the nearest hospital. No one confessed to the push, and no one could—or would—say they'd seen anything at all. It seemed that a group of diners had walked by on their way out of the restaurant just at that time. Maybe one of them did stumble.

It smelled fishy to Maryanne.

She remembered her mother, who'd said there was no such thing as coincidence. She'd believed in God-incidence. And although Maryanne knew without a doubt that God had nothing to do with any of the strange events of the past few days, she also knew there'd been nothing coincidental about them.

To make matters worse, her personal thundercloud materialized just as the maître d' showed Carlie and Maryanne to a new table.

"It's time to go," J.Z. said.

"I don't think so," Maryanne replied. "I'm hungry."

Carlie gave her a mischievous smile. "Why don't you join us, J.Z.? I'm sure Maryanne would like your company. She seems a little shaken still. That carving knife came awfully close to her arm."

Maryanne looked at J.Z.

J.Z.'s gaze speared toward her.

A battle of wills ensued, silent but decisive. He might get his way, but so would she.

He took one of the two empty chairs. "Tell me what happened."

Maryanne tried to keep it light. "It was just an accident. Someone bumped into our waiter, who had started to slice meat right behind me. He dropped his carving knife. Carlie warned me, I moved and the knife landed on the table. That's it. An accident."

"Again," he said. With his one word, Maryanne knew her suspicions were warranted. The knife had been meant for her.

Back at the Papparelli mansion, Carlie excused herself. "I'll let you two say good-night in private."

"Thanks a whole bunch," Maryanne muttered.

"You really know how to build up a guy's ego," J.Z. countered.

"Like yours needs building up." Then she grinned. "So. Here we are in the mobster's castle. Don't you want to thank me for getting us in?"

"Not particularly. You had another narrow escape."

"And you think it wouldn't have happened back in New Camden? Think again, J.Z. The first one did happen at Wal-Mart—"

"What?"

Maryanne groaned. "Forget I said that. I didn't really mean it."

"What happened at Wal-Mart?"

"I slipped and fell, lost my pretzel and my drink."

"Is that why you took so long, and then came back with nothing to show for it? You mean I stood there like an idiot holding a bunch of bags while someone tried to hurt you? And you said nothing about it?"

"Give me a break. What was I going to say? A bunch of teenagers were goofing around in line when I bought my snack, and one of them bumped into me? Does that sound life-threatening?"

"No, but mixing with the mob does."

"How many times am I going to have to tell you? I'm not mixing with the mob."

He took a long, slow look of the mansion's entry foyer. "Then what are we doing here?"

"Trying to convince you that I'm innocent of all crimes." She remembered his promise. "I thought you were going to help me. That's what you said earlier. Now you're back to the accusations. What's that all about?"

"I didn't promise to help you prove your innocence. I promised to keep you safe. That's my job, Maryanne, and I intend to do it—well, too. But if while I'm at it, I happen to somehow—miraculously—find out you're innocent...well, we'll see about that when—*if*—it happens. I'd still be ready to shop for an orange jumpsuit if I were you."

"You know, that's what's wrong with you. You asked me to trust you a little while ago. I think you meant it, too. But you've got to get real. You're trying your hardest to prove me guilty, so how can you expect me to trust you?"

"Because if you let me do my job, if you do what I say, then I can keep you safe."

"Safe for what? For locking me up and throwing away the key?"

"If that's how it breaks."

"And you wonder why I'd rather trust the Lord." She took the time to check out their luxurious surroundings. "This is pretty bad. To think the money that paid for it all came from all kinds of sin."

"*You* should know—"

"Just stop it! Little digs like that are why I'd rather take my chances with revenge-hungry mobsters than with an overzealous and terminally blind Fed."

"Don't talk like that here. Someone might be listening."

"I don't think I even care anymore. I'm tired of all this. In fact, I'm plain-old tired." She went to the massive front door and opened the one half. "Good night, J.Z. Get a good night's sleep and a better attitude. I suppose I can expect you bright and early, no matter what."

"'And, behold, I am with thee, and will keep thee in all places whither thou goest…'"

"Don't mock God, J.Z. Or my faith. Don't stoop that low."

He blanched, grimaced. "Good night, Maryanne. You should be safe here. We have the place under surveillance."

"I'm always under the Father's watchful care."

J.Z. left.

Maryanne thought about him as she inspected the cavernous entry to the house built with ill-gotten wealth. Her feelings for him were a jumbled mess. On the one hand, his suspicion made her mad. On the other, his determination to protect her seemed genuine. So did his commitment to fight crime. It didn't matter that he'd developed tunnel vision about organized crime. He was still a decent man.

It would be much easier if she could hate him. But she couldn't. As overzealous as he was, there was something genuine and real about him, too. The wounded soul he'd revealed touched her. Or maybe it was, plain and simple, that desire of his to fight crime. It didn't really matter. She just couldn't hate him.

She sighed. All she could hold against J.Z. was his refusal to listen to reason when it came to her. And she almost—almost—understood why.

Well, that and how he'd abandoned his faith.

He needed prayer.

"Maryanne?" Carlie called from the balcony on the second floor. "I thought I heard the door. Did your simmering volcano leave?"

"He's not mine, but J.Z. did leave."

"Good. Come on up and let me show you your room. My housekeeper, Leona, brought up your suitcase and unpacked for you."

Maryanne didn't know how she felt about someone else doing something so personal for her, but she hesitated to comment. That was just how things were done in Carlie's world. "I'm on my way."

"Unless you're too drained by this awful day you've had, I'd love to take a couple of minutes to draw up a battle plan. You know, too many stores, too little time."

On her way up the long, curved stairway, Maryanne began to dread the whole thing. She wasn't sure she wanted to invest in a whole new her. It had taken her—and her mother—years to come up with the professional, modest, unexceptional look she now appreciated.

Was she ready for a major overhaul? Or was she just wasting money and time on something she would later come to regret?

Who was the real Maryanne?

* * *

"*That* is you, really and truly you," Carlie said the next morning. "Moss-green is your color. It brings out the red highlights Sissy put in your hair."

Maryanne stared at her reflection in the mirror. The green linen dress fit her slim figure as though it had been made for her, and she liked the soft, muted color, too. The simple, classic lines were a far cry from some of the more flamboyant outfits she'd seen on mannequins around the store, and it was undeniably elegant.

She gave a slow nod. "I think this one's a keeper. It's even on sale."

"You look great," offered the third member of their party.

J.Z.'s gray eyes glowed with sincere appreciation.

Her cheeks warmed. "Thanks."

She gathered up another armful of clothes and darted back into the dressing room. She'd never shopped with a man before. Even Dad hadn't joined her and Mother on the few occasions when they'd gone to a store. They'd preferred to shop from catalogs that specialized in good quality, sturdy if plain, basic clothes.

An hour later, she stood at the cash register, credit card in hand. "I'm beat. How about we call it a day?"

Carlie's shock made Maryanne laugh. "What? You don't think two dresses, a pair of pants and two pairs of shoes are enough?"

"We've barely scratched the surface," her fashion tour guide said with a shake of her newly tawny mane. "So go on. Pay already. We have a lot of territory to cover before we call it a day."

J.Z.'s heartfelt groan echoed Maryanne's dismay.

Carlie laughed. "Hey, Vesuvius. You invited yourself along. No comments allowed from the peanut gallery."

His dark brows shot together in a frown. "Vesuvius?"

Maryanne rolled her eyes. "Don't ask—"

"Sure," Carlie cut in, mischief in her eyes. "You look like you're about to blow your top."

J.Z. snorted. "First she calls me Shadow, now you name me after a volcano. What's wrong with my name?"

Maryanne looked at him in disbelief. "You're the one who goes by a pair of letters. What's wrong with a more normal nickname?"

"You think Shadow and Vesuvius are normal?"

"They're better than J.Z."

"Oh, yeah. Lots better."

The salesclerk ran the card through, and in the time it took to verify her account, Maryanne gave J.Z. a long, measuring look. "Better yet. What's wrong with Jeremiah?"

He flinched. "Everything. Call me whatever you want. Just don't call me that."

A story lurked behind his name. Maryanne stored that bit of data in a mental file. She'd ask him about it some other time, when they weren't in a store, when Carlie wasn't around.

True to his word, J.Z. collected Maryanne's bags, and the three of them left the store. Outside, he asked Carlie, "Where to next? Do we need the car?"

"Oh, no. There's the neatest boutique just around the corner. They sell the best button-down shirts in the world. They're made-to-order, and they're ridiculously affordable."

Although Carlie hadn't pointed her in the direction of the more exorbitant designer stuff, Maryanne wondered if the widow's idea of affordable came anywhere near hers.

"Why don't you take the bags to the car, J.Z.?" she suggested. "Carlie and I can go ahead. Meet us when you're done."

For a moment, he looked ready to argue, but then he shrugged. "I'll be right—"

Whizzzzzz-CRASH!

Maryanne gasped. The sound of breaking glass… another *whizz*…

J.Z. lunged at her. "Down! Everybody down. NOW!"

A dozen more strange *whizzes*.

People screamed. Cars honked. Time slowed.

Maryanne prayed.

J.Z.'s breath was harsh in her ear, his body heavy against hers. Then blessed silence prevailed.

She whispered, "It was a gun, wasn't it?"

"With a silencer."

"The bullets were meant for me."

He didn't reply. He didn't have to. She hadn't asked but rather stated what they both knew.

"Did he hit you?" J.Z. asked.

"No. You?"

"I'm fine."

"Anyone else get hurt?"

"I don't know."

She wriggled under his weight. "Can you call for help on your cell phone?"

"I guarantee you the store already called."

"So when are you going to get off me? You're no feather, you know."

"When we have enough cops around us that even a swarm of bees couldn't get at you."

Maryanne groaned. But then the welcome shriek of

sirens rang out, and she counted the minutes until the cavalry arrived.

Although she'd never get used to it, by now she knew the drill. She stood, made sure all body parts were still attached and functional then reassured J.Z. about a million times that yes, she was fine. Minutes later, she did the same for the benefit of the police.

"Did you see anything unusual, ma'am?"

"No."

"Did you see where the bullets came from?"

"No."

And so it went, until she glanced sideways and saw Carlie's stricken face. "Excuse me, Officer…" She checked his name badge. "Officer Randall. My friend doesn't look well. I saw nothing and heard nothing until the bullet went by me. Then J.Z. knocked me over, and he landed on top. I saw nothing more after that. So there you have it, and now my friend needs me."

She reached Carlie at the same time J.Z. did. One look at the woman, frozen in place, horror in her expression, fear in her brown eyes, and Maryanne knew she had to do whatever she could.

"Let me," she told J.Z. Then she laid a hand on Carlie's shoulder. "Carlie? It's Maryanne. You're okay now. It's all over, and you're okay."

For a moment, she feared Carlie wouldn't respond. But then she blinked. Her eyes focused on Maryanne. She shuddered and moaned.

"Were you hit?" Maryanne asked, even though she saw no sign of injury.

"No," Carlie whispered, her eyes still wide and scared.

"I'm sorry I have to ask," J.Z. said, "but did you see anything?"

Carlie turned toward him in what struck Maryanne like slow motion. "I saw the car drive by. I saw Mat fall. I saw the blood. It went all over me. I couldn't wipe it off. He didn't move…."

J.Z. said something in a rough, guttural voice. Maryanne didn't quite make out the actual words, but by his expression she figured it was just as well.

He looked ready to kill.

"She's in shock," he said a moment later. "I'm going for a paramedic. They're treating some people who were hit by glass."

Then Maryanne saw Carlie's silent tears bathe her cheeks. The widow began to rock back and forth where she sat on the sidewalk. She painted a picture of acute misery.

Maryanne enveloped her in a hug. The gesture seemed to open up the floodgates, because as soon as Carlie's face met Maryanne's shoulder, she burst into sobs, hard, wracking, convulsive.

A little later, Carlie returned the hug, and the two women held each other. It occurred to Maryanne that in a weird way it was fitting for them to have met, to comfort each other in this nightmare situation. In her own particular way, each was a victim of the mob.

Out the corner of her eye, Maryanne saw J.Z. speak with a paramedic. After an exchange of words, probably information about the shooting, the men began to walk in their direction.

"Help is coming," she murmured.

Carlie shivered. "I don't think anyone can help."

Thank You, Lord. At least Carlie had begun to respond. "Why is that?"

"Because I think the newspapers had it right. I think Mat was with the mob. And I think they're after me now."

If she only knew.

Then something clicked in Maryanne's mind. Maybe they were after Carlie. Just as they were after her. Had she made matters worse by befriending the widow? Had she put them both in greater danger than they would have been otherwise?

Had J.Z. been right after all?

Not about her guilt, but about the danger she was in?

God alone knew the truth.

TEN

Carlie's words gave Maryanne hope. She'd been right to seek out the widow, the only known witness to Carlo Papparelli's shooting. The deaths of the seniors didn't belong in J.Z.'s investigation. They weren't part of any inheritance scam. Each one of the Peaceful Meadows' residents had died from one of a handful of illnesses. Only the Laundromat mattered; he'd been shot—nothing natural about that. Then, after the shooting, word had gone out that he'd been killed. But he hadn't died, not right after the shooting. He actually died days later at Peaceful Meadows.

How and why had he wound up at Peaceful Meadows? That stroke? She had questions about that, too. And the coffin that went to Sicily was just plain sick.

What had the family shipped in it? Not Carlo "Laundromat" Papparelli's corpse—Maryanne knew that for a fact. Although he had been shot, and was admitted to the nursing home for those injuries in a…hmm…shady way, the cause of death was a stroke. Or so the doctors at the nursing home and the autopsy had said.

"I want to get out of here," Carlie said. "I've had all I can stomach for today. The cops know where to find me. I'm not going anywhere."

Maryanne helped her stand. "Let me look for J.Z. He has my car keys. We'll get you home."

Carlie gave her a teary smile. "You look worse than I do. If I need a break, and I do, then you need one, too. You keep having accidents."

With a downward glance, Maryanne took note of the torn knees in her jeans. "Great. Just as I was getting to like them." She looked back at Carlie. "My accidents weren't accidents."

"What do you mean?"

"Come on. This isn't the place to talk. Let's head back to your house. I'll tell you everything there."

They found J.Z. with the cop who'd taken his statement. He asked for a minimum of detail from the two women then told them to expect additional questions in the immediate future. No matter how determined the officer was to have Carlie checked out at the hospital, she insisted all she needed was rest at home.

Carlie and Maryanne each grabbed a shopping bag and left the rest for J.Z. Then they all went to Maryanne's car. They rode to the Papparelli mansion in silence, during which Maryanne took advantage of the time to pray.

Carlie went in first. She dropped her shopping bag in the foyer, and waved Maryanne and J.Z. toward the adjacent living room. "Make yourselves comfortable. I'll be right back. I don't know about you guys, but I'm dying of thirst. How about some lemonade? I'll have Leona make a pitcher—I'm practically addicted to the stuff."

J.Z. led the way into the vast, airy room. Maryanne took note of the sunny-yellow walls, the blue-and-white toile drapes, the sky-blue sofa and white armchairs, the eight-foot-tall leaded glass windows. "This is beautiful. Carlie has excellent taste."

"I guess." He sat on the sofa and gestured for her to join him. "Now that you've had a chance to walk out the kinks, are you okay?"

She sank into the lush upholstery at the corner opposite him. "I'm as well as a hunted woman can be."

"I'm glad you're ready to accept what I told you. Those weren't accidents."

"You're right. They weren't. Not even the pretzel incident. I don't know if I mentioned it, and I don't know if it's relevant, but as I fell that day, I heard someone say 'Payback time.'"

He crossed his arms. "You didn't think that might be important?"

"I didn't think much of the whole thing at the time. I thought one of the teens in line for the pretzels bumped into me. I figured the payback comment was meant for another kid."

Carlie brought a large silver tray to the wide upholstered ottoman that did double duty as a coffee table between the chairs and the couch. On it she'd stacked glasses, a pitcher of lemonade, an ice-cube bucket, spoons, plates and a dish of cookies.

"Leona's making a light lunch, but please, help yourselves." She started back toward the foyer. "Let me get the bags. I want another look at everything we bought—"

CRASH!

The force of the explosion shook the house.

Carlie fell back into the living room.

Maryanne screamed.

J.Z. ordered them down to the floor.

A wall of flame shot up just beyond the doorway. It made a horrific noise, a mixture of sizzling hisses and brittle crackling. The sound almost drowned out Carlie's sobs as she crawled back toward Maryanne and J.Z.

"We have to get out of here." Maryanne's voice was shrill.

J.Z. punched numbers into his cell phone. "I'm working on it."

"What was that?"

He barely paused his conversation to add, "A bomb."

Maryanne cried, "A bomb!"

"In my house?" Carlie asked.

The women traded glances. Maryanne recognized the fear in Carlie's face, voice and response. It mirrored hers. Praying, she helped Carlie stand. "It's getting hot in here. Where's the door?"

Carlie pointed toward the blazing foyer. "The only one."

Maryanne groaned.

"Come on," J.Z. said. "I'm going to break a window. We have to get out of here. Those flames won't just sit there, and that wool rug runs from two feet beyond the foyer and straight through the room. It'll work like a wick and burn fast."

"You can't," Carlie said.

He frowned. "I can't what?"

"Break a window. You can break the glass, but see the lead between the panes of glass?" At his nod, she went on. "That's not really lead. They're reinforced steel bars. We can't get out that way. Mat had a thing about safety."

Maryanne met J.Z.'s gaze. A mobster might have reason for paranoia.

Carlie's chuckle bore a tinge of hysteria. "Now I know why. I was married to the mob. Only it wasn't a movie. It was my life."

Sobs shook her, and J.Z. ran a hand through his hair.

Maryanne didn't know what to do, how to comfort her friend, how to help J.Z. She, too, felt as though she'd stepped onto the set of a horror movie, but the bullets and the bomb had been way too real. And she wished she knew whether this film would have a happy ending or not.

First, though, they had to get out of the inferno. She was drenched in sweat. The heat grew greater by the second. Smoke had started to fill the room. She prayed some more then turned to J.Z. "What are we going to do?"

"We're stuck until help gets here," J.Z. answered, anger in his face. "If you're so sure about that God of yours, even after this, then I suggest you start to pray."

"What do you think I've been doing?"

"Pray harder. We need serious help to get out of here alive."

She did pray, harder. She asked for wisdom and strength and help.

When she realized Carlie and J.Z. were both staring at her, she looked around the lovely prison the Papparelli's living room had become. "Let's go to that far corner. And we should probably break the glass in the windows, even if there's nothing we can do about the bars. We need fresh air, and the smoke has to get out somehow."

They shoved the furniture to a side, and J.Z. hurled a small, sturdy side table at one tall window after another. Maryanne winced at the sound of breaking glass—she'd heard it only a short while ago, caused by bullets, and she doubted she'd ever forget the fear it brought. *Help me, Father. Give me strength.*

"About time," J.Z. said. "They're almost here."

Sirens screamed over the crackle of flames. "That was the fire department you called."

"And Dan and my office. I had to report this latest attack."

"Attack…" Carlie echoed.

Maryanne swallowed hard. She might never have another chance—literally—to ask for Carlie's help. And if they died, she didn't want J.Z. to do so without knowing the truth about her. "Remember I said earlier that I would tell you everything?"

Carlie nodded.

"Well, we're stuck here until someone gets us out, and if they don't…" She shuddered. "I might as well start while I can still talk."

With J.Z.'s solid bulk at her side, Maryanne recounted the events of her last few weeks in brief, direct and graphic terms. She left nothing out, not even J.Z.'s ridiculous suspicions. At the end, she saw anguish in Carlie's face. She reached out and clasped her friend's hand, gave it a squeeze for encouragement.

"Hey!" a man called from outside. "You in there. Move away from the bars. We're gonna cut through them to get you out."

"Thank You, Jesus," Maryanne murmured.

She and Carlie scooted a couple of feet over to the large, empty stone fireplace and crawled inside the only space that offered any protection. The flames had begun to eat the lush wool carpet as fast as J.Z. had said. Its threat marched right at them.

Outside the window, an engine sputtered to life. Maryanne watched in fascination as a yellow-garbed firefighter slipped what looked like giant claws around two of the steel bars. She heard a *whoosh,* the claws flexed and they snapped the bars as if they'd been slivers of butter. The firefighter repeated the operation at a spot higher on the steel rods. Chunks of metal dropped down on the inside and the outside. The Jaws of Life was doing its job.

J.Z. dodged pieces of severed metal to direct their rescuers' efforts.

The fire burned closer. Maryanne turned to Carlie. "I need your help. You're the only witness to your husband's murder. You're the only person who can vouch for me, who can say I wasn't there, that I didn't kill him." Maryanne took a deep breath and pressed ahead. "You're the only one who might know who would have wanted him dead."

Carlie seemed to shrink. "You want me to—"

"We want you to consider turning state's evidence," J.Z. said as he avoided another chunk of steel, his voice gentle and encouraging. Maryanne smiled in gratitude. A second later, he was back to the task at hand, inspecting the firefighter's progress, the hardened G-man attitude back in place.

But Maryanne knew better than to buy it anymore. She'd been given a glimpse beyond that shell a time or two. There was much more to J.Z. Prophet than even he probably knew.

"Will you help me?" she asked Carlie.

The widow struggled with the question. "I don't know that I can. Mat did business with my family. J.Z. can't hear me right now, so I'll tell you my reasons. That way, if someone asks, it'll be your word against mine."

"But—"

She swallowed hard. "My father may be involved. Maybe even my brother Tony. I can't turn against them."

Maryanne's stomach sank. She wiped the sweat from her cheeks, glanced toward the window, and saw the hole the Jaws had chomped out. She didn't have much time to press her case.

"You won't help me even now that you know someone's trying to kill me?" At Carlie's nod, she prayed for strength and played her last card. "Even now that they've tried to kill you, too?"

Two more steel rods crashed in. J.Z. yelled, "Come on! Move! The fire's almost to the hearth."

Maryanne stared at Carlie for a second…two. Nothing was said. No agreement was reached.

The women ran, their future undecided, their present in ruins like the room they left behind.

J.Z. helped Maryanne and Carlie drop down to the paramedics. He jumped after them, and the firefighters went in to battle this rear flank of flames. The sight of Eliza Roberts ten feet away almost drove him back into the burning house. "What are you doing here?"

"I'm your Supervising Agent, aren't I?"

He shrugged.

"It doesn't look to me as though you've done a very good job protecting our suspect. Until I got here and spoke with Maddox, I only knew of two attempts, this one being one of them. Now I find out there was a third, at a restaurant last night."

"I didn't get a chance to check in."

"That doesn't cut it, J.Z. It goes against policy and gives me grounds to yank your badge."

"Got it." He narrowed his eyes. "Is that why you came? To warn me again? In person? Should I feel honored?"

Eliza glared, blue eyes icy in the warm summer sun. "Don't be an idiot. Unless you do a better job and keep her alive, I'm going to have to lock her up. For her safety, if nothing else."

"You're excited. Is there something special about this case?"

"It's my first big one as a Supervising Agent."

"Ah…you want more brownie points."

"Just do your job."

"That's what I'm doing."

"I also came to tell you that you won't be doing it around here anymore. I've arranged for you to take Wellborn to a safe house. I want her alive and kicking for the trial. I also want her to name names. She's not the only fish I want to catch. When she finally talks, we can take down the bigger ones, too."

"You might like to know she's trying to talk Carlotta Papparelli to turn state's evidence. If you remember, the widow's the only witness to Mat's murder."

Eliza's eyes widened. "Are you serious? You really think she'll testify? Do you have any idea who Carlotta Papparelli is?"

"The Laundromat's wife."

"She's also Antonio Verdi's daughter. Tony the Toe's baby sister."

The names were unforgettably familiar. The old rage simmered in his gut. He glanced at the intuitive librarian. "Chalk one up for Maryanne, then. Even with all I know about the Verdis, I somehow failed to learn about the daughter. How could that be?"

Eliza's smug smile made him madder still. "Antonio, and later Papparelli, made sure they kept her in the background, to protect her. Even society-page reports of the wedding didn't draw the connection, and I'm sure it wasn't an oversight. Since there's more than one Verdi family in the U.S., it went under the radar."

It shouldn't have—not under his. It galled J.Z. to face his failure to uncover such an important detail, but there was nothing he could do about it right then. "Maybe Maryanne will get Carlie to turn."

Eliza bit her lower lip. "We'll see. She might be helping the widow cover up whatever tracks might be left." She looked around, saw the women speaking to a cop, and then faced him again. "I have a packet for you. It has directions, cash, everything you'll need for the assignment."

She rummaged in her briefcase and came up with a thick nine-by-twelve envelope. "Zelda's going to meet you there. She's got data questions for the suspect."

Even though Eliza's premise put Maryanne's innocence in question again—how had she zeroed in on a big mob fish and his family if she hadn't known about them in the first place?—it grated to hear his boss refer to Maryanne that way. "She has a name."

"Don't get too used to it. Make sure you keep everything on a professional level. You can't let yourself care—"

"Give me that." He held out his hand, more than ready to get away. "The sooner we leave, the sooner we can close this case."

She held out the packet. "Remember. I've got my eye on you."

"And it feels like a knife in the back."

She gaped.

He walked away.

"Who's that?" Maryanne asked when he walked up to her and Dan.

"Our boss."

"She doesn't look happy. No love lost between you, I take it."

Dan had the gall to laugh. "Once upon a time, they were tighter than glue."

Maryanne's eyebrows rose. "Can't see it—can't see *them*."

"I warned him," Dan added.

J.Z. took Maryanne's elbow. "Now that you've both had your fun, it's time to go. She ordered me to get you to a safe house."

She shivered.

His grip on her arm tightened.

"So you're getting your way after all," she murmured. "You're locking me up."

"Not permanently. At least not yet."

"Then for how long?"

"Until we have a solid case."

She pulled away. "No way. I have to get back to my dad. He's not well, and he needs me."

"I thought you took vacation for your makeover blitz. He won't expect you back for a while. We might have the case sewn up by then."

She looked scared. J.Z.'s chest tightened. He wished he could do something to comfort her, but Eliza did have one thing right. It had to stay professional. Even though he wished he could assure her that everything would be okay.

He wanted her to be innocent.

But he didn't know if she was. Not for sure. Not after what Eliza had told him.

"Say goodbye to Carlie," he suggested. "We do have to leave. You're not safe around here."

She squared her shoulders and tipped up her chin. Her eyes sparkled as she walked away.

"Be careful," Dan said. "This is getting ugly."

"I know. I don't like anything about how it's coming down."

"Maybe that's because you're finally figuring out that Maryanne's innocent."

As Dan voiced the possibility J.Z. had fought since the first bullet flew past them, his conscience kicked in. "I'm not ready to go that far, but I am willing to consider the likelihood. In spite of her connections."

"What led you to this brilliant, if easy, conclusion?"

He slipped the envelope under one arm and ran his other hand through his hair. "This morning's bullets were hard to miss. Then the bomb—it was a bomb, wasn't it? While she could be a target because she took out the Laundromat, she could also be their target because we brought her to their attention and she makes a convenient scapegoat."

Dan nodded.

"The bomb made it clear that someone's at the end of his patience. He wants her dead, maybe Carlie, too. Any idea where they planted it?"

"The firefighters found little to check. The only thing they have is a handful of scraps of cream-colored linen mixed with the remains of the explosive. They don't know what it is yet."

J.Z. did. He remembered Maryanne trying on the pants at the store. They'd looked good on her when she'd paired them with a gold silk blouse. He also remembered Carlie on her way back to the foyer for the shopping bags.

"We had a closer call than I realized," he said. "Carlie

and Maryanne wanted to look over their purchases, and Carlie was on her way to the foyer for the shopping bags. She'd almost reached them when the device went off. I think the cream fabric's from a pair of pants Maryanne bought this morning. Someone must have planted the bomb during the chaos at the shooting."

Dan's smile kicked up on one side. "Exploding pants...the mob's creativity knows no bounds."

"I wouldn't kid about it. We almost died in there. The bomb was probably on a timer. If they'd had it on remote control, they would have detonated it while we were in the car. We'd have had no chance then."

Dan grew thoughtful for a moment. "Seeing who Carlie really is, do you think maybe they meant it only as a warning? If they'd wanted to kill them, and you, it would make more sense to set it off in the car, like you said. I wonder if Carlie's family is behind the Laundromat's death after all? I don't think her father or that Tony the Toe brother of hers would really want to kill her."

J.Z. had no illusions about the Verdi family. He knew too much about them. "That could explain it. You might want to see who else was in the house besides the three of us—and the housekeeper, of course. Although she bears checking out, too."

"I'll take care of it."

"Thanks."

"I just want you to keep your mind on staying alive. A good partner's hard to break in." He raised his hands to shoulder height. "I know, I know. No kidding allowed. Anyway, keep Maryanne safe. She's a neat lady. Don't want anything to happen to her."

J.Z. looked around for the neat lady, and found her with

Carlie. Both were in tears, but their hands were clasped. "I better get over there. I wonder what that's all about."

Dan chuckled. "Weeping women. Better you than me."

"J.Z.!" Maryanne called when she saw him approach. "Guess what?"

She looked ready to pop. "Tell me what."

Her smile glowed through her tears, and she shocked him by throwing her arms around his neck. "Carlie's agreed to cooperate. Everything's going to be all right."

He froze. Maryanne's unusual exuberance had caught him by surprise. Then her words sank in. He placed his hands at her waist and shifted his gaze to Carlie.

"Are you sure?" he asked.

The widow, misery on her face, nodded. "I have to know the truth. I spent years hiding from it, refusing to question the strange things I saw. I wanted to claim ignorance, but I can't do that anymore. I'm not sure how much help I can be, but I do know some of the men my father, Tony and Mat do business with. I'll help any way I can. I can't let them kill Maryanne."

"See?" his armful of librarian asked, her face radiant.

Her enthusiasm was contagious. He gave her a hug. He again realized how good it felt to hold her close, to see her smile, to hear her animated voice.

"I do see," he answered. "And if Carlie's sure about this, then we have a lot to do. And fast. We have to make sure she's safe, too, because now she's really going to be a target, all on her own. If there's one thing organized crime doesn't tolerate it's betrayal."

With a final gentle squeeze for Maryanne, he looked to see if Eliza had left. He found her with Dan near her car. Their expressions were a study in contrast. They'd seen him hug Maryanne. While Dan's grin had canary feathers all over it, Eliza's rage left no doubt where she stood. Jealousy was just as ugly as revenge.

He approached, his steps slow, reluctant. He had no choice. She was his boss. "We have to make some changes."

"How so?" Dan asked.

Eliza glared. But not at him. At Maryanne.

"Carlie agreed to cooperate. She's going to need protection. I'm not sure that bomb was meant for Maryanne alone. Carlie may know more than she realizes."

Eliza dragged her attention from Maryanne. "I'll say things have changed. I haven't heard either of you mention the most important development."

J.Z. and Dan exchanged bewildered looks.

"A witness to a mob hit is pretty major in my book," J.Z. said.

Eliza waved his comment aside. "I hate to have to give you credit, J.Z.—"

"That's gotta stick in your craw," he countered, fed up with her attitude. "But you'll get over it because I'm sure you're going to try and one-up me on this most important development of yours."

"It's not my development. You're the one who was clear on it right from the start."

A sick feeling roiled in the pit of his gut. But he didn't speak. He'd wait Eliza out.

Her triumphant smile was not pretty. "Just look at them, J.Z." She pointed toward Maryanne and Carlie. "Don't play dumb, because I know better. Can't you see she's played you for a fool?"

He only saw two women saying goodbye. "How so?"

"You said all along she was one of *them*. It's obvious

she's tight with the mobster's wife—not to mention an Oscar-worthy actress. It's no big leap to think she's threatened Carlotta Verdi Papparelli. Wellborn's just hung herself with this little twist. Her power over the Verdis' baby girl proves the strength of her ties to the mob. A new acquaintance, a perfect stranger, as she would have you believe she is, would never convince one of them to turn against the others. I want to know what she has on Carlotta."

Eliza shot another venomous glare at Maryanne. "She's smart, all right. Look how she's twisted your common sense in her effort to divert attention from herself. I'm bringing her in before she takes the next logical step—run."

His stomach sank. He'd tried to block all these possibilities from his thoughts after Eliza revealed Carlie's maiden name. He was no longer sure of anything. One moment he was certain Maryanne was guilty, then the next he couldn't say so with any measure of confidence.

"Just because she's persuasive doesn't mean she's also guilty," he argued. "Besides, we don't have to do anything drastic. I'm already going to keep her out of sight. No judge who hears your logic will bite. We don't have enough on Maryanne Wellborn."

Where had *that* come from? Had he really said that? J.Z. frowned, but knew he couldn't back down. Why couldn't he? He didn't know. Not yet.

"You might get a warrant," he added, "but you won't get anything to stick. You won't get an indictment, so she'll walk."

Hate blazed in her eyes. "That's not the song you sang a couple of weeks ago. You were sure she was guilty as sin.

What about the e-mails? And her fingerprints on Mat's IV stand? Did you suddenly forget those?"

J.Z. couldn't collect his thoughts soon enough to respond. So Eliza went on.

"What's wrong?" she taunted. "Did she get to you? How cozy are you with your witness, Agent Prophet?"

He couldn't deny her accusations. He was guilty as charged, on his early suspicions and the coziness, too. Maryanne had gotten to him. And if she was innocent, as he was beginning to fear, he could be guilty of a lot more. He refused to bear the guilt of a wrongful arrest, as well. He wouldn't humor Eliza.

"You need something more than jealousy—"

"This has nothing to do with me." Her cheeks reddened, and she seethed. "It has everything to do with the case. I want Maryanne Wellborn under arrest—the prints place her at the scene, the expensive digs for her dad give her the motive and her frequent trips to Peaceful Meadows give her the opportunity. What more do you want? You can't refute the fingerprints. Any judge will bite."

A car door slammed, and a speeding vehicle's tires squealed.

The boring beige Escort sped around the corner, Carlie at the wheel, Maryanne at her side.

J.Z. groaned and ran to Dan's car.

"Go get them," Eliza said, surprisingly cheery. "Add fleeing the law to her other crimes—and we don't need a warrant to nab her for that."

ELEVEN

In almost the same breath, Eliza charged Dan with Carlie's protection. The men, aware of the need to catch the fugitives, if for no other reason than to keep them alive, jumped into Dan's car and followed.

Sooner or later, the newest edition of *Thelma and Louise* would have to stop. The Escort got excellent mileage, but every now and then it would need a drink.

Carlie drove like a race-car driver. Only difference was that race cars stuck to a track; she was on the loose on America's roadways. If, after this episode in her life, she ever wanted a career, J.Z. would be sure to suggest NASCAR. Dan kept the beige car in sight by virtue of determination and his excellent driving skills.

He also kept up a steady stream of muttered gripes. "When I get hold of that maniac…"

J.Z. chuckled. "What? Can't take a taste of your own medicine? Riding with you is a nail-biting experience."

"Yeah, but I know what I'm doing. She's just running wild. I'll be amazed if she doesn't hit someone."

The last time he thought of prayer was right before Maryanne began to pray inside the burning Papparelli home. Moments later, the fire squad arrived. He could only hope that Maryanne was praying right then. They needed all the help they could get.

He opened the envelope to see what Eliza had arranged. He scanned the pages, counted the cash and checked out the map. If nothing else, Eliza was efficient.

"What'll you do with your half of that team when we catch up?" he asked Dan.

Dan changed lanes right behind Carlie. "Beats me. I don't have a clue where Eliza'll want me to stash her. We can hang with you two for a couple of days, at least until our fearless leader comes up with a plan. Unless you intend to take Maryanne back to lock her up."

Just then, Carlie veered off the main road onto the skinny side of a fork up ahead. J.Z. hung on to the handle over the door as Dan slammed the brakes and spun the wheel. They plowed up onto and crashed down from a curb and missed a road sign by inches. The arrow indicated they were headed toward Berks County, PA.

J.Z. gave Dan a sideways look. "Did you forget Eliza's warning?"

"*You're* going to play by the book *now?* When this woman's freedom is at stake, and Eliza doesn't care?"

He considered his options. If he went with his gut, he'd take the women somewhere relatively safe, where Eliza wouldn't find them right away, until he had a firm grasp on what Carlie really knew. Then he'd plan his next step.

But if he went with his head, he'd go back and keep his job.

J.Z. sighed. "I don't know. And I'm not sure it's a good idea to keep those two together for any length of time."

"I know what you mean."

They drove. And drove. Then drove some more.

After a while, Dan asked, "Did you get a chance to check how much gas that tin can had in the tank?"

"Less than half, but it's no gas guzzler."

"Neither is this, but I'm going to need a fill-up pretty soon."

"They must be close to empty, too. I doubt they can go much farther."

Sure enough, shortly after they crossed into Lancaster County, Thelma—or was Carlie playing Louise?—pulled into a gas station and stopped at the single vacant pump out of six.

Dan nosed up between the Escort and the car at the next pump over. The women stepped out, crossed their arms and stared.

J.Z. opened his door. He unfolded himself to his full height, and leveled a look at Maryanne, who now bore no resemblance to the librarian he'd first met. She looked like a mess—a pretty mess—but her spine was straight, her shoulders squared, her head high.

She held his gaze. "I'm not going to jail."

"What you just did pretty much sealed your fate. It's called resisting arrest, as Eliza so kindly pointed out."

"She's nasty."

"Don't you forget it."

"I can't believe you once—"

"Get over it. I did. It's history." He slid a glance at Dan, and saw his partner engaged in a similar verbal tussle with his charge. Served him right.

"What matters now is that I have to keep you safe while I get to the truth. I'm not sure how I'm going to do it yet, since Eliza changed her mind about the safe house. I doubt it would be very safe for you anymore. It'll be the first place she checks. And believe me. She wants you behind bars."

She tipped up her chin. "I'm not going with you. All you want to do is lock me up."

Did he? "You won't believe it, but I want to find out what really happened even more. Although, after that race down Pennsylvania's not-so-fine back roads, you and your pal deserve a few hours of solitary confinement to consider your sins."

A strange expression crossed her face.

"What?"

"Ah…er…nothing. I…um…wonder how you plan to find out the truth."

"Give me a break. I've spent the past two hours hoping to survive the neo-Thelma-and-Louise chase. I need time to plan."

"Hey! That's kind of cool. No one's ever thought of me as either Thelma or Louise."

Had he just given her more ideas? "Well, I've got news for you. The spree's over. Dan's new assignment is Carlie's safety, so we've decided to split up by car. One of us will drive one of you. To start out with, though, we'll travel together."

"And you don't know where you're taking me."

"I'll think of something. I always do."

"I don't doubt it."

That didn't sound like a compliment. "I've been trying to make a phone call for the last ten minutes, but my cell phone gets no service in this backwater cornfield. Don't even think of moving before I get back."

Zelda was nearly frantic when he reached her. "Where've you been? Are you hurt? What's this I hear about knives, bombs and run-amok Mercedes? I thought you were tailing a librarian, J.Z." She took a breath for more fuel. "I oughta pull your ears, boy! Didja catch the mobster gals? What're you gonna do with them? What kind of mess have you cooked up this time?"

"I see Eliza called you."

"Yeah. So what? Now are you going to tell me what's coming down or do I have to guess? Twenty questions isn't going to be half enough to get me any answers. Do you have the killer e-mail queen with you?"

"I do, but I'm not talking until I'm sure you won't rat me out."

Zelda snorted. "To Eliza? That girl's no more a Supervising Agent than my cousin Toliver's tabby tomcat."

"That's what I love about you, Zelda. You cut right to the bone. But this time, you got one thing wrong. Whether we like her or not, Eliza *is* calling the shots. That's why I have to know you'll give me the time I need to get some things straight."

"Awright! The half-cocked shotgun's at it again."

"Would you believe me if I told you I really meant to toe the line this time?"

"No."

"Well, I did. But things changed."

"What happened?"

"The librarian's the one who wigged out. She's just dragging me in her wake."

Zelda guffawed. "About time someone got the better of you, boy. So. You gonna give me a crack at her? I've some questions that need answers."

"Are you calling Eliza?"

"No! Haven't you figured that one out yet? I trust a Center City rat more'n I'll ever trust that Eliza Roberts.

She's snide and catty and too protective of her hoity-toity job, and too high-and-mighty by half. If you think you need to run, then I'm gonna help you run. But you have to promise me time with the girl."

"You got a deal. But you have to know we're not heading your way anymore. And I can't tell you where we'll wind up—"

"Sounds to me like you're flying by the seat of your pants and haven't got a clue where you're going."

"Something like that."

"Tell you what. I'll find me a way to get word to you as to what I need and how you can get it to me. I don't know yet how, but kinda like you, I'll figure it out as I go."

"Do you have something solid?"

"Nah. Not really. Just some details I want to clear up. Far as I can see, she's clean, J.Z. These e-mails went right to the library's membership clerk, and only to him."

"You're sure, now?"

"Just as sure as I was when I told Eliza. She didn't like it any more'n you do."

So Eliza knew Maryanne's e-mails appeared innocent. What was the reason for her decision to press for Maryanne's arrest? Could it be the jealousy he thought he'd sensed, the jealousy that immediately crossed his mind? That'd be stupid. Was there something else?

"Gotta go, Zelda. I'll be in touch. And thanks."

"No prob. Stay safe and God bless."

Now that he thought about it, this wasn't the first time Zelda offered him a blessing. Why had he never noticed it before? And why had he done so now? Could it have anything to do with the company he was keeping these days? Maryanne had a potent effect.

He returned the phone to its cradle, and went back to the cars. Another thought occurred to him. If Zelda could prove with any certainty that Maryanne's e-mails were innocent, and Eliza already knew it, then he was not about to follow her contradictory order to arrest Maryanne.

Even if it cost him his job.

First, though, he had to find somewhere to stash her where the Gemmellis and the Verdis wouldn't find her—or Carlie either, for that matter.

"I've got mostly good news," he said.

Hope lit up Maryanne's eyes. "Can I go home?"

"Sorry. It's not that good. Not yet." He popped open the trunk of Dan's car and retrieved his duffel. "Zelda—our computer analyst—vouches for your e-mails. I may be able to negotiate with Eliza and get her to back off on the arrest. That should buy us some time."

He slammed the trunk shut then opened the back door of the Escort and threw in his bag. He faced Maryanne again.

"It doesn't mean you're home free. There's the crowd that shatters store windows and bombs expensive homes. I doubt they'll be happy to learn you've been cleared. In their eyes, if you didn't whack Mat, then you make the perfect scapegoat. There's at least one of them who wants you to take the fall."

Carlie waved. "Helloooo! I'm here, too. Where do I come in?"

Dan pointed to his car. "You're under protective custody, or at least you're going to be once everything's set up. For the time being, you get in my car and we head out somewhere safe."

"Have any ideas?" J.Z. asked.

"Only one," Dan replied. "Remember Norm's wreck of a money pit?"

Norman Griffiths, Dan's uncle, restored old homes for a living. J.Z. had spent a memorable weekend helping uncle and nephew haul trash out of the rickety place last summer. "Didn't he give up on that one?"

"Yeah. But he hasn't been able to sell it—wonder why, huh?" He shook his head. "Anyway, it's still standing, and he's still paying water and electric, too."

"Sounds good."

"Where are you taking me?" Maryanne asked. She didn't look meek, mild or cooperative.

Dan chuckled. "Gentlemen, start your engines. We're taking us a road trip to West Virginia."

They agreed on separate routes. No reason to help those who were after Maryanne and Carlie and give them a two-for-one-hit deal. J.Z. and Maryanne would go due west then south, while Dan and Carlie would go east first.

J.Z. turned the Escort out of the gas station and onto the country road on which they'd intersect Route 30 west in about twenty minutes or so. They'd grab a burger at a drive-through in Lancaster, then pass through York, Hanover, Gettysburg. The key here was to keep going. They'd make as few stops as possible.

About fifteen minutes later, J.Z. stole a look at Maryanne. She had her head back against the rest, and she'd closed her eyes. She really didn't look like a mobster. She never had.

Was he ready to believe her?

If she was innocent, then why was someone—a mobster—so intent on killing her? What could an innocent bystander have done to enrage the Gemmellis or the Verdis or both? How would she have come to the attention of the mob? If she was innocent, that was.

The only thing that occurred to J.Z. was that his investigation into the nursing home scam and the Laundromat's murder, with his laser-like focus on Maryanne, had put her on someone's radar. He suspected Tony the Toe rather than Joey-O. Joey was behind bars for shooting Mat.

Yes, Joey was a Gemmelli man, and the Gemmellis had long wanted Mat dead, but Tony and the Verdi family had a number of shady deals going with Carlo Papparelli. Mobsters were notorious for falling out with even their closest cronies. J.Z. didn't think Carlie's brother had actually tried to kill Maryanne and Carlie, but the Verdis had more connections than America had power lines. And they'd be awfully unhappy about Mat's untimely death.

They'd be out to get Mat's killer.

If that was the case, then J.Z. was to blame for the danger Maryanne was in. Because he'd been so certain in his suspicion, she'd set out on her quest to prove him wrong. Then, that quest had led her to Carlie, a connection to the Papparellis he believed made her an even greater target for the mob. For more reasons than he cared to consider, he was responsible for her. He had to stay ahead of the killers. He had to right his latest wrong.

He squeezed the steering wheel and tried to focus on the road. His insides twisted and churned; guilt ate him alive. He drove in a kind of autopilot mental mode, his thoughts on the past. His past...

"Look out!" Maryanne yelled as an oncoming box truck hurtled across the divider line straight at them.

J.Z. yanked the wheel to the left. The car clattered onto

a gravel side road. A large wooden sign by a dirt drive said they'd just driven past Dirt Mound Chicken Farm.

When a tire crashed into a pothole the size of Australia, J.Z. bounced and hit his head on the roof. "Ooof!"

Maryanne turned in her seat. "They're behind us, J.Z."

The rearview mirror gave him a clear view of a hand out the passenger side of the truck, gun trained on the Escort. He hit the gas. They bumped and thudded over the rutted road, his heart beating loud enough to deafen him.

But it didn't. Not quite. He heard metal strike metal on the back of the car.

Maryanne grabbed his arm. "They're catching up!"

The car swerved to the right.

He spun the wheel to the left. The Escort jounced some more. "They will if you do that again. Let go of my arm, and sit tight. By the way, this would be a good time to pray some more."

Another *ding* rang out.

J.Z. weighed his options. He could continue down this sad excuse of a road, no idea where it might lead. He could pull into one of the many driveways, but that would only endanger innocent bystanders. Or maybe—

He ran out of options. The sign up ahead read Dead End. A third *ding* sounded against the left rear side of the car. The truck and the killers were gaining ground.

Their only chance to get out of this alive was if he used the Escort's small size and greater maneuverability to their advantage. He could do a 180 and, in the time it took the truck to recover, speed back to the larger road. The sooner they reached Route 30, the better. There was safety in its volume of traffic; he could more easily slip away under that cover.

It'd be touch and go, since they'd have only inches between them and the truck. On the upside, the shooter was in the passenger seat. The Escort would pass on the driver's side. For a moment, he felt the urge to ask for help, to trust, to believe in something—Someone—greater than him.

But he pushed the urge aside. The years of stored bitterness had taken their toll. He was all they could count on.

Ahead, he noticed the upward slope at the end of the dirt road. Just before the incline began, the road narrowed to a single lane. It was time to go for broke. J.Z. eased the pressure on the gas.

"Are you crazy?" Maryanne asked. "They're going to hit us."

He yanked the wheel to the left. "Hang on."

"What are you doing?"

"Turning around."

"Why? They're going to ram right into us…shoot us…"

The car's tires spun on the gravel and dirt. J.Z. kept his gaze on the truck as it plunged toward them.

"Lord Jesus, into your hands…," Maryanne cried.

He kept the wheel turned all the way. The car slid, the tires grabbed, they slid again. He applied the brakes to temper their speed. Gravel flew up against the car, its impact different from that of the bullet that followed.

He held tight to the wheel. Then, with a wobble, the car fishtailed one last time and faced the opposite way. J.Z. hit the pedal again. They flew past the truck, whose brakes squealed as the driver tried to avoid the mound and turn to follow. But it couldn't; its size and momentum played against it.

The Escort careened back down the bumpy road and

seconds later broke through onto the paved road again. J.Z. swerved in between a van full of women with white caps on their heads and a souped-up classic car determined to share its bass-heavy rap with the world outside.

He didn't care. He'd pulled them through. Now he had to get away from where the killers in the truck could catch them.

"Take the map out of that brown envelope."

She did.

"Find the quickest way to West Virginia. And forget Route 30. I just want to get us out of the Keystone State ASAP."

With a heightened sense of urgency, J.Z. let Maryanne assume the navigator's job. She handled it with her librarian's efficiency. She gave him clear, concise directions that kept them on a less visible approach to the Mason-Dixon line, West Virginia, and Ron Griffiths' house. When not giving directions, she kept quiet, and J.Z. was glad she wasn't a nervous chatterer. That would drive him nuts.

He slid a sideways look at her. She'd closed her eyes again, leaned her head on the rest, but she hadn't fallen asleep. He knew without a shadow of a doubt that Maryanne was praying.

For a moment, he remembered the sudden urge to believe he'd experienced when the truck was nearly upon them. In contrast, Maryanne seemed to maintain a constant and ongoing conversation with her Lord. He'd seen her scared, witnessed the depth of her fear, but somehow she always returned to that certain sense of peace. Most women he knew would find it impossible to stay calm as they fled from would-be assassins.

He could only attribute this to her faith, a faith that sustained her through horrifying experiences, that peace that was supposed to surpass all understanding. His momentary need in the face of imminent danger hinted at something greater, deeper. His spiritual emptiness might be catching up with him.

But he was who he was. He couldn't change the past. For a multitude of reasons, he wished it were different, that he didn't bear the Prophet family shame, that it hadn't ruined his relationship with God. But how could it not? His family's shame went too deep, and his father's crimes cast too long a shadow for a perfect God.

"J.Z.?"

"Yes."

"Will you tell me about it?"

Was she a mind reader, too? "What do you mean?"

She turned in her seat. "A couple of times you've brought up your father, and I understand his situation is difficult for you, but I think there's a lot more you haven't said that's hurting you still."

He scoffed. "There's not much to be said. He was an operative of an organized-crime family. He got caught, was prosecuted and is doing life for murder one. It doesn't get much clearer than that. Or much worse."

"Then tell me this: how'd you wind up with the Bible-to-the-max name? You said something that leads me to believe he might have used an assumed name."

"The trial showed that before my mother met good ol' Dad, he didn't exist. He could produce a birth certificate, Social Security number and driver's license, but there was no record of them anywhere. No one could trace Obadiah Prophet's roots, and he sure wasn't talking."

"That must have been hard."

"Not as hard as watching what it did to my mother."

Her warm hand came to rest on his forearm. "It must have crushed her. I know it would have me."

He shot her a glance. Her sadness and compassion met his gaze. "In every sense of the word. She collapsed during the trial, and never recovered. She died the day after the jury read the verdict."

"You believe your father's actions killed her."

"Wouldn't you?"

She fell silent.

He waited her out.

"I know how my emotions would respond, but I also know that I can't put myself in a position to judge. I leave that to the Lord."

"Then it's just as well he's been locked up for the past fifteen years."

"I understand," she said. "I also think I understand your commitment to justice."

"I've got to make a difference and make up for my father's crimes. He chose to hurt and steal and lie, but I refuse to be tarred with the same brush. No one's ever going to say "like father, like son" about me."

"You don't have to, you know."

"I don't have to what?"

"Try and atone for your father's sins. Jesus did that on the Cross. The Father loved us so much that He provided atonement when He allowed His son to be sacrificed for us—for you and your father and me."

The familiar words threatened to ignite the flame of hope in his heart. But he knew better, so he quashed the spark. "I wish I could believe, but I've never seen evidence of that kind of love. I've never seen God's face, felt His touch, heard His voice."

"Look closely, J.Z. God imprints His face in each one of His children. We're all created in His image."

"Not Obadiah Prophet."

Maryanne made a gentle, compassionate sound. "I think you need to see beyond your earthly father's flaws. You can't measure your heavenly Father by that same measure—you can't measure Him at all."

"All I know is what I know."

"You might know more than you think. What about your mother?"

J.Z. sucked in a sharp breath. "What about her?"

"From what you told me, she didn't take part in your father's crimes. Is there a reason why you choose to forget her love for you?"

"Of course, she didn't participate! And I don't forget her love. What I also don't forget is that God let my father make a victim of her. God let good ol' Dad kill her. If God's so powerful and loving, why didn't He do something to stop that crime, my father's other crimes—any crime, for that matter? She did nothing to deserve what she got."

"I don't know."

Her simple response caught him by surprise. "Then how can you ask me to believe in some supernatural kind of love that's supposed to be greater than my understanding but that lets something like that go on? That gives me nowhere to hang my trust."

"It's called faith, J.Z. God loves us without strings attached, and that's the kind of love He wants from us. To Love Him just on His word, without conditions, demands or trade-offs."

That long-dead flame tried to flicker to life in his heart again, but he couldn't let it take hold. "Yeah, sure. At times

I wish I could believe like that, but I just can't get a handle on that kind of unconditional love. I have nothing to measure it by, to give me a sense of what it might be like."

She fell silent for a while. Then, about ten miles farther down the road, she said, "Why don't you focus on your memories of your mother's love instead of your father's sin? You might remember that you felt God's touch in her love."

Her words caught him off guard. Was it a matter of his focus? Had he only looked at his past in one way? It was something he'd have to consider. But this wasn't the time.

He gave a noncommittal shrug. "Maybe. But right now I need to focus on my job. Besides, I got you into this, so I have to get you out."

"What do you mean?"

His cheeks burned. "I…ah…well, I was wrong. About you."

"How so?" she asked, a touch of humor in her voice.

"You're gonna make me say it, aren't you?"

"I think you owe me at least that much."

"Okay, fine. You're not a hit woman with the mob. You're a librarian from New Camden, PA, with an elderly father who lives in a nursing home. There. Are you satisfied?"

Out the corner of his eye, he saw her lips try to twitch into a smile, but her willpower prevailed. "Yes, J.Z. Thank you very much. It takes a big man to recognize his mistakes."

He shot her a disgusted look. "I'm just being honest. And since I made a mess of your life, I have to fix it for you. I don't know how I'll do that quite yet, but I can promise you I'm going to make sure you're cleared of any suspicion and can go home to your dad as soon as possible."

She placed that soft, warm hand on his arm again. "I'm

sorry I teased you, J.Z. I know you'll do your best. I want you to know that although I didn't trust you for a while, I think the Lord sent you to me for a reason. He has given me the peace I needed to place my trust in you."

Her words moved him more than they should have. Warmth filled his heart and spread, giving him a sense of strength, competence, triumph. He stole another glance at her. He smiled.

Maryanne Wellborn was an amazing woman. From the very beginning, and during the height of his suspicion, she'd persevered until she proved her point. In a very short period of time, he'd come to admire and respect her.

Hey, he'd even started to…*like* her. A lot.

TWELVE

The day turned into a tar-black night. J.Z. didn't let the lack of light lull him into a sense of security. To clear Maryanne and come out the other side of this mess alive, he'd practically have to grow eyes in the back of his head.

At a quarter to nine, J.Z. felt his right leg might be forever frozen into position on the gas pedal. And they were low on gas; he had to fill up. The ma and pa gas station/convenience stores on the back roads they were forced to take closed early. He pulled into the next one, glad to see a refrigerated case inside. He was parched.

"Where are we?" Maryanne asked when he stopped the car.

"Beats me. You're the one with the map."

She gave him a sheepish grin. "Sorry. I fell asleep. But we can ask the guy inside. I'll need to find the best route to…I don't know. You tell me."

"Tell you what. I'm going in there to grab something cold with caffeine. I'll ask the guy where we are. When I get back we can check the map."

J.Z. pumped gas, ran in and paid for his Mountain Dew, and then pumped the clerk for information. He sat back at the wheel and turned the key. "We're almost to Harpers

Ferry. I'm going over to that lamppost so we can get a better look at the map."

"That works. I have to use the ladies' room before we leave, but let's see where we're going first."

He helped her unfold the map of Pennsylvania, glad that it showed part of adjacent states. They found Harpers Ferry right away.

"We're not that far from Norm's wreck," he said. He pointed to a flyspeck of a dot. "Ridley's Branch is the name of the town—if you can call twelve houses, a twenty-by-thirty foot church, a gas pump and a goat farm a town. From what I can tell, it's only about fifty or sixty miles away. We'll be there in about an hour and a half. Depending on the roads—"

A tinny version of "Ode to Joy" burst out from somewhere under Maryanne's feet.

"My cell phone!" she cried. "I didn't know it was here. It must have fallen out of my bag earlier today." She flipped it open. "Hello?"

J.Z. winced. Thanks to satellite technology, Eliza could now trace them through her cell phone records—which she probably had already obtained the order to do.

"What!" She leaned forward and grabbed his forearm. Her fingers dug deep.

In the yellow glow of the lamppost, he saw the color drain from her face. "Who is it?"

She drew in a sharp breath…shook her head. With obvious effort, she asked, "What do you want?"

In the ensuing silence, she closed her eyes. Her expressive face reflected a depth of misery that struck him deep. A terrible idea began to take shape in his mind.

He felt the urge to rip the phone from her hand, but if

he were right, that would only make matters worse. He had to let her finish the call.

She went on. "But I don't know—"

Her caller must have cut her off.

J.Z. opened his Mountain Dew and drained half the bottle. He tried to stay calm, but his pulse picked up speed with each beat. He had yet to take his gaze from Maryanne.

She locked her eyes on his. "How do I know you're telling the truth?"

The hand on his arm convulsed. Maryanne's body stiffened. A tear rolled down her cheek. "Dad…"

He'd been right. And he hated being right this time. Which pointed out in graphic reality how truly wrong he'd been at the start. But none of his earlier mistakes compared with this. He had no idea how he would ever right this one.

"I understand," Maryanne said. "I will be there."

In a jerky motion, she snapped the phone shut. She took a deep breath, closed her eyes and prayed. When she again met his gaze, he saw the return of that peaceful determination he had come to know…and admire.

"Turn around, J.Z. We're meeting Carlie's brother Tony somewhere in the Pocono Mountain area. He'll call to let us know exactly where tomorrow at noon."

When J.Z. didn't argue, Maryanne let out a sigh of relief. They had no alternative. Tony Verdi had her dad, and he wanted Maryanne and Carlie. He didn't care about J.Z. and Dan, but if they got in the way, he'd take them, too, as a bonus.

But when J.Z. also didn't budge, she knew it wouldn't be that easy to head out and make the trade for her dad. "Didn't you hear me?"

"Of course, I heard you. I heard every word you said."

"So why aren't you driving us out of here?"

"Because I can't be responsible for your death."

"You prefer to be responsible for my father's, then."

He winced. Good.

"No," he said. "I'm going to figure out how to get the two of you out of this mess I got you into."

"And how do you figure you're going to do that, Superman?"

"Give it up, Maryanne. I've gone through something called training, have…oh…maybe six years working for the Bureau. Remember? This *is* what I do for a living, you know."

She rolled her eyes; his sarcasm didn't help. "And you're good at it. You already told me once. But at that time, a bunch of creepy gangsters weren't holding a gun to my dad's head. Oh, I should tell you I heard a woman yelling in the background. They're holding her, too, until I get up there with Carlie, so you'd better get hold of Dan. I won't let them hurt Dad. He has to get back to Peaceful Meadows. He needs his meds, or else…or else he'll—"

A sob stopped her.

"You said you trusted me just a while ago," J.Z. said. "Now you'll have to put that trust to the test. I won't let them hurt your dad *or* you. I promise."

She gave him a sad smile. "That's a promise you can't keep. You have no control over what those men do. All you can do is help me protect my dad. Then you can do whatever you want to catch them."

"It'd be better if you let me take care of catching them. We can rescue your dad, too."

"Won't work. If they even suspect I've brought you

along they'll shoot Dad and the lady. And I believe this guy." She shuddered. "He had the freakiest voice."

He ran a hand through his hair; drained the rest of his soda; crunched the plastic bottle flat in his hand.

"Look," she said. "I know you're frustrated. But this is something I have to do. It's more important than your job or your pride or anything else."

"It's not about my pride—"

"Hear me out," she said, her urgency growing. "I understand everything you said, how capable you are, and all that. But I answer to God. He calls me to honor my earthly father, and if it means that I have to lay down my life for Dad's sake, then that's what I have to do. I trust the Lord."

In response, he rolled down his window and lobbed the flattened soda bottle into a nearby steel drum that served as a trash can. It clanked at the bottom, the sound loud and harsh in the night.

"I really don't need you to get back there," she said. "I don't want to go alone—I'm not stupid—but if that's the only way I can get there, then I will find a way to do it. I will be there tomorrow at noon."

He started the car, backed up and turned onto the road they'd driven here. "You do what you have to do," he said, "and I'll do what I have to do."

"Thank you for turning around." She sighed. "But don't interfere. Please. At least, not until Dad's safe. Then you can do whatever you want."

He didn't speak.

"J.Z., I mean it. Don't interfere. They'll kill Dad and that lady—"

"Tell me about the woman. Who is she?"

"Beats me. Tony just said she was in Dad's suite when

he got there. He took them both. I figure it must be another Peaceful Meadows resident, but I didn't recognize her voice."

"So we have to add another senior citizen to the mix."

"Tony said he'd let her go with Dad once he has Carlie and me."

"And you're ready to take Tony's word," he said, disbelief and something else in his words. "You'll trust him before you trust me."

"No, that's not it at all." The hurt in his voice surprised her. "I know you'll get Tony. I just don't want to give Carlie's brother any reason to pull that trigger. Let me make sure Dad and that woman get away, and then you and your fellow agents can grab all the mobsters you want."

He shot her an exasperated look. "I didn't want to say it because I didn't want to upset you any more than you already are, but you have to think this all the way through. How can you think they'll let your dad go? He's seen them, they've held him at gunpoint. He's a witness, Maryanne. Just like Carlie."

Tears fell down her cheeks again. He'd voiced the thought that had hovered in the back of her mind but that she hadn't wanted to face. Still, it made no difference.

"I have to do it. It's the chance I have to take. I can't just sit and wait for you and the FBI to plan and argue and brainstorm and finally stomp your way into wherever Tony and his pals are holed up. Once I'm in there, I'll figure something out. Dad's pretty sharp, and Carlie knows her brother."

As they drove under a rare light pole, it illuminated the car enough to let her see his grip tighten on the steering wheel. His knuckles shone white.

"This isn't getting us anywhere," he said, his voice just as tight. "So tell me about the woman. You said you heard her?"

"In the background. It wasn't very clear. And what I heard didn't make much sense." Maryanne concentrated for a moment. "She yelled something about Tony, that he had to…tow something? I don't know."

J.Z. barked out a rough laugh. "That's Tony's nickname, Maryanne. They call him Tony the Toe."

"You mean…like on a foot?"

"Yep."

"Why would they do that? That's really weird."

"For a while, about five years ago, he had to wear a big cushioned brace on one of his feet, like the ones doctors give patients who've had foot surgery. Rumor has it he shot off one of his toes by accident."

Maryanne shuddered. "That's awful. But I think the woman knows him, or at least knows he's gun-happy. She yelled some strange stuff, something about a sawed-off shotgun that was only half-cocked—"

"Zelda! He's got Zelda Mathers."

"Who's she?"

"She's one of us. A computer specialist. What she doesn't know about those stupid machines isn't worth knowing. She's the one who checked out your e-mails."

Maryanne frowned. "Why would she be in Dad's room?"

J.Z. hit the gas pedal. "She told me she'd try to get in touch with me somehow. Maybe she figured you'd check in with him, and that way she could get a message to you—to us."

"That's great! When I get there, I won't be on my own. We have an agent on the inside. The Lord's taking care of us. You'll see."

"Maryanne, Zelda is sixty-two years old, and she's a computer geek, not Rambo."

"You're no Rambo, either, but you keep telling me how good you are at your job. Zelda must be pretty sharp if she's a computer expert and still working for the FBI at her age. I'm sure the four of us will figure something out."

"Four?"

"Sure. We have to get Carlie up there, too. Tony made that perfectly clear."

"Forget it. Three victims are three too many."

"No way. Carlie has to come."

"I'm the senior agent on this case, and I'm not dragging my partner and his witness into this mess."

"But it's my father whose life hangs in the balance." She flipped open her phone, hit a couple of buttons and pressed it to her ear.

He reached over. "Give me that!"

She scrunched up against the door. "Hey, Carlie. It's me, Maryanne. I know we're late. Something's come up, and we won't be going to the money pit after all—"

J.Z. made another stab at the phone. "You're putting your friend in danger."

Maryanne rolled down the window and stuck her head out. "Your brother Tony somehow got my cell phone number. I'm sorry to tell you, but he's a pretty nasty piece of business. He's got my dad, and unless you and I go meet him, he'll…" She took a deep breath. "He'll kill my father. We have to—"

"Hurry," Carlie finished. "We'll be right behind you. This was my biggest fear all my life, what I tried to avoid and never faced. But now it's caught up with me, and I'm not going to let them get away with it. Where are we supposed to meet them?"

J.Z. lunged one more time.

Maryanne leaned out farther. "You may have a hard time talking Dan into doing the right thing." She undid her seatbelt so she could keep the phone out of J.Z.'s reach. "Anyway, he said we're to go to the Pocono Mountain area. He'll call me tomorrow morning to let me know where we're supposed to meet."

J.Z. took a corner then hit the brakes.

Uh-oh. "I can't talk much longer—"

"Listen," Carlie said, "I've a good idea where he is. There are homes still sealed for the winter in the East Stroudsburg, Marshalls Creek area. Sometimes snowbirds don't come up until late June or early July. Meet us at the Pocono Raceway exit."

The car stopped. J.Z. opened the door.

"Sounds good. Gotta go. This G-man's not cooperating—"

Agent Prophet took the phone from her hand and closed it. "That wasn't smart."

"Maybe not, but I gave Carlie the choice. She agreed with me. We can't let Tony the Tiger—no, Tony the Toe—get away with one more crime."

She held his gaze. "With the help and by the grace of God, we're going to stop him."

Six hours later they reached the Poconos. They got off the freeway, and decided to spend the last few hours of the night in the car at the Raceway parking lot. It was conveniently deserted.

Maryanne tried to lie down in the backseat, but this was an Escort, and even though she wasn't particularly tall, five foot five was too long for comfort. She didn't want to know how J.Z. handled sitting in the driver's seat for so many hours on end.

If her calculations were correct, Carlie and Dan would meet them in about two hours' time. She hoped she could relax, even if for a short while.

But just as she closed her eyes after a fervent prayer for her dad's safety, J.Z. muttered something angry under his breath and started the car. He hit the gas, the tires spun then caught and they took a sharp turn out of the parking lot.

"What's wrong?" she asked.

"Dave Latham and Tom Hardy were waiting in the dark for us."

"Who're they?"

"A couple of agents from our unit. Remember Eliza? She's not about to forget you."

"How'd they know where to find us?"

"Maybe Dan had better luck taking over Carlie's phone than I did yours. He might have called the office."

"There's one way to find out." She grabbed her phone from the driving console, where J.Z. earlier dropped it in frustration. A moment later, she heard her friend's voice.

"I can't talk long," Maryanne said. "I have to save my battery. Did Dan use your phone? Did you guys call the FBI and tell them where we planned to meet?"

"No. Why would we do that? That cranky boss of theirs wants you in jail. I wouldn't let Dan do that to you, especially since Tony has your dad."

"Well, they found out because two agents were waiting for us. J.Z. said they were a Dave Something and a Tom Whatever."

"That's bad. But listen. Get to Marshalls Creek. It's a

tiny town past East Stroudsburg. Meet us at the shopping center in the middle of town. You can't miss it."

"Marshalls Creek. Got it. See you soon." She turned to J.Z. "They weren't the ones who called—"

"That doesn't matter now. We have to get to a gas station. We're almost on fumes, and we won't get anywhere if we don't fill up."

"What? What are you talking about?"

He mimed a zipper closing his lips.

Maryanne opened her eyes wider and stared. He couldn't be right. Could he?

She mouthed the word *bug*.

He nodded. "Have you looked at the gas gauge lately?"

She closed her eyes. "Great," she whispered. Then, in a louder voice, she added, "No, I hadn't, but it does look low. And I need to use the ladies' room, so it's just as well we're stopping soon."

They drove in silence for a while. They kept to the side roads, concerned as to what might lie in wait for them wherever they went.

Then, he pulled into a gas station. They really needed to fill up. Maryanne stepped out of the car and stretched. The ladies' room had become a necessity, too. "I'll be right back."

J.Z. nodded and started to pump gas.

In the locked cubicle, Maryanne prayed. "Lord, I'm scared. We have killers after us, and now the ones who're supposed to be the good guys are after us, too. I don't know what to do, but I do know that if I don't get Dad back home soon, his blood sugar'll go crazy."

She went to the rust-stained porcelain sink with its ugly, chrome stick legs. She splashed her face with cold water again and again. The brown paper towels in the chipped, white enamel dispenser scratched her skin, but that was a small price to pay for the sensation of fresh water on her face.

She returned to her humble "throne." "Please help me, Father. Show me what to do. And keep after J.Z. I think he's begun to see how much he needs You. He's just a little stubborn—he's a man."

By then, her bladder threatened mutiny, so she took care of that, too. She returned to the sink, washed her hands and studied herself in the pitted mirror. She winced.

"Ugh!" The reddish-brown corkscrews sproinged all over her head. Her eyes wore an underscore of purplish-blue, and her skin was red from the rough paper towel.

"Oh, yes, Maryanne Wellborn. You're the picture of feminine loveliness, all right. No wonder J.Z. is so indifferent to you."

Was that really how she felt? Did she want him to *not* be indifferent? How could that have happened? They had less than nothing in common, and that mattered in a relationship between a man and a woman.

He even rejected God. And that was one thing she believed: a couple had to share a common faith. If they shared that, they could weather just about anything that came their way.

"Oh, Father. I'm in trouble here. I need even more help than I thought. Guard my heart, just as I pray you'll guard my dad." She sighed. "In Jesus' precious name, Amen."

She walked back to the car, reluctant to face J.Z. after that moment of discovery in the dingy bathroom. But her discomfort never had a chance to materialize. J.Z. took care of that.

"About time," he groused. "I'd begun to think you'd found a way to run off and rendezvous with the mob."

Even though he hadn't intended them that way, his words gave her an idea. She kept her response light. "I'm baaaaack! And ready to roll. Unless you need to use the bathroom, too."

"Yeah, I do. I figured I'd better wait for you to get back since I didn't want to leave the car alone. I thought about the bug while you were gone, and I checked the car everywhere I could. I didn't find anything, so I think it might be Dan's car they bugged."

Maryanne considered the possibility. "You did say he went to the office while we went shopping with Carlie. Your boss could have had someone plant it then."

"That's what I think. But if she did, I don't know why. She knows I'll get to the bottom of the scam, and finger the boss and lieutenants who're killing the seniors for their money. She knows I'll call in enough backup to take them all down."

"Maybe Dan's right," Maryanne said with a mischievous smile. "Maybe she's just jealous, and wants you back in her clutches as soon as possible."

He blushed. "Give me a break. Eliza's a pain, but she wouldn't use the Bureau for her own games."

Maryanne shrugged. "I can't imagine your supervisor bugging your car, either."

"I have a bad feeling about this. They knew where to find us. A bug is bad news. It means someone wants more than what we've told. The best thing to do is to wait for Tony's call, then get reinforcements. I'll deal with the eavesdropping later."

Maryanne went to argue, but realized she'd get nowhere. Besides, he'd given her that idea a couple of minutes earlier. And she was about to carry it out.

"I disagree," she said, knowing he would've thought it

strange if she didn't. "Go ahead, though, and use the bathroom. We can argue some more once you're back."

He snorted, but went ahead and made for the men's room. Maryanne waited until the door closed. Then she knelt by the muffler and reached for the extra key she kept hidden under a thick layer of duct tape.

She sat, started up the Escort and whispered an apology to J.Z. Then, as she put the car in gear, the bathroom door opened again. She hit the gas pedal and met J.Z.'s steely stare in the rearview mirror, his anger clear in his rigid stance.

At the first red light, she pulled out the phone and dialed Carlie. "I think you and Dan had better rescue J.Z. He was determined to call for backup, and that would have sealed my father's fate. I left him at a gas station."

When Carlie stopped laughing, Maryanne gave her directions. "He won't be a happy camper," she added. "He looked meaner than a tornado on a stormy night."

"Don't worry about it. Dan can deal with his partner. And I'll take care of calling my dear, darling brother Tony."

Her sudden bitterness shocked Maryanne. But she could understand Carlie's sense of outrage.

Carlie added, "I'll be right behind you. We're going to make sure your dad is safe."

Maryanne thanked Carlie, closed the phone, and focused on the road. She had no idea where to go. She only knew she couldn't let J.Z. bring in the troops. That would seal her father's fate.

Tony didn't make her wait long for his call. His harsh, icy voice gave her clear, concise directions. Then, when he figured she knew how to find the meeting place, he added, "Just you and my sister, you got that? No cops, no one else. You, and you alone."

Maryanne's stomach knotted tighter. "I got it, Tony. I just ditched the Fed. It'll be me. And Carlie said she'd call—"

"She did. And she better dump her goon, too."

"I can only speak for myself, and I'm doing what you asked. I'm on my way—alone. It's just me."

And God.

THIRTEEN

Rage served no purpose after Maryanne sped away. Especially since J.Z. wasn't sure his anger was aimed at Maryanne as much as at himself. He'd come to know her pretty well in the last couple of weeks, and her readiness to postpone a disagreement—one that affected her father's safety—should have raised his suspicions. Nothing about Maryanne Wellborn was ever that easy.

Now he was stuck in the middle of Who-Knew-Where, West Virginia, without a way to catch up to her, while she rushed straight to a confrontation with a killer.

J.Z. was sure now that Tony the Toe had played a part in Laundromat's death—he was more than likely the one who made sure the deed was done at Peaceful Meadows. Where a pact between Tony and Joey-O came in, he didn't know. But he would find out. No matter what.

And he would also keep Maryanne safe. Somehow.

First thing he had to do was get out of here. While he'd hesitated to use his cell phone earlier, now he had no choice. He hoped he could get a signal in this forgotten corner of the world.

He opened the phone and noticed the battery had little charge left—just enough to at least give Dan directions.

But when he spoke with his partner, he learned that Dan already knew all about his humbling at Maryanne's hands. Dan and Carlie were fast on their way to his rescue, and his partner found J.Z.'s comedown rather funny.

"If you crack even one lousy joke," J.Z. warned, "you'll pay for it."

Dan chuckled. "I told you Maryanne's a neat lady. I also told you she's innocent. You should've listened, pard."

"I'm listening now. And we have to follow her. I hope Carlie can help us track down that brother of hers."

"She thinks she knows where Tony might be. We're close to the gas station, so you don't have long to wait. Then we'll head back to the Poconos. See ya."

No matter how close Dan was, he wouldn't get to the gas station soon enough for J.Z. He couldn't help but worry about Maryanne. The choice she'd made led her to certain disaster, and she'd gone with no protection. Tony the Toe Verdi knew no mercy.

He sat on the step outside the men's room and tried to calm his fear. But no matter what he told himself, one fact remained. He couldn't stand to think that someone might hurt Maryanne—he refused to consider the other, more sinister possibility.

There was nothing he wouldn't do to keep her safe. He'd come to accept her innocence, that she belonged in New Camden, at the library, at church functions, with her father. He wanted to make sure she continued to bring books to the residents at Peaceful Meadows.

The joy he'd seen her display was genuine. As was her faith—the faith she claimed called her to risk her life for her father's sake. A woman like Maryanne didn't come along every day. She was as "neat" as Dan had said, and

J.Z. couldn't stand the thought that he might never get another chance to hold her in his arms.

That dream…it had left a permanent vision in his mind, a longing in his heart. If he couldn't keep her safe, he'd never share with her the joy of a newborn child. And he realized he wanted that. A lot.

He had fallen in love with her. It was that simple.

He checked his watch. Time seemed to have entered a bizarre warp. At alternating moments, it either flew by faster than ever before, or it seeped by in a lazy crawl. Either way put Maryanne closer to her encounter with Tony, and J.Z. had to get there in time to keep him from hurting her. He'd gladly take whatever Tony had in mind for her.

His life wouldn't be worth much if he failed to save her.

And then he knew. He understood what she'd tried to tell him earlier that night. She'd said God called her to honor her earthly father, even if that meant giving up her own life. He'd marveled at the depth of her love. Now he also understood the strength of her conviction. He understood her willingness to sacrifice herself for her father's sake.

On the heels of that thought, words, phrases from his past returned. *For God so loved…He gave His one and only Son…whoever believes in Him shall not perish….*

God's sacrificial love was at the heart of the Christian faith, the faith that sustained Maryanne. That faith filled her with a peace he'd never understood. That faith assured her of her Father's care, even among mobsters.

He loved her. He was willing to die in her place.

Love…because of God's love, Jesus became a sacrifice. God let His Son be killed for the sake of His Creation. God had loved that much.

Maryanne had been right about another thing. J.Z. had known love without strings, his mother's love. Bitterness born of shame at his sleazy father's actions had made him turn his back on those good memories. It had been easier to feed his anger and hate than to accept a love he didn't understand, a love that allowed the loved one to choose right or wrong, a love strong enough to forgive and to wait for the loved one to love in return.

Yet another phrase from his long-rejected faith surfaced. *God is love….*

"He's not a puppeteer that pulls strings," Maryanne had said. "People can and often do choose to turn away from Him. That's when things get nasty down here."

She'd also said that God wanted the same total, unconditional love He offered in return. Had God loved and waited for him all along? Was He still waiting for J.Z. to return that love?

J.Z. glanced to either side, and when he saw no one else in the dark, he dropped to his knees. "God? If You're really like Scripture says, like Maryanne believes, and if You've loved me all the time I blamed You for my father's crimes, then I'm sorry."

He was rusty at this prayer thing. "Um…I guess feeling sorry is never going to be enough, but since You're in the business of forgiveness, please forgive me. I realize now how much I'd blocked out what I knew all along. I'm ready to see more, to see what I should see and not to look only for what I want to find. I love Maryanne, and I don't even know if she cares for me. It's not a good way to feel, so I understand how my anger must have felt to You."

It felt pretty strange to kneel on cracked concrete

outside a gas station bathroom, too. But if God really was who He was supposed to be, who J.Z. once knew Him to be, then God knew exactly where J.Z. was.

In more ways than one.

"I'm not asking for me," he prayed, "but for Maryanne. She loves so much, and she's loved You all along. Now she's gone nuts and is heading toward more danger than she should have to face. Help her out. Help me help her."

His eloquence would win him no prizes, but his clumsy prayer came straight from the heart. "Help me see You, and help me trust. Thanks. Oh, yeah...Amen."

"What are you doing down there?" Dan asked.

J.Z. scrambled to his feet. "Uh...I didn't realize you were here. I was...ah...I guess you could say I was patching up a friendship I ruined years ago."

His partner gave him a strange look. "I'm surprised your cell phone still had enough juice for a call. Mine's dead."

"You could say I have all the juice I need to reach this friend." He was glad about that. For Maryanne's sake, and for the sorry state of his heart, he was going to need a ready connection to that source of power and strength from here on in.

He clapped Dan's shoulder. "Let's go. Maryanne's got too big a head start on us. I don't want her near Tony the Toe without some kind of help."

Although he now accepted that Maryanne had the best help there was, he also knew there was no reason to tempt Tony with one of those choices that brought nasty consequences, as Maryanne had called them.

J.Z. didn't want Tony, someone who'd turned his back on God years ago, to choose to kill.

* * *

Hours later, J.Z. turned in the seat to look at Carlie. "Are you sure you know where you're taking us?"

"I know where Tony hangs out when he's out here," she replied. "He's a big-time gambler, and he has friends who run private high-stakes games. He also knows which cabins belong to New Yorkers who only come out here on weekends, and he knows which ones belong to snowbirds."

"The season's over," Dan said. "The snowbirds are back."

Carlie shrugged. "I know at least three places whose owners spend June down south so their grandkids can visit after school's out."

"I buy it," J.Z. said. "Is that where Tony told you to meet him?"

"No. He said to call him from the grocery store across the fire department in Marshalls Creek. Maryanne's the one he sent to the cabin."

J.Z. narrowed his eyes. "You are taking us to Maryanne, aren't you?"

Anger flared in Carlie's brown eyes. "Of course, I am. She called and told me where she was headed. You'd better not think I'd help Tony hurt her."

Her indignation seemed genuine. He shook his head, and hoped it wasn't a mistake to trust her.

Carlie leaned forward, and J.Z. could almost feel the strength of her sincerity. "If she says Tony is holding her father, and if Tony really is holding her father and not just saying that to scare her, then she's in as much trouble as she thinks her dad is. Tony's a snake. Anyone who would take an old man from his nursing home will do just about anything."

"Would he have killed your husband, too?" Dan asked.

She leveled those dark eyes on Dan. "*Especially* Mat—if he got in Tony's way. Tony's my big brother and, I'll always love him, but I've always had a hard time *liking* him, you know? Even when we were kids, he never could stand for anyone to get in his way—even when it came to his toys."

J.Z. took a chance. "Was Tony in the car?"

Carlie faced him. "You mean, when Mat got shot?"

"Of course."

"No. But I did see two men. The one with the gun was this crazy guy they call Joey-O. Tony and my father hate him. Back when I was interviewed, the cops told me they'd arrested Joey. He's in jail awaiting trial. I said over and over again that I only saw a man in the driver's seat. I didn't get a good look at his face."

"How can you be sure the other one wasn't your brother?"

"I am sure. We'd just had dinner with Tony and his latest fling. He stayed behind in the restaurant while she used the bathroom. Now I have to wonder if he put her up to it so they'd be inside when Joey-O shot Mat."

"Do you think Tony was in on the hit?"

"I told you Tony can't stand Joey-O. Joey works for Larry Gemmelli, and that's enough reason for Tony to hate him. As far back as I can remember my family has had problems with the Gemmellis. But I guess they might decide to work together if for some reason they wanted the same thing. It'd have to be something pretty big, though."

The more things changed, the more they stayed the same. "So the Gemmellis and the Verdis are still at war after all these years."

"I guess."

"Then how would Tony know the Gemmellis were going to hit Mat?"

"About six weeks ago, Tony said Mat messed up some business deal. Larry came over, and the three off them did a lot of yelling and screaming about it. I tried to ignore the whole thing, but they were way too loud to ignore. Even my father wouldn't talk to Mat after that."

J.Z. thought back. Six weeks set the argument at a time when he'd been investigating two nursing homes close to the New Jersey border. All along, he'd known in his gut that the Verdis were involved in the kill-the-old-folks-at-the-home-for-their-money scam. It was their kind of deal. He'd have to check and see if anything significant had happened.

"Wasn't it about six weeks ago that the attorney general shut down that one nursing home?" Dan asked. "You know, the one where eight residents died in less than three months' time. Each one of them left close to half a million to the place."

"I remember," J.Z. said. "Four mill in three months. That's a lot of money—money that disappeared mysteriously from escrow accounts just days later. But we couldn't pin anything on anyone. Why would both the Verdis and the Gemmellis feel that Mat had wronged them?"

Dan laughed. "You're asking the wrong guy—remember, I was with you." He fell silent for a moment, and then he shook his head. "Four million's more money than I can imagine. Maybe Mat kept the dough? Or maybe they felt he moved too fast, and that's what made the AG shut down their cash cow. The AG's involvement would make those goons pretty mad."

"It's possible. But we won't know for sure until we

get those guys in an interrogation room. How much longer, Carlie?"

"We're about twenty minutes away from Marshalls Creek."

"I thought that's where Tony told you to meet him. You said you were taking us to where we'd find Maryanne—"

"The cabin's in Marshalls Creek. Tony's in one of the other vacant ones, or he's waiting at the Castle in the Sky."

J.Z. frowned. "What's a castle in the sky?"

"An old casino—I don't think it was ever a legal place. The building's been condemned for a couple of years now, but since no one's bought the land, it's vacant."

"I take it the Castle in the Sky is also in Marshalls Creek."

She pursed her lips, drew her brows together and considered his question. "As far as I can remember, it's just on the far edge. It could be in the next little town. You've got to understand, Marshalls Creek is a tiny place."

"Good enough for me." He glanced at his watch. "Fifteen minutes, then?"

She waggled her hand. "More or less."

He sat back and tried to plan. But he couldn't. His emotions got in the way. All he came up with was a series of scenarios, each one worse than the last. But his resolve didn't waver.

Maryanne would come out of this safe and sound.

He would make sure she did.

No matter what the cost.

"Marshalls Creek," J.Z. murmured fifteen minutes later. It was as small as Carlie had said. "How much farther?"

Carlie leaned forward and pointed to the left. "Turn here, Dan. It's only a couple of miles down this road."

Tall trees lined both sides of the narrow, twisty strip that seemed to melt into more trees at the edge of the headlights' glow. J.Z. had begun to feel as though the night would never end.

The creek ran to their right. A handful of narrow bridges spanned its modest width and led to neat, small cabins. Most were dark, since sane people were still sleeping, but the odd one here and there did have lights on inside.

"Slow down," Carlie said. "We're almost there. You don't want to miss it."

Moments later, they rattled over a wooden bridge. But instead of leading to a particular cabin, this one ended at a gravel lane. They turned onto the lane, then rolled past half a dozen cottages.

"Turn off the engine," Carlie said. "The drive slopes down, so we can coast in. I don't think you want to scare Maryanne. She might run again."

J.Z. smiled. "She's easy to figure out, isn't she?"

Carlie gave him an odd look. "She's just who she says she is. What's so hard about that?"

Dan chuckled. "Some of us have a harder time than others figuring out the easy stuff."

J.Z. chose to ignore the comment. "Let me go in first. If she sees you both, she might think she can bargain for your support. We don't have time to argue with her."

Carlie made a face. "Just go easy on her. She's scared."

"I'm not going to hurt her, but I won't let her hurt herself, either."

He hurried down the gravel drive to an attractive A-frame right on the creek. In the quiet night, he heard the water bubble over rocks. No lights showed through the white curtains. He hadn't expected to see any.

The steps to the front porch didn't creak under his weight, and the front door was ajar—the lock had been broken. He couldn't see Maryanne breaking and entering, so it looked like Tony had thought of everything so far.

Once inside, J.Z. made a quick visual sweep of the tiny kitchen, smaller bathroom and the large living area with its tall, soaring pitched roof straight ahead. He noticed attractive furniture, simple curtains at the creek-side floor-to-ceiling windows, and a large collection of blue-and-white plates on the far right wall. The one thing he didn't see was a certain librarian.

Steep stairs rose against the wall at his left. In the cozy loft, a large television set, leather recliner and wooden rocker filled a small sitting area. To the right of the recliner, a door opened to a bedroom.

That's where J.Z. found Maryanne.

She'd crawled under the silky looking floral cover, but he could still see the curve of her cheek and the spill of outrageous auburn curls. A swell of emotion filled him, and J.Z. took a moment to watch her sleep.

God, if You wouldn't mind, I'd really like the privilege of watching her sleep for a long, long time. So I'm going to trust You and do my best for her. Thanks. Amen.

"You're here," she murmured in a sleepy voice.

"Didn't you know I'd follow?"

She bolted upright. She blinked and stared. "What are you doing here? I told you not to come. You've made things worse for my dad."

"I liked your first response a whole lot better."

"That one doesn't count. I was mostly asleep. I'm awake now. You've made a mess of things."

"I see you're as ready to argue as ever." He sat by her side. "But I'm just as determined as you are. We have to work together. I can't let you walk into the bullet Tony has waiting for you."

His harsh words had their desired effect. She shuddered. "You'd rather I let my dad take that bullet."

"You know I don't. I want to save you both, and I can. But you have to cooperate with me and the Bureau—"

"Tony's not stupid. He's probably watching. And if he kills my dad because you showed up here—"

"I doubt Tony's done anything yet. He wants you, and he wants Carlie. Your father and Zelda are probably safe until Tony gets what he wants, so don't try and put that guilt on me. You know how I feel about that. I take responsibility for my actions."

"And for actions that aren't yours. I know about your misguided need to atone for your father's crimes. And even though I admire that you recognize your mistakes and how you want to fix them, that doesn't matter in this case. Your father had nothing to do with what Tony's done. Even if he had, God took care of atonement on the Cross of Calvary. That's why the Father forgives a sinner who confesses and repents."

His father had everything to do with his thoughts, choices and decisions, even in this case. Maybe most especially in this case—one that involved his father's old pals, the Verdis. Still, her words of forgiveness made hope sputter to life in his heart. "It'd be wrong for me to count on confession and forgiveness after I let you walk into certain suicide. If I did, I'd be no better than Tony or my father."

Her expression softened, and she laid a hand on his arm. "No, you wouldn't, J.Z. It's my choice to make. And

I choose to put my life in God's hands. I'm ready to go home to the Father, if that's what happens in the end."

"I could never forgive myself—"

"There's your problem." She tightened her hold. "You're the one who needs to forgive. Forgive your father. Let go of the past. Ask God's forgiveness for your anger and bitterness and lack of faith. Then forgive yourself."

He chuckled without humor. "Would you agree to work with me if I told you I already asked God's forgiveness?"

Golden hazel eyes opened wide. "You did?"

"You may have done me a favor by leaving me in that crummy gas station with nothing better to do than talk to God."

"Oh, J.Z." Her expression turned kind and compassionate. "I'm so glad. You needed to make peace with Him."

"How much peace do you think I'll have if I don't try to save your father, Zelda and you?"

"Your relationship with God has nothing to do with that."

"But it does. It has everything to do with you. You showed me what love was all about. You found a way to break through the shell I'd built around my heart."

She looked down at her hands, clasped on top of the bedspread. "I'm glad you heard what I said."

"It wasn't so much what you said, but what you did— what you do and who you are."

"How so?"

"It's the love you give everyone around you." J.Z. didn't know if it would make a difference, but he had to let her know. "I thought I'd never known that kind of love, but I knew I wanted it. Still do. With you."

She met his gaze. "What are you saying?"

He took her hands in his, looked into her eyes. "I'm

new at this, but I think I love you. I want a chance to let that love grow. Give me a chance to save your dad and Zelda. Let me protect you, too."

Her breath hitched. "Oh, J.Z. My feelings run deeper than just attraction and respect for you, too. And I'd like to see if our feelings grow into something deep and real. But I can't ignore God's call to honor my father. I can't turn my back on him."

"But you're ready to turn your back on me."

She gasped. "It's not the same thing. His life is in the balance."

"And you think mine will be anything if I let you die?"

With smooth, easy gestures, she untangled herself from the bedcovers. "That's something you'll have to take up with the Lord. Your choices are yours, and mine are mine. I will honor my dad."

He stood. "If it's honor you want to consider, then you have to respect mine. It calls me to save both of you."

"If you charge in after me, then at least one of us will die for sure. If I go in with Carlie, the four of us stand a chance to beat Tony at his game. She's his sister, and she has to know him pretty well."

He wanted to argue, but she was right on at least one point. He'd feared all along that no matter how determined he was to save both Wellborns, reality would likely lead to the death of at least one—probably Maryanne.

"Just so you know," he said, helpless to prevent the cynical note in his voice. "I've done a successful bust or two, and Tony's no smarter than others we've caught. I will call for backup, and I will do my best to prevent the worst."

"I have no choice." She walked out to the loft sitting room. "I'm going as soon as Tony calls."

"I'll be right behind."

He followed her down the steps, but turned toward the front door. She went to the living room, and curled up on the leather couch.

He left.

Anger carried J.Z. to the waiting car. "You'd better go with her," he told Carlie. "She has some crazy idea that between the two of you, plus her father and Zelda, you'll come up with some grand scheme to beat Tony and get away."

Carlie stepped out of the car. "Who knows? She could be right. There will be four of us."

"Swell," he muttered. "She's got you thinking like her. Don't count on Tony being all by his lonesome. Just go. Maybe Tony will experience a rare attack of brotherly love when he sees you."

"Don't count on it," she said as she started down the gravel drive. "Make sure you bring an army when you come."

J.Z. dropped onto the passenger seat and leaned back against the headrest. "I'm calling Latham and Hardy," he told Dan. "They were around here just hours ago. They may wind up arresting me, but I know they'll do everything to nail Tony and his pals. They might be able to help you prevent disaster."

"My phone's dead," Dan said.

"I think mine's got one call left in it."

Once David Latham got over his surprise at J.Z.'s call, he agreed to ask for backup. The men chose to regroup at the by-now-infamous grocery store parking lot. Since Tony expected his sister to be there, they would hide the cars and walk.

As they drove back over the wooden bridge, Dan shot

him a sideways look. "Do you think that was smart? I suspect someone's bugged us. Has that occurred to you?"

"I had a pretty strong feeling last night. What's the difference? We need all the help we can get—you hear that, Eliza or whoever's on the other end?—don't know where you put the bug, but I know you can hear us. It's time to set up the bust."

They drove by the fire station, turned and went past the grocery store. Five hundred yards down the road they saw an empty commercial building. They parked behind it and hurried back to the meeting place.

As they looked for David and Tom, J.Z. gave Dan a sideways look. "We've got more than just mobsters and a jealous boss to deal with, you know."

Dan met his gaze. "You really think…?"

"I'm not sure Eliza would bug us out of spite. I'm afraid someone's turned. There must be a mole in the office, so until we know for sure what's going on and why, we'd better grow eyes in the back of our heads."

FOURTEEN

Maryanne's stomach did a flip when J.Z. closed the door on his way out. He was a good man—troubled, a decent, honorable person, but on the path to restored faith. And he wanted to give their feelings a chance to grow.

To her amazement—and dismay—she was falling in love with a man with whom she had nothing in common. And he had said he thought he loved her, too.

Lord Jesus, I didn't look for someone like him. You know that. I always hoped and prayed for a man who thinks as I do, who likes the things I like. J.Z.'s a G-man, and there's nothing peaceful or comforting about that. He's not even a book person!

During those first few days when J.Z. began to shadow her back home in New Camden, she'd noticed his reading choices. Without fail, he went for the car magazines. What would they have to talk about? She knew nothing about cars.

And his job…

She shuddered. How could she ever live with the anxiety it created? She'd never be able to sleep knowing a loved one was just a step away from death—

Maryanne sucked in a sharp breath. She had to face the

truth. She'd asked J.Z. to do just that, to stand by while she risked her life. And yet she was afraid to consider a life with him for that same reason.

Did she dare call him back? Did she dare risk her father's safety?

She didn't think so.

She didn't know.

She was torn.

"Oh, Father…I haven't taken J.Z.'s feelings into consideration. I only thought of my fear for Dad. But if I've decided I can't live a life where I stand by his side as he performs his job, how can I expect him to sit and wait while I try and save Dad?" She shook her head. "And what about my pride? I wrapped myself in it, didn't I?"

She'd wanted to see herself as the only one who could save her father. She'd bought into Tony's fear-inducing threats. And J.Z. did have a point. He was a trained agent, used to dealing with the worst kind of criminal element. She'd rejected his help. She'd withheld the trust she'd promised him.

"Lord God, forgive me. I need Your help, and I need to trust You. For all I know, You sent J.Z. to provide that help. And in my blindness, I sent him away. I'd like another chance."

It was too late to catch him. She'd heard the car drive away. And because she didn't know what Tony had in mind, she had to stay and wait for his call.

"Maryanne?"

She jumped. From Carlie's expression, Maryanne gathered this wasn't the first time her friend had called her name. "I didn't realize you were here. I'm sorry."

Carlie still looked confused. "You were pretty deep

in those thoughts, and I think you were even talking to yourself."

Maryanne stood. "No. I was praying. I realized I had a bundle of sins to confess, and some other things to ask God. I've been so busy thinking I'm so smart that I couldn't see how dumb I've really been."

"Okay. Now you lost me."

"Your brother's the scariest person I've ever come across. I let his threats get to me. In my fear, I relied on myself. I fell into the trap pride sets for people, and decided I was the only one who could save Dad, just because that's what Tony said. I went so far as to send away an expert. How dumb is that?"

"I'm not so sure I follow. Tony *is* scary. The one thing I remember growing up is how mean he can be. And if he told you to come alone, he meant it. The last thing he wants you to bring along is an FBI agent."

Maryanne stepped closer. "That's my point. I let fear blind me to common sense. Of course Tony doesn't want FBI agents. He's in trouble, and they'll bring him down. Pride always gets you, and I let it get me."

"You're not a proud woman." Carlie reached out and touched her arm. "You're humble and quiet and live a simple life. If anyone's guilty of pride around here, it's me. Look at the way I live."

"But I'm the one who got us into this mess."

"J.Z. would disagree. Dan says he blames himself for drawing Tony's attention to you. That's why J.Z.'s so determined to protect you."

Maryanne let out an exasperated sigh. "There's that need again to atone for every bit of guilt he can find to put on himself." She checked her watch, and began to pace.

"Father God, please hurry and take away J.Z.'s blinders. Show him that forgiveness is a gift of Your grace through Your Son. And get Tony to hurry up and call."

She came to a halt before she rammed into Carlie. "Whoa! Sorry. I'm tired of waiting for Tony. I'm getting antsy."

"Do you do that a lot?"

"What? Walk into people? Not usually."

"No. Talk to God like that. As if He was here in the room with us."

Maryanne lifted a shoulder. "I guess I do talk to Him all the time. He is here, Carlie. He's everywhere. And He listens to the prayers of His people. I'm His. I gave Him my life years ago."

A wistful look crossed Carlie's face. "I wish…"

"I told you to ditch the goons." The harsh, male voice cut off Carlie's words.

Maryanne spun and took her first look at Tony Verdi. Although she could see the family resemblance to his sister, anger distorted his features.

Fear began an icy crawl through her blood, but she remembered her promise. She would trust the Lord.

Head held high, she said, "I sent them away. It's just Carlie and me here. I did my part, and was waiting for your call. Where are Zelda and Dad?"

"That's none of your business. They're fine. And you didn't do what I told you to do. You and Carlie brought the goons, and they're calling in more. So if you want your dad and that wild woman back, you better give me the cash."

A glance at Carlie told Maryanne her friend was as in the dark as she. "I don't have any cash. I don't know what you're talking about."

His jaw jutted. "Don't act dumb, lady. It's no coincidence the Feds are all over you. How'd you get the money away from Mat?"

She really *had* entered the *Twilight Zone*. "I never knew the man. He died before I had a chance to bring the library cart to his room."

He rolled his eyes. "Stop with the library cart stuff. The FBI doesn't waste its time following librarians without a good reason. Where's the money?"

"I don't—"

"Tony," Carlie said, her hand on Maryanne's shoulder. "If Maryanne says she doesn't know, then she doesn't know. I don't, either. Did Mat owe you money? Maybe I can pay you back. You don't have to hurt anyone."

He had an ugly laugh. "You have four million bucks handy?"

Maryanne's stomach lurched. "No one has that much money."

Carlie crossed her arms and stared through narrowed eyes. "Does this have anything to do with that big fight you and Dad had with Mat and Larry six weeks ago?"

"See?" Triumph didn't improve Tony's expression. "I knew one of you had the money."

"I don't have four million dollars," Carlie said. "I don't even know if Mat had it. But I think this has something to do with that nursing home in New Jersey. Am I right?"

Her brother didn't like her question. "That's none of your business, Carlie. This is men's business. What do you know about the cash?"

"Nothing." She blew out an exasperated sigh. "I just know what I heard you guys yell. You and Dad said Mat cheated you in some deal on that nursing home. Is that why you killed him?"

If Maryanne had thought Tony's initial anger alarming, she now revised that assessment. It was nothing compared to this.

He took slow, deliberate step after step toward his sister. "Don't stick your nose in this, kid. Just give me the money."

"*I* didn't stick my nose in anything." Carlie met his gaze, her stance firm. "You had Mat killed right in front of me, and then you took a man in a wheelchair from his nursing home. He happens to be my friend's father. *You* stuck me in it."

He stepped back, hands in the air. "I didn't kill that weasel Dad married you to. Joey-O did that—he's in jail, remember? I was in the restaurant waiting for Lillibeth. Don't you try to stick that one on me, okay?"

"Oh, yeah, big brother. Sure. Whatever you say. Mat 'died' outside the restaurant. Then what was all that about the phony coffin and the nursing home, huh? Huh?" Carlie didn't let up. "Are you going to tell me that Mat came back from the dead to just croak all over again of so-called natural causes?"

Maryanne wondered if J.Z. was really bringing backup, if they'd get here in time. At the rate they were going—if she were to continue to add fuel to the siblings' argument—she might be able to distract Tony long enough to let the agents nab him. Then, if it wasn't too late, they could get back to looking for Dad.

As J.Z. had wanted to do all along.

Lord, bring him here in time.

She gave Tony a measuring look. "You don't need Carlie to pin any crime on you. You've done a good enough job of it yourself."

"I'm clean!" He wagged a finger at her. "I haven't done

a thing. It's her husband who took me to the cleaners on an investment we made together."

Carlie glanced at Maryanne, and then checked her watch. Maryanne nodded. Both women hoped their help would arrive soon.

"When did you start 'investing' in nursing homes?" Carlie asked.

"About a year ago—" He cut off his words and glared. "Don't you go and get cute here, Carlie. I can't tell you any more. I just want the dough. Where'd Mat stash it? Or was it your little friend there who hid it?"

Maryanne's thoughts spun through a myriad of possibilities. Four million dollars was a lot of money to misplace. From what she'd learned in her reading, mob families specialized in sanitizing ill-gotten gains. And Carlie's husband went by the name Laundromat. What *had* happened to all the money?

An idea began to gel. "Are you related to Larry? Or maybe to Joey-O?"

The Verdi siblings faced her. "No way!" Carlie wrinkled her nose. "The Gemmellis are not the nicest people."

"Was Mat related to them?"

Tony frowned. "What is this, twenty questions?"

"No. I'm just curious. You have my dad, you think I stole a fortune, plus you're threatening me, so I think the very least you can do is answer a couple of questions for me. Was Mat related to the Gemmellis? Is Larry his brother, his cousin, his nephew?"

"It's none of your—"

"I heard you," Maryanne said. "But you didn't hear me. I know nothing about any money, Carlie says she never bothered to ask Mat about his work and you keep telling us your 'business' dealings aren't our business. How can you expect us to know what happened to any money matters between you and Mat? It seems to me you've gone to a lot of trouble to grab and scare the wrong people."

"What's that got to do with family?"

Everything, if it's a mob family you're talking about.

"Well, I think—"

"What's the holdup in there, Tony?" a man called from outside the cabin. "Need help with them?"

Tony swallowed hard. He darted a glance at Carlie. "Nah. Give me five, Larry, will ya?"

"Why are you hanging out with Larry Gemmelli again?" Carlie asked. "Since when did you two become such good pals?"

"Since we made a deal with your husband, and then he stiffed us. Now, are you going to tell me what Mat did with the cash, or am I gonna have to let Larry take over? It won't be pretty if he does."

Carlie blanched.

Maryanne didn't like the sound of that, either.

And she had no way of knowing her father's condition. "Where's my dad, Tony? You said you'd let him go once I got here. Well, here I am. So where is he?"

"He's okay with that crazy old broad." He shook his head. "Man, she's something else."

"Did you let them go?"

Tony looked over his shoulder. "Larry's running the show. He'll decide what to do when he has the cash."

Maryanne's stomach plummeted. Another thing J.Z. had predicted. Mobsters didn't leave witnesses.

And she'd thought she knew what to do. "Forgive me, Father."

Tony glared. "What are you doing? Do you have a mike to your old man? Is that why he stayed so calm? Talking to you or something?"

"No. I'm praying. You might try asking forgiveness yourself."

"Bah! Churchy stuff." He bobbed his head toward the door. "Let's go. We gotta move."

Carlie gave her brother an indignant look. "You're nuts. I'm not going anywhere with you and Larry Gemmelli. Look what happened to Mat."

As the siblings argued on, a faint shadow crossed the width of the tall window that faced the creek. Maryanne would have missed it if she hadn't been straight across from the expanse of glass. No sooner did she notice the outline, than it was gone. And it looked familiar.

She gave Tony a measuring look. She had to word her questions well. "So how many people 'invested' with Mat? How many ways were you going to slice the four million?"

He shrugged. "It was just us—Dad and me—Mat, and Larry."

"Is Larry self-employed? Does he work all on his own?"

Tony broke out another of his ugly, grating laughs. "*Self-employed*…that's good." He shook his head. "Nah. Larry's got a bunch of guys who do stuff for him."

Maryanne caught another faint movement on the other side of the glass. *Hurry up!*

She arched a brow. "They're the ones who do his dirty work."

"You could say that."

"And how about you, Tony?" Carlie asked. "Who does yours? Joey-O? Was killing Mat some of your dirty work?"

Heavy footsteps stomped across the wooden floors,

letting Tony off the hook for that answer. The short, stocky man who walked in didn't look happy. "I told you talking wasn't going to work, Toe."

Maryanne shuddered. This guy made Tony the Toe look like a pussycat. Cold dark eyes peered from under heavy brows. A thin mouth gave him a cold, harsh look. But most alarming was the thick scar across his left cheek. Who knew what he'd done to earn that wound?

"Hey. She's my sister." Tony's eyes darted from Carlie to the new arrival. "You can't just—"

"I do what I have to do. And right now, I want to know who's got the four million."

Maryanne took a deep breath and extended her hand. "Larry Gemmelli, right?"

He stared at her fingers as if he'd never seen any before. "Why do you care? All you have to do is tell me where the money went after you knocked off the rat. And after all the trouble I went through to hide him long enough to get the dough."

So that was how Carlo Papparelli had wound up at Peaceful Meadows. "I care because Tony says you have my father. I didn't kill the Laundromat. A stroke did that. And I don't have the money, either. I don't know where it is."

"Oh, yeah, you whacked off Mat, all right. The Feds got your prints on that thingy with his meds. That's why they've been after you all this time. And he had the cash. So where'd you stash it?"

There they went again. Why was everyone so ready to see her as a killer? "I'll say it again. I had nothing to do with Carlie's husband's death."

"So did the Feds suddenly turn stupid? Why'd they come running after you if you didn't do him in?" He shook his head, and Maryanne thought of a testy bull. Before she could answer, he went on. "Nah. Give it up. It might go easier on you." He narrowed his eyes, and gave her a cold stare. "It might go easier on your old man."

Father, help!

"Larry!" a man called from outside. "What's taking you guys so long? I told you I could take care of them for ya. Want a hand?"

Tony and Larry traded looks.

Tony shook his head.

Larry shrugged. "Yeah, Paul. Get in here. And bring Louie with you."

Fear made Maryanne look toward the big window again. Dawn was breaking, and J.Z. and his reinforcements wouldn't be able to count on the dark to conceal them much longer. They'd better get in here soon.

More footsteps approached. Two men, one tall and skinny, the other medium in every way—hair, height, weight—walked in. But it wasn't the men that made Maryanne flinch—it was the shotguns they carried.

Tony stepped closer to Carlie. Maryanne supposed that was his idea of filial love. Just dandy.

Larry crossed his arms. "Well, ladies. What's it gonna be? My four million bucks—"

"*Our* four million bucks," Tony said. "A deal's a deal, Larry."

"Yeah, yeah. But if they don't tell us where they—"

"FREEZE!"

The four men jumped in surprise.

A gun went off.

Carlie screamed.

Maryanne thanked God. The Feds had made their move.

"We have you surrounded." She knew that voice and it gave her hope. He was the most determined man she'd ever known.

"Come on out here," J.Z. said, "and keep those guns down."

Larry laughed. "You think I'm stupid? We got the geezers, the girls and the guns. Either you guys get out of the way, or the geezers and the girls are toast."

Maryanne's heartbeat raced. "Dear Lord…"

"There's only four of you," J.Z. said, his voice firm, "and more than twenty of us. You're not going to get away with anything."

Larry looked around the room. He smiled when he noticed the size of the windows. "You asked for it," he yelled. "Say goodbye to the girls."

Paul and Louie stepped up to either side of Larry.

Tony turned green. "Come on, Larry, she's my kid sister—"

"Shut up and grab that chair," Larry said, pointing to one of six around a dining table. "When I tell you, pitch it at that window as hard as you can." He turned to the goon on his right. "And Louie, make sure you don't screw this up— Hey!"

A small, black projectile flew right at him. He flapped his hands and swatted it, but it dodged his efforts, then swooped upward, only to dive down again.

"Help!" Larry shrieked. "What is it? Just shoot it, already, willya?"

"It's a bat!" Carlie screamed.

Tony backed up against the far wall.

Paul and Louie stared from Larry to the bat.

Larry's panic grew. "Get it off of me! Get rid of it!"

Dawn had arrived, and in the doorway behind Larry and friends, Maryanne saw an elongated shadow. She measured the distance from the door to the guns, and she feared that either Paul or Louie would get off another shot before J.Z. could get to them.

She took another look at the two guns, figured she could cover the distance faster than he could, and offered a prayer.

As she leaped, she yelled a warning. "Carlie!"

Louie pulled the trigger, but Maryanne hit him at just the right time. The bullet missed her, and the goon went down. The shotgun clattered across the wood floor.

Maryanne clung to her victim's legs. She had him where she wanted him, and she wasn't going to let him go.

More shots rang out.

A man yowled in pain.

Larry kept up his cry. "Get the bat off of me! I'm gonna get rabies! Help!"

When her captive didn't try to fight her off, Maryanne risked a glance at him. He was out cold. It seemed his head had caught a corner of the cast-iron stove on his way down.

She let go and looked around. She saw Dan clap handcuffs on Tony's wrists. One of the men who'd lain in wait for her and J.Z. at the Raceway grabbed the back of Larry's shirt, while another agent struggled to slap a set of cuffs on him, too.

Larry whined on about the bat.

The bat fluttered wildly, blinded by the daylight seeping through the curtained wall of window.

Then Maryanne's heart stood still. J.Z. was locked in battle with Paul, who fought like a man possessed. The gun was between them, and they rolled and bucked and tugged to gain advantage.

But after waiting and worrying and praying for so many hours, Maryanne refused to let anything happen to J.Z. It had worked with Louie, so she figured she'd try it with Paul. The man under J.Z. twisted and reared like a mad horse, and in a sudden burst of strength, managed to roll them both to a side.

If he pinned J.Z. to the ground, Maryanne feared he'd—

"No!" she yelled and flew at the men.

Another shot rang out.

The kick of the gun jolted her off, and J.Z. fell away, too.

She feared the worst. Tears filled her eyes. *Lord Jesus, give me strength.*

Heart in her throat, she looked at the man she loved. As she watched, he sat, the shotgun in his hands. *Thank You, Father.*

An agent grabbed Paul's legs, and another his hands. The mobster looked dazed.

Silence filled the cabin.

Maryanne began to shake, but a pair of hands, warm, strong and steady, took hold of hers, and helped her sit.

"Are you okay?" J.Z. asked. "Did the bullet get you?"

"No. How…how about you?"

He cupped her chin in one of those sturdy hands. "I'm fine, now that I know you're okay."

Tears flowed down her cheeks. "I'm sorry," she said. "You were right, and I was wrong. I should have listened to you, helped you plan and do this right. Please forgive me."

He shook his head. "I'm the one who needs forgiveness. I decided you were guilty on the basis of questionable evidence, and I was influenced by my past. I brought trouble to you."

"You were doing your job."

"Not very well."

She looked around. Dan had cuffed Louie, and the two were engaged in a clumsy dance toward the door. The creep didn't want to go where J.Z.'s partner meant to take him.

Another agent, one she'd never seen, spread something over one of the guns with a fine brush. Outside, she heard male voices calling instructions, while other ones, those of Tony, Larry and friends, argued—without success.

Moments later, the room emptied and they were the only ones left. "Hey, but you got your man—men."

"I might have lost you." He placed his hands on her shoulders. "And if it wasn't for you, I'd still be lost. I'd still be blaming God for everything that's ever gone wrong. I blamed him for so long, that I made it impossible to recognize anything but bitterness and hate."

She looked into his grey eyes and saw more emotion there than she could have imagined. "And now?"

"Now I have to get a handle on this forgiveness thing. I don't know how or even if I can do it. At least now I can accept that my father chose a life of crime. God had nothing to do with it."

Maryanne smiled through her tears, these happier ones. "Blaming God does no good."

"I know that now. But it was easier than dealing with the shame. If I blamed God, I could hold on to my anger and my pain."

"Have you let it all go now?"

He gave her a crooked smile. "I'm working on it. And I'm working on forgiving myself—just as you said."

She touched his cheek. "And your father?"

"I'm getting there." He placed a kiss on the palm of her hand, then wrapped it in one of his. "Thanks. For showing me the way back."

"The Father's the one who did it. I may have been the tool He used, but I let my pride and stubbornness get in the way. I wasn't very cooperative."

"You did great. I saw how you live, and that made a big impression on me. Then you made the comparison that cleared things up in my mind. You said I couldn't judge the heavenly Father by my earthly father's failings."

She smiled. "You're moving down the path to reconciliation at a pretty good clip, here."

"I have a lot of lost time to make up. And I'm starting right now." He tipped up her chin, pressed his lips to hers. Her heart filled with joy, and she wrapped her arms around him.

"Woo-hoo! Good to see all your bug spray didn't keep the lovebug away, Cookie!"

"Awright! Take a look at the half-cocked shotgun go!" J.Z. pulled back and scrambled to his feet.

Maryanne cried, "Dad! What are *you* doing here?"

He rolled his wheelchair into the middle of the room. "What? Did you think I was going to miss all the fun?" He looked outraged. "Zelda and I got out of that dump where that Tony fellow locked us up. We make a pretty good team."

The look the two seniors exchanged was one of complicity. But it also held promise and something more.

Maryanne gaped.

It looked as though that lovebug had been working overtime.

"Hey, J.Z.!" Dan called from the front yard. "I know Maryanne's really great and all that, but we really could use a hand here. There's this thing called work, you know?

We've got these guys to get under lock and key, and then there's mountains of paperwork we need to get going on to bring this case to a close."

J.Z. held a hand out to her. "Here. Let me help you."

"Thanks." Although only moments earlier she'd been in his arms, now with an audience made up of Carlie, her father and Zelda—not to mention the three FBI agents and four mobsters who were waiting outside—she felt awkward. "You'd better go."

"Are you going to be okay?" J.Z. asked, his eyes warm, his smile tender.

She nodded. "I have to get Dad back home."

"I guess I have loose ends to tie up in Philly, myself."

"I know." He seemed reluctant to leave, as reluctant as she was to see him leave. "Go on. You don't want Eliza on your case, do you?"

He rolled his eyes.

Dan, who'd slipped back into the room, twirled a roll of yellow crime-scene tape and laughed.

J.Z. glared at his partner, then faced her again. "I'll be back soon."

"You know where I'll be."

He tapped the tip of her nose. "Don't write any more killer e-mails, okay?"

She gave him a pointed stare. "Watch those leaps—to conclusions, that is."

He grinned, then pressed a kiss to her forehead. "Be careful."

As he walked out of the room, she said, "God bless you, J.Z."

"He already has," he said. "More than I ever expected. More than I knew He could."

He left. As she turned to her father, a thought crossed her mind. J.Z. had said he'd see her again soon, but he hadn't said another word about love.

Were his words a promise or an easy out?

Only God knew.

FIFTEEN

Leaving Maryanne at the cabin was one of the hardest things J.Z. had ever done. But he was in no position to change their circumstances. At least, not yet.

He had work to do to close the case. And there was the matter of the bug. He had to know what exactly had happened. So, in spite of his reluctance, he headed to Eliza's office once he'd plowed his way through the unavoidable mountains of paperwork.

"Come in," she said, an unspoken question in her voice.

"I've a couple of things on my mind I need to clear up," he said as he entered her office.

She gestured to the battered wooden chair in front of her fine desk. "Take a seat."

He did. "After Larry Gemmelli bombed the Papparelli place, you were pretty gung-ho to arrest Maryanne. Did you want it bad enough to bug Dan's car?"

Eliza's eyebrows rose. "This is the first I've heard of a listening device. Are you accusing me?"

"No. I'm asking if you felt you needed to eavesdrop on us. Did you think we wouldn't get the job done?"

"For a while there, I had my doubts," she said with an airy wave. "But you're too obsessed by your quest for revenge. I knew you'd come through. Are you happy now that you've nailed a couple of Verdis? After all, your father was part of their organization."

J.Z. narrowed his eyes. He'd never shared with Eliza any details about his father's crimes. "I know the Bureau investigated every one of my father's crimes and his trial before they hired me, but that was well before you came on board. It's not exactly a raging topic these days. Did you see the need to use your position to investigate me?"

"Not exactly. In the process of the investigation, I pulled all our records on the Verdis, and lo and behold, the name Prophet popped up. It put your obsession in a whole new light for me."

J.Z. neither missed nor appreciated her sarcasm. But he chose not to comment.

Her smile said she knew just how he felt. "Face it, J.Z. There aren't many people with your last name, especially in jail."

He shrugged. "Well, I've never made a secret of it any more than I've made a big deal of it. So let's get back to my original question. Did you think I wouldn't do my job?"

"When you left for New Camden, I was pretty sure you'd do fine—as long as you didn't break any laws. But then your attitude toward the librarian changed. You didn't drop your suspicions, but something was different. I don't know. It was subtle and I had my worries."

"Enough worries for you to bug a car?"

"Enough that I felt the need to go to the bombing site. But that was it." She tapped her long, red-polished nails on the desktop. "I guess it wasn't the librarian after all, was it?"

This was going nowhere. J.Z. stood. "You needed to know that Dan and I are afraid we might have a mole in the office. Someone here knew to send David and Tom to trap us. Last I heard, you're still the boss. I wonder how you knew where we planned to meet."

When Eliza didn't speak, didn't react, J.Z. went on. "At the same time, someone alerted Tony and Larry."

"That's a strong accusation, J.Z."

He was sick of Eliza's attitude. "Look, someone might be dirty. That's pretty bad in my book. I talked to Dan, David and Tom. We can't let it slide. If we do, someone'll die, maybe a lot of someones. We have to make sure we can trust those who're supposed to watch our backs when we're out on the field."

She waved in dismissal. "I'd never tolerate that kind of treachery in my unit. I run a tight, clean ship. So don't go making wild accusations. I don't want a civil war in my office."

"I don't want another trap—one that could turn deadly."

"Do your job and you'll be fine. Don't let paranoia send you off on another of your wild-goose chases."

"I'll remember that, Eliza. And I suggest you make sure that ship of yours stays clean and on its correct course. Think about it. Anybody around this place who goes on the mob's payroll could have you in his sights, too."

"None of my people have turned. I *know* they're clean."

Eliza's words carried such conviction, and her personality was such that J.Z. had to reconsider. Had he let the stress of the investigation get to him? Maybe. He had been emotionally invested in this case.

He sighed and turned to go. A mole in the office wasn't all that likely. The vindictive Eliza Roberts would not only not tolerate one, but she probably also served as a potent deterrent against betrayal.

He left somewhat relieved. He might not like Eliza that much anymore, but he knew how tough and efficient she was. He could consider the case closed.

Three days later, J.Z. forced himself to walk into a place he'd sworn he'd never go. Those three days had flown by, filled with work and prayer. He had sought God's wisdom, and he knew he had to see his father again.

Maryanne had opened his eyes. He'd needed forgiveness, and he'd asked for God's, but she'd also urged him to forgive his father, and that had proven a harder thing to do.

After meeting Maryanne, he saw a love between her and her father that reminded him of long-forgotten days. Up until the arrest, Obadiah Prophet had been a devoted husband and father. The contrast between the father he'd known and the killer Obadiah turned out to be had been too great for a kid to reconcile.

How could a man who cared so much for his wife and who spent so much time with his son also be a killer for hire? It hadn't made sense to the fourteen-year-old who'd only wanted his dad.

J.Z. wasn't sure he'd ever understand what drove his father to the murderous choices he'd made. He couldn't imagine a life of crime, and he doubted Obadiah would ever explain. J.Z. had heard that to this day, the man remained unrepentant. Worse yet, he'd never taken responsibility for his crimes, even when faced with irrefutable proof.

Still, that didn't change what J.Z. had to do. He'd picked up his mother's old Bible, dusted it off and taken time to see what God had to say about forgiveness.

The bottom line was that J.Z. had to forgive his father. That night at the gas station, he'd asked God's forgiveness. But that was only one part. In order to move forward with the rest of his life, J.Z. had to forgive. He had to face his father one more time.

And he had to share with him the truth, God's gift of forgiveness, of redemption, of atonement through the death of his Son. Even though Obadiah had talked a good faith game all those years ago, and knew chapter and verse by heart. Even though J.Z. doubted his father would listen no matter what and how hard he tried. He knew what he had to do.

With a prayer on his lips, he went in.

With another prayer, and a heavy heart, he came back out.

Obadiah had rejected J.Z.'s words. He'd insisted he needed no forgiveness, since he hadn't done a thing. Redemption was for others, he said, for those who'd sinned. He was innocent. He'd been framed, set up to take the fall for someone else.

He'd belittled the forgiveness his son extended.

J.Z. wondered, if after all those years of sitting in a cell, repeating the excuses and denying the truth, Obadiah had begun to believe his lies.

"Forgive him, Father," J.Z. said. He turned the key in the ignition, and headed for the turnpike. "I couldn't make him see, but maybe someone else might. Bring him a Maryanne, someone who will show him the way back."

The sadness he felt at the miserable condition of his father's soul was tempered by the joy he'd found in his other gift from God. Forgiveness first: he'd taken care of that. Maryanne second: he was on his way.

Finally putting his past behind him, J.Z. paused at the toll-booth, took the card, and got on the road toward his future.

Maryanne waited at the other end.

"Would you please explain to me why you've put these ugly things back on?" Trudy asked.

"They're my work clothes. No big deal."

"Yes, it's a big deal." Trudy plucked at the sleeve of Maryanne's black-pin-striped white shirt. "You look great in your jeans. You wore them with a jacket and tailored shirt the first day you came back to work. And you wore them again last night to the youth ministry meeting. Now you're back at this stuff. I want to know why."

Maryanne didn't know if she could put into words all she'd learned about herself in a few short weeks. "They're what I'd rather wear to work. I feel more comfortable here like this. This is the professional me. The other's the non-business me."

Trudy waved her arms in exasperation. "I give up. I have better luck with my husband and sons than I have with you."

Maryanne watched her friend close the door to her office. Trudy had a point. She'd only worn her jeans to work once—they'd felt wrong. But her older, plainer clothes didn't feel right all the time, either. Just as the rigid routine of her pre-mob days no longer felt right.

A part of her needed stability. And there was nothing wrong with that. But another part of her now agreed with Trudy's assessment of Maryanne's former life. She'd always rejected anything that didn't fit within the tight pa-rameters she and her mother had established, and she had lived a boring life.

She stood and began to pace. "Have I really figured out

who I am now, Lord? You showed me that there's more to me than just the narrow slice Mother taught me to see. I'm not just Maryanne-the-library-anne, like J.Z. called me. But I'm also not just the wild woman who chased after mobsters in some crazy, misguided effort to prove herself. I'm a little of both."

She'd had a lot of time to consider all these things. She'd found evenings very long these days. An ornery cat didn't fill them very well. And Dad had a new lease on life. Zelda, the FBI's computer whiz, had decided to retire. They wanted to spend as much time together as possible.

Maryanne missed J.Z.

She had prayed, sought God, read His Word, prayed some more. God had revealed some mistakes she'd made and some flawed positions she'd held.

"I'm a little nervous about this, Father, so I'm going to need Your help." But she *was* going to trust God.

And just as she'd accepted the different nuances that made up the whole of who she was, she was going to have to do something she really didn't much like. She was going to have to shop.

Without her shopping buddy.

Carlie had been placed in the Witness Protection Program since she'd agreed to testify. Although Tony, Larry, Joey-O and her father were behind bars, there were others who didn't want her to tell all she knew.

Maryanne was going to miss the brave widow.

Especially when she went to choose new clothes. That new wardrobe had to work with all the facets of her life. She still wanted a subdued, tailored look for work, but for after-hours she was ready to let the more spontaneous part of her take the lead.

J.Z. had been right about another thing. By forcing herself into such a tight mold, Maryanne had let herself become a caricature. And she was no Olive Oyl. She was a woman with all the depth of personality that only a truly creative God could design.

She missed J.Z.

She'd done everything to avoid thinking of him. He'd said he'd be back soon, but she hadn't heard a word. True, he had to take care of who knew what about the case, but if Carlie had found the time to visit before she did her vanishing act, then he certainly must have had the time to call. Or come back.

What if he'd decided he *hadn't* fallen in love after all? She'd have to deal with the sadness, then. But she wanted to know either way.

Her office phone rang. "Hello?"

"It's me," Carlie said. "I wanted a last chance to talk, since I won't be able to stay in touch. This is my goodbye call, and Dan's not happy with me, since he's afraid I'm not 'hiding' enough. Can you believe they stuck me with that guy again?"

"What do you mean *stuck you?* Isn't he J.Z.'s partner? Shouldn't he be chasing mobsters in Philly?"

"He's my whatever-they-call-them in the Witness Protection Program. He's the one who's taking me to wherever I'm going, and he's become some kind of glorified bodyguard until I testify."

Maryanne grinned. She couldn't wait for the day when Carlie could tell her about the experience. Poor Dan. "Good luck. You two didn't see eye-to-eye a whole lot."

"Nope. We don't." Then Carlie fell silent.

A knot filled Maryanne's throat. She really liked Carlie.

"I wanted to thank you," Carlie said. "For your friendship, the prayers and the Bible. I'm taking baby steps, but I know I want to talk to God like you do. I want to hear His voice, too."

"He's there, Carlie. Ask Him, and He'll answer."

"That's what I'm doing, I'm asking. And I'm waiting."

Maryanne heard Dan in the background. Carlie said, "I gotta go. Keep me in your prayers, okay?"

"Always. God bless you, Carlie. I'll be waiting for you when you come back."

"God bless you, too."

After she hung up, Maryanne sat back at her desk. She tried to focus on work, but tears blinded her and the sadness refused to lift. She wished J.Z. hadn't vanished.

She tried to pray, but couldn't focus on that either.

Then she got a call from Dean Ross, Peaceful Meadows' director. A new resident in the retirement complex needed library privileges. "What's the name, Dean?"

"Zelda. Zelda Mathers. She moved in this morning. Seems your father knows her."

Maryanne laughed. "Oh, yes, he does. And you'd better watch out. Those two might prove too much for your place. I can't wait for the next senate meeting. Expect fireworks or mutiny, at least."

Still chuckling, she booted up her computer. As she wrote the memo to Sandy, the membership clerk, she heard the distinctive ding that signaled receipt of e-mail. She sent the one, and opened the other.

She gasped.

I know I'm no great prize, but I do love you. And I've been gone longer than I wanted to be, so you have every reason to be angry. I had unfinished business with my earthly father, and my Heavenly Father wouldn't let me off the hook.

I love you, Maryanne. Will you give me a chance?

A knock sounded at the door. She looked up through the flood of tears. It was the former Internet-phobe, skinny laptop in hand.

"How about it?" he asked, uncertainty in his gray eyes. "Will you give me that chance?"

She tried to speak, but the lump in her throat was too big. She nodded instead.

J.Z.'s long legs brought him to her side in three or four strides. He wrapped her in his arms.

She held his gaze, looking into those intense gray eyes, eyes that showed every emotion he so often tried to hide.

He wasn't hiding anything right then. "I love you, Maryanne. I want forever with you. And if you say yes, there's no going back. For better or for worse, and by God's redeeming grace, I'm terminally yours."

"Yes!" she cried. "Yes, yes, yes, yes, yes."

They sealed their promise with a kiss.

* * * * *

Look for Ginny Aiken's next book,
MIXED UP WITH THE MOB,
Coming in September 2006
from Love Inspired Suspense.

Dear Reader,

As a writer, wife, mother of four sons, one daughter-in-law, two dogs, grandmother to one Sun Conure parrot (think parents who wind up with kid's pet) and herder of my children's numerous friends, I crave peaceful time for myself. Reading has always been a refuge, and I especially love books that tell a great story and strengthen my faith for my daily walk—I also like to laugh. That's what I try to bring you through my books. Enjoy *Mistaken for the Mob!*

Blessings,

Ginny Aiken

QUESTIONS FOR DISCUSSION

1. As an only child, Maryanne struggles to relinquish the home where she grew up. What memories bind you to the past and prevent your walk into the future?

2. J.Z. has shut the door on God for years as a result of his earthly father's crimes. How did that distort his view of life?

3. Because of J.Z.'s determination to avoid the "like-father-like-son" label, he blinds himself to evidence. How does a near-obsession endanger more than Maryanne's well-being?

4. Carlie has refused to acknowledge her family's and husband's activities. Does her refusal contribute to their crimes? How would you respond if you discovered wrongdoing by a loved one?

5. J.Z. is attracted by Maryanne's faith, but again, memories of his father convince him she's a sham. Have any events in your life made it difficult for you to trust and follow God?

6. Maryanne's love for her father leads her to risk her life in order to save his. God's love led him to sacrifice his Son. How would/do you live out this kind of love in your life?

7. J.Z. visits his father in prison, but the older man rejects his son as well as God. Has a loved one responded like this to your efforts at reconciliation? How have you handled the aftermath of the rejection?

8. Maryanne has held a distorted idea of what "appropriate" dress should be, denying various aspects of her personality. Her mother left her with a heavy dose of fear of change. Are you denying a part of the person God meant you to be? Why or why not?

9. When J.Z. and Maryanne drop the blinders they've both worn, they experience freedom, and can move forward toward God's blessings. Is there something holding you in the past? How will you break those bonds and step forward in faith?

Love Inspired

SECRETS OF THE ROSE

BY
**LOIS
RICHER**

FINDERS, INC.

**Recovering lost items and
mending broken hearts.**

She'd had the perfect life,
until her husband was killed
in a mysterious accident.
But when Shelby Kinkaid's
little girl was kidnapped, she
would have to use her
investigative skills, with the
help of supportive neighbor
Tim Austen, to save her
daughter's life...and her own.

**Available August 2006
wherever you buy books.**

**Steeple
Hill**®

www.SteepleHill.com

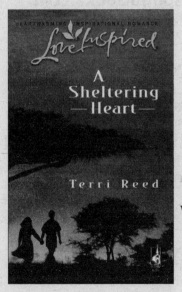

A SHELTERING HEART

BY

TERRI REED

Showing handsome Derek Harper that Healing Missions International healed hearts, not just bodies, was the promise Gwen Yates had made to her boss, because Derek was more interested in the organization's numbers. That her own heart was vulnerable to Derek had somehow escaped Gwen's notice.

Available August 2006 wherever you buy books.

Steeple Hill®

www.SteepleHill.com

LIASH

2 Love Inspired novels and a mystery gift... Absolutely FREE!

Visit
www.LoveInspiredBooks.com
for your two FREE books, sent directly to you!

BONUS: Choose between regular print or our NEW larger print format!

There's no catch! You're under no obligation to buy anything. We charge nothing—ZERO—for your first shipment. And you don't have to make any minimum number of purchases.

You'll like the convenience of home delivery at our special discount prices, and you'll love your free subscription to Steeple Hill News, our members-only newsletter.

We hope that after receiving your free books, you'll want to remain a subscriber. But the choice is yours— to continue or cancel, anytime at all! So why not take us up on our invitation, with no risk of any kind!